I WANT IT THAT WAY

A RETRO ROMANTIC COMEDY

CAROLINA CLASSICS
BOOK 3

KAREN GREY

Published by HOME COOKED BOOKS
A division of Jasper Productions, LLC
www.homecookedbooks.com

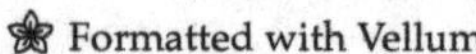 Formatted with Vellum

PRAISE CAROLINA CLASSICS

★★★★★ "Dust off your old Nokia phones and brush up on your snake game because we're going back to the 90s!" - *Jojo Reads Romance*

★★★★★ "After finishing this story, I want to load up the 5 CD changer and take a road trip to the beach. A fun, sweet and a zigazig-ahmazing 90's retro story that brings all the feels in the best possible ways." - *Bookbub review*

★★★★★ "With perfectly placed pop-culture references, expressions, and music, Karen Grey has a magical way of making her stories a visceral experience and transporting readers back to the nineties." - *Bookbub review*

★★★★★ "So heartfelt and relatable - I was drawn in and hooked from the first page." - *Goodreads review*

★★★★★ "Made me laugh, tugged at my heartstrings, and threw in some steam for the triple crown win." - *Bookbub review*

★★★★★ "Bursting with nineties pop culture references, complex characters, and delightful storytelling!" – *Goodreads review*

★★★★★ "This romance has all the feels, it's romantic, and funny, and it's full of sizzling chemistry with wonderful characters you can't help loving." – *Bookbub review*

★★★★★ "Reading this is like immersing yourself in your favorite dramedy." - *Bookbub review*

CONTENT GUIDANCE

The content notes below are meant to give readers a generalized view of potentially triggering subjects within this novel.

- Use of expletives: frequent but not mean-spirited
- Sex/Nudity: several sex scenes on page
- Violence: none
- Alcohol use: multiple characters on page

If you'd like a more detailed list of content warnings (which may include spoilers) they are available at:

https://www.karengrey.com/contentguidance

"Prove yourself brave, truthful, and unselfish, and someday, you will be a real boy."

—The Blue Fairy, *Pinocchio*

"Perhaps the greatest risk any of us will ever take is to be seen as we really are."

—Cinderella , *Cinderella*

PROLOGUE

DANI

I'm disappointed by the real Lukas Keith.

When I signed on to this made-for-TV-movie production as personal driver for the guy—as in *the* Lukas Keith, aka the actor famous for his role as Joey in *Our House*—it wasn't like I expected him to be exactly like his character.

You know, cheeky but adorable, beloved by all.

I've been driving for movies and TV shows here in Wallington for a few years now. I've had plenty of opportunities to be disenchanted by famous people. I get that an actor's personality is likely to be very different from the roles they play.

I'm still disappointed by the real Lukas Keith.

Maybe, because Lukas was Joey right there in our living room for most of my childhood, I felt like I knew him already.

Maybe, because my friend Violet—a casting assistant on the movie—told me Lukas would be playing a role just like Joey, I assumed he always plays himself.

Or maybe it's because he's even better-looking in person.

It's not that he's been obnoxious. He hasn't hit on me, or asked me to buy him drugs, or thrown up in the car—all things that have happened with previous clients. He's just been borderline rude. Every single day it's the same. He gets in the car, mumbles a greeting without making eye contact, and then slumps down in the back seat to bury his nose in a script.

When we arrive at his destination, he mutters a thank you and practically runs away from the car. Like I've got the plague or something. He never says anything else, not even to arrange the next pickup. The second AD does it for him.

I don't know what is up with the guy, but the tension he carries around with him is exhausting. So, even though I'll miss the extra income, I have to say I'm relieved as I pull into the driveway of his rental house for the final pickup. Once I drop the guy off at the Wallington airport, I'll never have to deal with him again.

When I arrive at his rental house, I turn off the stereo, Smashmouth's "Walkin' on the Sun" still ringing in my ears. I don't play music unless clients request it, and he never has. He appears at the top of the stairs as soon as I park and insists on loading his own bags into the trunk, but after I shut the passenger door behind him, he hides behind a script again.

His body language made it clear from the very first day of this gig that conversation between us is not welcome. But he can't be learning lines now. The movie wrapped yesterday.

"Already preparing for the next role?" I ask, against my better judgment.

"Yep."

He pops the *P* at the end of the word so aggressively, I know I should just let it go, but instead, I poke the bear. "Is it any good?"

He doesn't answer, and when I glance in the rearview mirror, he's white-knuckling the script. Reminding myself that my only job is to get him to the airport, I keep my mouth shut for the rest of the drive.

After I park under the Departures sign, I pop the trunk

and paste on a professional smile, counting the seconds until this job is over.

He's out of the car and dealing with the Skycap by the time I turn off the ignition, and I debate whether I should even get out. It's not like the time when I drove the actress who shared every detail of her mother's battle with cancer, who cried as she hugged me before she went through those doors. Or even the aging British cinematographer, who told me so many hilarious stories that I wanted to adopt him as my grandpa. Who invited me to visit anytime I was "over the pond."

I'm not even sure Lukas Keith knows my full name, and I'll be doing my best to forget him once those sliding doors close behind his very fine ass. He proves the truism: not all pretty faces have personalities to match.

"Danielle?"

The pretty face in question, dominated by soulful blue eyes framed by chestnut brown brows, suddenly appears in the open passenger side window. He's never looked at me directly when he says my name, and the force of his attention pins me to my seat.

"Sir?" a man calls. "Your baggage claim ticket?"

"Can you wait a sec, Danielle?" he asks me. "I have something for you."

He jogs away, and it's like the sun disappearing behind a cloud. Everything dims a little bit for a few moments. When he returns, sliding into the front seat and turning that intense gaze back on me, I'm not only blinded by its force, but I suddenly don't know what to do with my hands.

Meanwhile, my heart's like the rabbit my dog Skye chased around the backyard last week, desperate to get away, racing from one side of my chest to the other. I don't know whether it's his movie star presence, or what, but the blood pumping through my veins is so loud, I have to lean closer to hear what he's saying. This puts me in range of his intoxicating scent, which riles up parts of me that have been dormant so long I thought they'd expired.

I'm not sure how long he's been holding out the wrapped package before I take it from him, but once my eyes have something else to focus on, I can at least breathe again.

"You can open it." His hushed tone wraps around my shoulders like a favorite sweater on the first chilly day of autumn, making me want to snuggle closer.

"If you want. You don't have to," he continues, almost like he's nervous. "I usually get my driver a nice bottle of booze or something, but I don't know. I thought you might appreciate these. I actually had fun hunting them down."

My cheeks could set fire to an ice cube, but curiosity is going to kill this cat if I don't open the gift, so I just rip into the paper. When I see what's inside, I literally gasp.

"I hope you like them." His voice now tentative, he leans closer to lift the collection of neon sticky notes from the box, only to reveal another in pastels.

"Wow," is the only response I seem capable of uttering.

"Maybe it's dumb." He sounds so vulnerable that my gaze shifts to his face, where his expression is equally unsure. "But I noticed how you use sticky notes to organize your planner, and I thought the different colors would be useful."

He's waiting for a response, I know he is, but I'm afraid if I say anything I might cry. I mean, it's just paper, but it's like the guy *sees* me. The guy who I thought didn't even know my name has peered into my heart, examined my soul, and given me the perfect gift.

"But, like, feel free to toss them if you don't like them." He reaches for the box, like he's going to take it away from me, and I clasp it to my chest before he can.

His hands go up in surrender, and he laughs, the sound like rain in spring. "I was going to point out that I did leave you a tip in the box as well. In case you were going to throw it away."

A car beeps behind us, and he looks back like he, too, forgot where we were. "Okay, well"—he hooks a thumb behind him—"I gotta catch my flight."

He climbs out of the passenger seat, closes the door, and then leans down, meeting my gaze again. "You take care, Dani."

I'd planned to pull away from this drop-off with a *good riddance*, but now, I can't stop watching as he walks away. When he reaches the automatic doors, the idea that I'll never see him again hits me like a rogue wave.

He raises his hand to stop the doors from closing, turns around, and waves. He waits to pass through until I wave back. Only then does his hand drop.

And then he's gone.

CHAPTER ONE

DANI

Just suck it up, Dani, I tell myself as I hoof it through the swampy Carolina heat from my car to the shrink's office. *If this one says no, you can always go to another one.*

As I press the button to let the doctor know I'm here, I acknowledge that I can hardly blame her if she thinks I'm a lunatic. If the definition of insanity is doing the same thing over and over again, expecting a different result, the number of times I've paid someone to tell me I don't get to make decisions about my own body would qualify me as wacked.

What is *a sex life worth?* you might ask.

Let's add up what I've spent so far.

Appointments with gynecologists *not* resulting in the tubal ligation I asked for: six hundred dollars. A visit to this shrink so I can get a letter attesting to the fact that I'm capable of making my own damn decisions: another hundred and fifty dollars.

The door to Dr. Rangel's office opens, startling me. "Come on in, Danielle."

Pasting on a cheerful smile, I do as she says. I do not,

however, head for the couch and lie down like a patient. Instead, I take the chair by her desk.

Following my lead, she crosses to its other side and taps an envelope sitting on her desk. "After our last session, I'm happy to give you a letter stating that you are lacking any psychological impediments that would affect your decision-making process."

An audible sigh of relief whooshes past my lips. "Great, thank you so much."

When I reach for the envelope, however, she slides it out of my reach. "I do have a couple more questions for you."

Eyes on the prize, Dani, eyes on the prize. "Okay."

"I am curious as to why it is that you're opting for sterilization."

"Do you need to know to give me the letter?"

Her lips twist to the side slightly and her gaze shifts toward the window. "Technically, no. But I can't help but wonder if there are underlying issues that require our attention. If you're seeking to solve a problem physically that may be more appropriately addressed emotionally."

I don't know where she's going with this, but I want that letter, so I hold up a hand in a Girl Scout promise. "I am not afraid of having children. I am also not going to be talked into having them. I helped raise half of my nine siblings. I have no interest in bringing any more Goodwins into the world. I believe we're full up as it is."

She takes a deep breath, and before she can ask what I'm pretty sure is next on her list, I add another hand to the first, so she's got two to look at. "And I swear, no uncle or cousin or stepdad diddled me. I just tense up when a penis gets near my vagina because all I can think about is that army of sperm coming for my poor little defenseless egg."

"Tense up?"

"Like, so tense that there's no way anything is getting in there. Sometimes I actually have the urge to run away."

"Are you saying you're a virgin?"

"Not exactly, but I've never been able to enjoy sex. And it's getting worse rather than better." I blow out a breath. "I get all sweaty. Sometimes even nauseous."

I'll give her credit, she looks curious, but not horrified. "These are classic fight/flight/freeze responses, like when your body believes it's in danger."

"The first gyno I went to told me I should just"—I make air quotes—"'relax, have a glass of wine before sex.' Like that's a good idea. I mean, don't more people get pregnant when they've been drinking?"

"If they're drinking to excess." She folds her hands and leans closer. "I wonder if unpacking some of your experiences might be beneficial. For many people, emotional intimacy can be necessary in order to feel sexual pleasure."

At this, my hands and my head give into gravity.

"Is that frightening to you?"

"No," I say, forcing myself to sit up and face her again. "Of course not. It sounds exhausting."

She tips her head to the side again. Very birdlike, this lady. "Exhausting?"

"Yeah. Another person wanting things from me. Another person to worry about."

And the head tips to the other side. "That's what you do for the people you care about? Worry about them?"

"Well, yeah. People leap without looking. Including two of my best friends. One married a total jerk just because she couldn't pick between two guys who have loved her forever. And the other one is pregnant with a guy she's only known for a year. They're not even married."

"Are your friends unhappy with these changes? Because life is about change."

"Who can tell? Whitney, the one who got married? I call her once a month but can't get her to talk about anything beyond what color she just painted her nails. And Violet, the one who's pregnant, *seems* happy. But she has no idea how her life is going to get turned upside down. She's an only child and doesn't know anything about raising kids."

"But wouldn't you agree that they should be able to make these choices for themselves, no matter the consequences?" Her chin lowers, and she waits until I make eye contact to continue. "The way you want to."

"But guess who they're going to expect to be there to pick up the pieces?" I point at my chest. "This girl."

She nods slowly and then gazes off to the side again, her hand still on my damn envelope. "I'm curious about the other thing that exhausts you. People wanting things from you."

Damn, this woman must have a tape recorder in her head. "What about it?"

"I'm wondering if you experience relationships as transactional."

"Like, you scratch my back, I'll scratch yours? I mean, yeah. That's how most people are."

"Do you ever do things for people you're close to, just because you care about them?"

"Well, sure. But the problem with most people is that they run around trying to get things they don't really need, and they're never satisfied. From the latest gadgets to the next baby."

"And what about you?"

"I am never going to be like that. Which is why I'm here." I'm doing my best to hang on to my temper, but I feel like she's trying to catch me out. "I take care of my own needs, if you know what I mean, but from what I hear, it can also be nice to have someone else make you feel good."

"Which takes us back to my original premise. Sterilization may be a solution that solves some of your problems, but it may not be the magic wand you're hoping for. For many, many people, for most women, in fact, a certain level of attachment and trust is required before they can relax enough to, say, climax with a partner present."

"Well, hopefully I'm not like most women."

"And what if you are?"

"What about all those folks out there having sex for fun? All those women looking for tips in *Cosmo* magazine?"

The skin around her eyes and mouth tightens. "I think there are fewer of them than we are led to believe."

"I guess I'll just have to hope I'm not one of them. Now can I have my letter or what?"

Two days later, I'm painting the back bedroom of my house when the phone rings. Setting the roller in the tray, I sprint to the hall nook, hoping to pick up before the machine gets it, since I've been playing phone tag with a gynecologist who refuses to leave a message.

"Hello? Danielle Goodwin speaking."

"Is this Danny?" an unfamiliar female voice asks.

"Uh, yeah. That's me."

"Oh, sorry. I thought Danny would be a guy. My bad." She clears her throat. "I'm a transpo PA on *Lawson's Reach*, and I have the airline information for your pick up Monday?"

Like way too many young women these days, her voice goes up at the end of every sentence, as if she's not sure of what she's saying. Drives me nuts, but she's not one of my cousins or siblings, so I let it go. Besides, I've got my own shit to deal with. Including figuring out how to deal with the child star-turned-TV producer that I get to ferry around town for the next two weeks.

The guy who, for the past two years, has popped into my head every single time I pull out my vibrator.

Lukas Keith is hands down the most attractive and the most confusing SOB I've ever met. Until the last five minutes of our time together when I was his driver on that Hallmark movie, I was pretty sure he hated me. I have no idea what to do with the feelings those final moments stirred up, especially because they are one hundred percent likely to be felt only in one direction. I mean, he's Hollywood royalty. I'm a nobody. Just a driver and locations scout in a backwater Southern town that just happens to get a lot of film and TV production. Not to mention the fact that he's been in love with his co-star from *Our House* since he was in short pants. No way could I compete with America's sweetheart, Kellie Kingston.

If I wasn't saving money for a tubal ligation—assuming someone will someday grant me one—I definitely would've turned down the job.

"Hello? Are you still there?" the PA asks.

"Yes, I'm—" At the call-waiting beep in my ear, I switch gears. "I have to take another call. Can you give me your number real quick, and I'll get right back to you?"

I scribble down her info as quickly as I can before connecting with the other call and repeating my greeting.

"Oh, I'm glad I caught you, Ms. Goodwin," another unfamiliar female voice says. "I'm calling for Dr. Jenner."

"Oh, great. I'm ready to schedule the procedure whenever he has an opening."

"Oh, I'm sorry. That's not—that is, he asked me to call and tell you that you're not a good candidate for a tubal at this time."

"Did he not get the letter from Dr. Rangel?"

She clears her throat. "He did, but there are other factors—"

"Can I speak to him?"

"He's very busy, I'm afraid. He said to tell you that he has seen too many women in your situation regret their decision and come back wanting a reversal he can't provide."

"What does that mean? My situation?"

"Under thirty and unmarried, dear. I mean, honey, what if

you meet the man of your dreams and he really wants kids? What would you do then?"

"Ma'am, the man of my dreams is one who, like me, doesn't want children," I grit out, squeezing the receiver the way I'd like to wring this lady's neck. "And how is it that turning thirty is going to magically make me mature enough to make the decision?"

"All I can say is," she says, her tone snippy, "this is his decision, and he told me to tell you that it's final."

When I don't say anything, she adds, "You have a good day now, you hear?"

After roaring my frustration into the void she leaves behind, I slam the phone into the cradle so hard the ringer jangles.

But it doesn't help.

Monday afternoon, when I flick through sticky notes and discover an open slot on the calendar between my last locations appointment for the day and my pickup for Lukas, I consider the best use of my time. My work as a location scout has grown steadily, but not enough to give up my other gigs. Driving Lukas will conflict with the bartending I usually do to fill in the gaps, but it's worth it because the pay is good. The days are equally long; I just spend more of them on my ass than on my feet.

For that reason, if I had a bigger window, I'd pick up my dog from my friend Vi's office and take her for a run. Skye spends her days at Vi's office, but I'm in charge of her exercise. When Vi was my roommate, it was easier to co-own a pet. Now that Vi's living with her boyfriend, we're always shuttling her back and forth, like divorced parents.

I can squeeze a run in after I drop Lukas at his place, so I swing by my house before going to the airport. As I jog past the kitchen on my way to grab shorts and sneakers, the blinking answering machine taunts me. Could be my mom or a sibling wanting something from me. It could also be a call-back from one of the many homeowners I left messages for this morning.

I keep moving toward my bedroom. As I gather running gear, it occurs to me that if I had a second phone line, I could separate business from family calls, so I select a bright-blue sticky note from the collection on my desk and use it to add a reminder to my color-coded to-do list.

As I do so, a note for a gynecologist appointment falls out of my planner. Wadding it into a ball and tossing it in the wastebasket does not change the fact if I were married, or even engaged, I could change the doctor's mind.

Not that I have any candidates lined up.

"Honey," my mom's voice is the first up after I push the play button on the machine, her saccharine tone a tell. She wants something. "I had an idea I want to talk to you about. There're some new condos going up out near us. Wouldn't it be great if you got out from under that falling-down old house in that awful neighborhood and moved out here? I hate having to worry about you all alone in that place."

This is mom-speak for: I'm spending all my time with my grandbabies and don't want to deal with the two teenagers I still have at home, and since you said no when I asked if they could take the extra bedrooms in your house, I've now decided you should leave the lovely house your aunt left you and move close to me where it'll be easier to offload them onto you.

The woman loses interest in her kids the moment they start to talk, which meant I helped raise most of my siblings until I moved in with my great aunt. Even as Aunt Gracie waged a battle with breast cancer, it was easier taking care of her than running after my siblings.

My mother's last volley: "I'll even help you with the down

payment. Then you'll have more money to buy nicer clothes so you can find yourself a man, Think about it, okay? Love you."

Yikes. She's on the hunt and serious. Probably sold off another chunk of her family's land and is feeling flush with cash.

"Hello, Dani-girl," the next message begins after a beep from the machine. "How are you doing, honey? I've got a new contact for the phone tree. A couple finally moved into the old Rogers place." My neighbor Ida's husky tone has the opposite effect of my mother's faux sweetness, and my shoulders relax back into place as I take down the information.

My aunt kept a neighborhood call list to organize everything from the yearly block party to casserole brigades, and I've been happy to keep it up. Knowing my neighbors and feeling a part of this community is one of the things I love about living here. My aunt never married or had kids, and she was happier than any of the other women in my family. I have no idea what her sex life was like—she may have been independent, but she was still Southern, and ladies don't talk about that kind of thing—but she never seemed lonely.

After putting the sticky note with the new neighbors' contact information on the wall cork board, I make another note to call Ida back when I get a chance. We're overdue for a visit.

The next few calls are from homeowners returning calls about shooting *Lawson's Reach* on their properties, and I jot down the times they're available to meet me. As I pick up the phone to call one of them back, the phone rings in my hand.

"Aunt Dani?"

It takes me a moment to put a name to the voice: Carrie, one of my many much-younger cousins that call me aunt. Every one of my mom's sisters is alike. That is, they look sideways at a guy, and nine months later they pop out another baby. "What's up, Carrie? I only have a minute or two."

"I was just wondering if you could lend me some money?"

I take a deep breath and count to five before answering. "What for?"

"I need a cell phone."

If she were knocked up, or in trouble some other way, that'd be one thing, but it's practically my job to say no to this child. "No one needs a cell phone in Wallington, sweetheart."

"But all my friends have one," she says, a whine creeping into her voice.

"How old are you again?"

"Seventeen."

"What did your mother say when you asked her?"

She pauses for a beat before answering. "She said to ask you. Said you have plenty of money."

I may have a good cushion of savings, but it's because I don't waste my money on frivolous crap. I don't have a cell phone. I haven't even replaced the rotary phone in my hand with a cordless. I put any extra funds in places even I can't get to the money, like an IRA and a health care savings account. Or into fixing up my aging but beautiful little bungalow in a neighborhood most of the town thinks is dangerous. The outcasts that share it, commonly referred to as "the freaks, the blacks, and the gays," are happy to let that reputation lie.

"Listen, Carrie," I say, forcing a smile, "You finish high school, get your associate's degree and a good job, and I'll help you with your first month's rent and deposit on an apartment."

"But I need a cell phone."

"I'll even throw in a box of condoms from Costco. But that's my final offer. Bye, now. Love you."

It's how my family always signs off, but to me the words have become meaningless.

CHAPTER TWO

LUKE

"Are you sure you don't want me to take the 405 instead of the canyon?" the cab driver asks as he pulls away from my house in Studio City. The one I won't be seeing for several months. "Traffic isn't bad."

"I prefer surface streets, thanks." Hopefully my tone is curt enough to prevent further discussion without being rude. I have my reasons for avoiding the highway—no easy feat in the City of Angels—but I'm not getting into them with a stranger.

Anyway, I've got plenty of time before my flight departs, and I've got phone calls to make. Goodbyes to say that will distract me from the drive as well as from my worries about my new job.

Just as I pull my cell from my jacket pocket, it vibrates. Seeing my buddy Max's name on the screen, I flip it open. "Don't worry, man, I'm on my way to the airport."

"I'm not checking up on you."

Max was my roommate at boarding school, so not only does he know most of my secrets, but I know when he's bull-shitting. "You sure about that?"

"Okay, I am checking up on you. But I'm also calling with news. Some good, some bad."

Max is the latest showrunner on the hit TV show *Lawson's Reach*. Number five, to be exact; the production hired and fired three in the second half of its first season. My old friend is taking a calculated risk in bringing me on as producing director. As showrunner, he has to be in LA full-time running the writers' room and would typically rely on the line producer or UPM to be his eyes and ears on location. But because this particular show has a history of drama both on and off camera, he wants someone he can really trust in Wallington.

By hiring a guy like me, Max is betting that our long personal history will be more beneficial than the relatively short length of the list of credits on my directing résumé.

"Bad news first," I say.

"New budget from the studio means we've got to cut costs. Which means you only get a driver for the first couple weeks."

The egg white and spinach omelet I had for breakfast suddenly threatens to come back up. "Well, that's a problem."

"You have a driver's license."

"That I haven't used in three years."

"I thought you said therapy was helping."

I slump down in the back seat and lower my voice to answer. "Only in terms of being a passenger."

"Maybe this is a chance to change that," he says, like it's no big deal. Even though he knows it is.

"Max, you know it's not—" Trying and failing to keep irritation out of my voice when just the thought of driving making my hands clammy and my heart race, I do my best to concentrate on my breathing.

"I mean, the town is tiny," he goes on. "It'd be a good place to work through things. Plus, you said you requested the same driver you had on that movie you shot there, right?"

"Yeah, so?"

"You liked her."

"What is this, eighth grade?"

"Not *liked* her, liked her, you idiot. You said she was super chill. Unimpressed by your famous ass."

"I'd argue that more than my ass is famous." Or *was*, anyway.

"My point is, instead of driving you around, she could help you get back to doing it yourself."

With an eye on the taxi driver, I swallow further argument. No need to air my dirty laundry in public. "I'll figure something out."

"I'm just saying, man. You could take this as an opportunity."

"Anything else?" I ask, my tone probably sharper than it should be with my boss.

"I'm about to fax the final budget to O'Neill, the line producer. I wanted you to know about the change before you went over it with her."

"Thanks, man. I do appreciate the heads-up." It wouldn't be a good look to wig out on my first day at the office.

"O'Neill's a ballbuster, but she's good people."

"Anything else? I owe Angie a call before I get on the plane."

"Ah, tell your lovely mother I said hi. You have the latest scripts?"

I pat my messenger bag, bulging with photocopies. "Yep. Plan to go over them on the plane."

"That's the good news, by the way. You've got the green light from the network to direct the first episode."

"Wow, that's great." Both Max and I were worried the powers that be might insist on bringing in a director with more experience.

"I had to beg a little bit, so don't fuck up."

"Thanks for the vote of confidence."

"You're welcome."

I open my mouth to tell him that I'll check in tomorrow, but before I can, he says, "Oh, shit. There's one more thing. Speaking of literally fucking up, we just got this memo, directly from the chairman of the board of Brothers Werner."

"Sounds ominous."

"It's a no-tolerance policy for quote-unquote 'fraternization among employees.' People are already calling it the Morality Memo."

"What is this, the 1950s?"

"My theory? It has to do with two things. You remember how I said it was all hush-hush why the last showrunner got fired?"

"Yeah," I answer, wondering where this is going. People get fired in Hollywood all the time for all kinds of reasons.

"When I cornered one of the writers who's been around from the beginning, he told me the previous showrunner had an affair with a writer."

"Why is that such a big deal?"

"Apparently, after they broke up, she had a huge meltdown in the studio commissary. Right after the show got that mention in *Ten Things I Hate About You*."

"You mean the dad character saying something about Lawson's *River* where the kids share beds 'and whatnot'?"

"It doesn't matter that they didn't quite get the name right. That line plus the woman's meltdown stirred up controversy all over again about the show being overly sexual. Long story short, they fired the writer and bought out of the showrunner's contract."

"Typically unfair."

"Meanwhile, we're still trying to sell the idea of a love story between two male characters to the suits." He clears his throat. "All this is to say that I need you to keep things squeaky clean over on the right coast. Keep those kids out of each other's beds."

When I groan, he echoes it. "My thoughts exactly. Good luck, brother."

After I hang up, I take a moment to digest all this information before calling my mother. Who also happens to be my manager. Ex-manager technically, though she's refusing to accept that I've fired her. Once her assistant puts me through, she starts right in. "Are you sure you can't put off leaving another day? Because I was just talking to casting at Universal and they've got a movie you'd be perfect for."

"Angie. We talked about this."

"I could get you a meeting later today. Then you could take the red-eye."

"For one thing, my first day is tomorrow. I'm not starting this gig by driving directly to work from the airport. And two, when are you going to get it? I quit."

My mother's acting career fizzled out when she had three kids back-to-back. After I booked a commercial that she lost out on, she shifted gears. I'll never know if leaving acting behind was a relief or a disappointment for her, but I do know she flourished as a manager. My brother and I were her first clients, but twenty-some years later, she's got more clients than I can keep track of.

My brother's career is booming, so I'm not sure why she takes my failures so seriously. Before she can launch into her usual arguments, like I just need to take a class from this guy, get a haircut from that woman, change my workout, yadda yadda yadda, I'm saved by the bell.

"Gotta go, Angie. Kellie's on the other line."

"Oh, tell her to call me. I have something to run by her."

Did I mention that my mother also represents my longtime co-star-slash-best friend with whom I have a complicated public relationship? Stifling a sigh, I promise to pass on the message and tell her I'll check in with her and my father once I'm settled.

"I hope you're not making a mistake. Running second-unit shoots and babysitting a bunch of teenage actors in the middle of nowhere," she tuts. "Are you sure you want to give up on your own career for that?"

Maybe it's because I was her first client. The one responsible for extinguishing her own rising star. But my mother can't quite accept that not every child phenom can cut it as an adult.

Too many hours and too little fresh air later, my feet finally hit the ground in Wallington, North Carolina. I'll be calling the beach town they call the Hollywood of the East home for the next nine months, assuming Max and I can manage to hang on to our jobs. After the very short walk from the gate to baggage claim, I begin to scan faces for my driver.

It doesn't take long before I catch the glint of her midnight-black hair. When I catch sight of her profile, my reaction is instantaneous. A spot between my shoulder blades —muscles so habitually tense I forget what it feels like to relax them—*poof*, lets go.

I've thought a lot about this woman in the past two years. She probably had no idea, but she helped me get through a pretty rough time. Between dealing with my fears of being in a car to facing the reality that my career was over, I barely said a word to her. It took everything in me to get through each day on that show. Pretending I was grateful to be there, even though it was obvious that my career had reached its nadir. I mean, not only was I working on a made-for-TV movie while my brother was bouncing from an Oscar-nominated art house film to a superhero franchise, but I couldn't even score a lead. I was just the snarky best friend.

At the time, I was terrified to quit because I'd never done anything else. But that job was the straw that broke the camel's back. Two things got me through it: Living right on the beach, where watching the sunrise over the water gave me some perspective, and my driver's calm, quiet presence at the beginning and end of each day.

Maybe Max is right. If anyone could help me get back in the driver's seat, it'd be her. She's so confident and competent, maybe it'd rub off.

She hasn't seen me yet, so I take a moment to appreciate the view. Not that I'd act on my attraction to her, even without a Morality Memo hanging over my head, but the woman is so effortlessly beautiful. I'm sure her tawny skin has never seen the inside of a tanning salon. Naturally dark lashes and high cheekbones draw attention to her wide-set, almond-colored eyes. There's nothing showy about her uniform of golf shirt and khakis, or her unfussy ponytail, but her presence commands attention.

The moment she sees me, a frown crosses her face briefly before being replaced with a professional smile. It's only when her gaze drops to the carrier in my hand and her brows come together in confusion that I remember Peanut.

"Is that a dog?" she asks.

"It is."

"Your dog?"

"Uh, yeah."

She raises a brow. "Does it need to relieve itself before we get your checked bags?"

"Probably?" I'd been able to take him out to pee when we changed planes in Charlotte, but the poor guy has been stuck in the carrier for most of the day.

She holds out a hand. "Why don't I take him—or her?"

"Him."

"Outside while you get your bags," she finishes.

"I'd appreciate that, but he's got some issues."

"Don't worry. I'm used to clients with issues."

I think that was probably an insult directed at me, but I hand her the carrier and tell her I'll meet her out front.

The Wallington airport ground crew takes its sweet time getting the bags to the carousel, but everyone is so friendly while they make you wait that you hardly notice. By the time I emerge from the cooled air of the terminal into the muggy early evening, Peanut—who is much more likely to cower than wag his tail at strangers—is on his back writhing in pleasure as Dani rubs his belly and whispers sweet nothings to him.

The green-eyed monster awakens within, and it takes several beats for me to shush it. Pretty pitiful to be jealous of a scrawny little dog.

She looks up when I roll my bag over to the grassy area where's she's squatting with the dog. Scooping him up, she juts her chin toward the parking lot. "I'm over here."

After spreading a towel on the back seat of the town car, she puts him on top of it, points, and delivers a firm "stay" before closing him inside. Picking up the pet carrier from the sidewalk, she peers at the suitcase I've already stowed in the trunk. "Just the one bag?"

I take the carrier and drop it next to my bag. "I've got some boxes coming with transpo."

One perk of having grown up in LA is that you know people everywhere. The uncle of a high school buddy is the head teamster on *Lawson's Reach*, so my belongings are taking the slow route across the country with the cameras, lights, and other production equipment that can't be rented locally.

She closes the trunk. "To production or your rental?"

"I'd like to check in at the office first, if that's okay with you."

"Do they know you brought a dog?"

"That is one of the things I need to check in with them about."

"Good luck with that."

"You don't think one of the beach houses will allow dogs?"

She shoots me a pitying look. "Honey, I doubt you're staying at the beach. It's summer. High tourist season. No one wants to rent a beach house to production when they can get triple the rate from tourists. Anyway, laws about dogs on the beach are pretty strict."

"Shit. I didn't think about that."

I still don't how I got talked into taking him in the first place. I've never had a dog and have no idea what to do with one. But when Kellie found out about this group of dogs that'd been rescued from a horrible hoarding situation, she convinced me that adopting him would be good for both of us.

More likely, this is yet another impulsive decision on my part that'll come back to bite me on the ass. Perhaps literally.

"We going, or what?" Dani asks, breaking into my thoughts.

"Sorry," I say, and fold my frame into the back seat next to the dog, who, surprisingly, leans against me. I set my hand on his flank and start the breathing exercises recommended by my therapist. In on four, hold for four, out for six. After a few rounds of those, I focus on the sensations around me. Whenever my thoughts swerve toward images from the accident, I do the breathing again.

The drive from the airport to the studios is short, but even so, having the little dog next to me is a comfort I hadn't expected. Probably not a good idea to walk in the office with him, though, so I ask Dani if he can stay with her while I pick up my housing information.

She agrees, but mumbles something that sounds like, *Don't get used to it.* When I pull out my cell phone and ask for her number, she shakes her head. "Those things still don't work here."

"Seriously?"

"It's not like I'm in charge."

"No, if you were in charge, the problem would be fixed."

She side-eyes me. "You're assuming I think it's a problem."

"You still use a pager then?"

She holds one up and hands me a business card. "I'll wait out here if you're not going to be too long."

After I get out of the car, I drop my phone in my briefcase and try to remember what it was like to not be constantly available.

I think I liked it.

DANI

Lukas is true to his word and is back at the car within fifteen minutes. He's actually spoken full sentences to me today, so I venture a direct question. "What's the news about keeping a dog at a rental?"

He holds up a key. "She wasn't happy about it, but the housing coordinator talked one of the landlords into it. I just have to make sure he doesn't disturb the neighbors. And I had to put down a big deposit."

After handing over the paperwork with the address, he gets in the car. I'm pretty sure I know where this place is, but I pull out a map to make sure. As I scan the grid for the location, I notice he's doing the same breathing thing he did on the drive from the airport to the studios .

Instead of ignoring me after I start the car, he asks, "Could I hire you to, uh, give me driving lessons before production starts up?"

I meet his gaze in the rearview briefly and determine that he's not joking. "You don't know how to drive? How is that possible?"

"I just… don't."

After stopping at a light, I turn to face him. "Tell me the

truth, or there's no way I'll even consider teaching you to drive."

He sighs heavily, but before he can spit out whatever crazy reason he has for skipping out on yet another step to adulthood, a beep from behind us has me turning my attention back to the road.

"It's a long story," he finally says. "I'd tell you if I could, but I can't."

"How do you get around in Los Angeles?"

"Drivers, friends, taxis."

Being dependent on others to get around is not something I could tolerate. I got my license the minute I turned sixteen. "Why now?"

"Things are different with this job. I'm not 'the talent' so the budget isn't there for me to have a driver past pre-production. I'm hoping driving here will be easier than it would be in LA."

An image of Lukas driving a car pops into my head, from some stupid movie he was in. "But I've seen you drive. On TV, I mean."

"You watch me on TV?"

Glancing in the mirror again, I'm surprised by the sheepish grin on his face. I can tell it's real, because it's much more endearing than what I've seen him employ on TV.

I shrug, not willing to stroke the guy's ego. "Not on purpose. I can't help it if you show up on the screen when I click the remote." Not that I change the channel, but I'll never admit that.

"In any case," he begins, like he's got my number, "what you saw was me behind the wheel of a process car."

"Right. Of course." I may not work directly on sets like my buddies Sully and Ford, but I have seen the setup where the camera is mounted on a vehicle that tows the car the actors pretend to be driving.

"I know it's a lot to ask," he says.

"Why not go to a driving school? Don't you want to learn from an expert?"

"You're a professional driver. Can't get more expert than that."

"I'm not trained to teach driving, just to get you from point A to point B safely." I mean, I've taught most of my younger siblings and half my cousins to drive, but still.

"It's more that… I trust you, Danielle."

His rental is downtown, much closer to the studio than he'd be at the beach. In fact, I'm pulling into the driveway when he says this. The sincerity in his tone has me forgetting what I'm doing momentarily, and I almost take out the mailbox. Pulling my attention back to the thing I'm supposedly so good at, I steer carefully up the slight hill, put the car in park, and set the emergency break before speaking. "You trust me? Why?"

I turn to face him, and my heart clenches when I see that he's got his arms around his little dog, like they're comforting each other.

Despite all my claims otherwise, I'm a sucker for a creature in need. And he seems to need this from me. Like, really need.

He hasn't answered my question, and his attention is elsewhere. Not just out the window, but somewhere deep inside. Neither of us says anything until Peanut breaks the spell with a whine from the back seat.

When Lukas doesn't move, I say, "Your dog might need a tree to pee on."

At my words, the man literally shakes himself back from wherever he'd retreated. "Right. Sorry."

He shifts to grab his messenger bag, and I catch a whiff of his scent. Some of my clients fill the car with heavy colognes and perfumes that take forever to clear out, even by driving along the water with the windows open. But his has always been refreshing. Clean and sharp, somehow. Like he doesn't tolerate any softness. That, I appreciate about the man.

"Dani?"

His voice brings me back to earth. "Uh, yeah? When do you want a pickup?"

"Does eight work? I've got meetings all day."

"Sure. That's fine."

"But that's not what I was saying."

When I meet his gaze, he's got that look again. That honest-to-god-I'm-up-shit's-creek-without-a-paddle look. "Please think about the driving thing? I'd do anything in return."

I nod, promising that I'll think about it, but even as the words leave my mouth, I get what seems like the best *and* worst idea in the entire world.

CHAPTER THREE

DANI

Lukas hits the ground running with his new job, even though *Lawson's Reach* is still in pre-production. His days aren't quite as long as they will be once primary shooting begins, but for the first two days, I pick him up at eight in the morning and he doesn't request a ride home until eight at night. I don't see him in between those hours until Thursday, when I take the show's department leads on a tour of potential exterior and interior locations.

A teamster drives us in a passenger van, and it's kind of weird being in a vehicle with Lukas when I'm not at the wheel. It does give me time to observe him, however. His trademark boyish charm seems to work about as well on the two women in charge—Helen, the line producer, or Glenda, the production coordinator—as it does on me.

That is, it doesn't.

Between the two of them, they question every single point he tries to make and literally bat away his attempts to open doors or precede him inside a building. After a few hours of this, I almost feel sorry for the guy. Not that I blame Helen and crew for being suspicious. You never know what you're going to get when an actor decides he wants to direct. Or a showrunner hires his friend to be a producer. With Lukas, we've got both in one handsome, but potentially useless, package.

I don't have time to dwell on all that, however, as it's my job to answer questions about each property. When I don't have answers, I make notes in my trusty planner so I can find them. To Lukas's credit, he's the one coming up with the most perceptive questions as well as thoughtful ideas for solutions.

I got into this work as a fluke after I started working on movies as a PA. My family life prepared me well for being asked to do all manner of ridiculous errands, being yelled at for no good reason, and having to cater to whiny brats. When I managed to regularly get an actress with a wee bit of a coke problem to set on time—basically, I treated her like a toddler—my reputation as a reliable, discreet driver was established.

The thing I've always loved most about driving movie people around is sharing Wallington with them—the places that most tourists don't know about or appreciate because they're not easy to get to. Like the restaurants too far away from the riverfront to walk to, or the quieter north end of Wrightsboro Beach. When a director I was driving suggested I'd be a good location scout, I found my calling.

It's not just my knowledge of and passion for Wallington and the surrounding countryside that makes me a natural for the work. My family is so big and has been here so long—as in, since we stole it from the Native Americans—I either know everybody in town or know someone who does. Which helps when you're trying to convince someone that it's a good idea to let a film crew take over their home for sixteen hours a day.

I love the work, but after a full day of touring the city and dealing with every department's concerns—whether it's a permit issue, or can we film in this neighborhood after ten at night, or where are we going to put base camp—I'm exhausted.

Unfortunately, I'm pulling double duty right now, so when we get back to the studio, I still have to drive Lukas back to his place. He wants to check his messages and emails, so I grab a quick dinner from catering and then stop by my desk in the production office to do the same. My brain enjoys ticking items off a to-do list and folding sticky notes over when tasks are completed, but this evening, I'm distracted by an idea—what is likely a really dumb idea—that won't seem to stay in the back corner of my brain where I shoved it.

Lukas hasn't mentioned the driving lessons again, but I can't stop thinking that we could trade services. He's an actor, after all. I'm sure he could manage to pretend to be in love with me for the length of a doctor's appointment. Still, when he pages me an hour later, and I swing by his office, I can't quite make myself say the words. Instead, a detail tickles the back of my brain. Something I noticed today for the first time. Once we pull out of the studio lot, I ask, "Hey, so what's with the different name on the call sheet?"

Peanut grunts when Lukas stops scratching behind his ears. "Oh, that's actually my real name. Whoever cast me in my first gig deemed Zelazny too difficult to pronounce, so they used my mom's maiden name instead. When my brother started working, they did the same thing. Thomas Keith is really Tomasz Zelazny."

"But you're listed as *Luke* Zela… well, I guess they were right," I say with a nervous laugh. "I can't get through that name myself."

"Zhuh-laz-nee," he says slowly. "It's easy once you get used to it."

"Says you. Not sure this American hick can do it."

"I'm sure you could get your mouth around it eventually."

Batting aside the thought that he's got other things I'd like to get my mouth around, I school my brain back to my original question. "But your first name—do you prefer Luke or Lukas?"

"My friends call me Luke," he says.

This puts me in my place I suppose, so I don't ask any more stupid questions. After I pull up in front of his rental, though, he doesn't move to get out of the car. He leans forward and asks, "Have you thought about it? Teaching me to drive?"

"I have," I begin, stretching out the vowels of the word as I wonder whether what I'm going to ask in return is insane.

"Seriously, Dani. Your competence is impressive. Anything you take on, you do it well. Handling a car, a dog, that homeowner who forgot we were coming today... I want to be you when I grow up."

When I roll my eyes at this, he lets out a sigh. "You know I need to learn. And I trust you. I mean, I know you won't take any shit. You'll just... get me through it."

I open my mouth, but before I can ask for what I want in return, he adds, "I'll pay you whatever you want."

Finally, I turn to face him. "That's the thing. I'm wondering if you'd trade the favor for another favor."

He nods rapidly. "Sure, anything you need."

LUKE

When Dani tells me what she wants from me in return for teaching me to drive, I can't help it. I groan. Loudly.

"Jesus," she says. "Way to make a girl feel like a joke. Forget I asked."

I shake my head, but I can't look her in the eye. "It's not you. It's me."

"Yeah. I've heard that before."

At her defeated tone, I sit up and place a hand on her arm.

When she flinches away, I retreat. "I'm sorry. I really am. It's … I can't explain why, but this is really… ironic."

She scrapes long fingers through her hair, which waterfalls right back into place. Any actress would kill for its natural texture and shine. Not to mention the way it frames her eyes.

Good thing she doesn't much like me, or I'd be tempted to take her offer seriously.

But, like the woman who's as much my sister as my biological one, she only needs me for one thing. To be her fake fiancé.

Which is just more evidence that my life is more fake than real. I even played a character in the transpo van today. Doing so served to keep my brain off the fact that I was in a motor vehicle, but the flirty rogue character fell flat with the female colleagues I was trying to impress.

Before I get sucked into that quicksand, I make myself focus on the woman in front of me. Like Kellie, Dani is super independent. She likely wouldn't ask if she didn't truly need my help. And as I've learned over the years of showmancing Kellie, I'm much better at pretending to be in love than I am at the real thing.

Still, an actor needs to know his motivation. "Can I ask why you'd need me to pretend to be your fiancé?"

When she just stares ahead, I'm pretty sure it's not because she's counting the number of gnomes decorating the pathway leading to the guesthouse production's renting for me. I could tell her that they number twenty-two, because I counted them yesterday while waiting for Peanut to do his business. Speaking of the devil, he's squirming like he needs to go right now.

"I really would like to know. But the dog—"

Before I can finish, she opens the driver's side door with a groan—she groans, not the vehicle—exits the car, and shoves her hands in her pockets.

After clipping the leash on the dog, I do the same. Peanut

sniffs around, looking for the absolute perfect place to pee. He's afraid to get too far from me and I don't want to drift too far away from the woman leaning against the car, arms crossed over her chest. Her serene, I've-got-everything-together mask is cracking, and I don't want to miss a peek beneath it.

Just when I think she's not actually going to tell me, she says something in a voice so soft I can't quite catch it. Pulling Peanut with me as I move closer to her, I ask, "Were you talking to me?"

When she meets my gaze, hers is so full of anger, I instinctively step back again. "I *said*, I want to get my tubes tied, but no doctor will do it until I'm thirty or married. Preferably both. I'm twenty-nine, so I'm hoping that if I show up with a fiancé, that'll be enough."

"You just need me to go to a doctor's appointment with you?"

"And pretend to be my soon-to-be husband who definitely doesn't want kids."

"That seems ridiculous in this day and age."

Her eyes flare. "That I don't want kids?"

"No, of course not. I don't really want kids either. What I can't believe is that in this day and age you'd need permission from your husband."

"Tell me about it." She kicks a pebble the way she'd probably like to kick her doctor's shins. "Their argument is that the procedure is not reversible, and they don't want me to have regrets. They just keep saying, *But what if you meet the man of your dreams and he wants kids?* They don't seem to get that the man of my dreams wouldn't want kids either."

It's possible the doctor is trying to protect her from a decision she'd regret, but it's more likely he's protecting himself from a lawsuit. But then it hits me. She's talking about more than one of them. "You keep saying *they*. How many doctors have you discussed this with?"

"Six. And I pay a hundred bucks to get the same answer every time. Plus, another hundred and fifty for the shrink I paid to write a letter attesting to my mental fitness. Not that it made any difference."

"Why does it cost so much to see the doctor?"

"I don't know. That's what it costs."

"Health insurance won't cover it?"

"I don't have insurance."

"What about the union?"

She shakes her head. "I'm a PA. I get a decent hourly rate because I've been doing it so long, but I haven't been able to join the union. North Carolina's a right-to-work state, so productions who come here use that to their advantage."

Peanut yelps at something under a bush before hiding behind me. "Hey, it's okay, bud."

After moving him to my side so I don't trip over him, I give him a few soothing pats as I consider her request. One thing's for sure: I'm not going to accidentally fall in love with a woman who has no interest in me *again*.

When I turn my attention back to Dani, the anguish on her face as she stares into the darkness is so out of character, my decision is made for me. I can't resist a damsel in distress. "Okay."

Her head jerks up. "Okay, you'll do it?"

"Sure," I say with a shrug. "One acting job at a doctor's office in exchange for driving lessons? I think you're getting the raw end of the deal."

DANI

When he says yes so quickly, I hold up a hand to stop him before he can slink off into the night with the dog that he is, admittedly, better at taking care of than I expected. "Just to be clear, this doesn't involve any hanky-panky."

He makes a pouty face. "You don't find me attractive?"

I roll my eyes. Actors are so damn needy. "Of course, you're attractive. It's been documented in a bazillion fan magazines."

"But do *you* find me attractive?"

"Why do you care? I'm asking you to pretend to be my fiancé for a gynecological appointment. Not a sexy situation."

"I find *you* attractive."

"Fine, you're attractive. But that's not relevant. We don't have to have any contact other than what's necessary to convince a doctor that we're in love."

"Along with whoever works at that doctor's office."

"Yeah, yeah. But not the general public. I'm not going to play the role of your rebound girlfriend. I don't want to get death threats in the mail because I'm the girl that broke up Loolie. That would be a disaster."

He shudders. "Man, I hate that portmanteau."

"What's a portmanteau?"

"When two names get combined into one. Like Lukas and Kellie into Loolie."

"Huh. I thought it was called a supercouple nickname."

"Either way, I hate it."

"What you think about it doesn't really matter, does it? It's a fact of your life." I narrow my eyes at him, now suspicious of his easy consent. "You're not going to use this as an opportunity to make her jealous and gin things up for your career, are you?"

He tips his head to the side. "Do you really think I'm the kind of guy who would do that?"

"How am I supposed to know? I hardly know you."

"We spent hours in the same car together two years ago."

"During which you probably spoke about ten words to me."

"You were hardly a chatterbox yourself."

"If you'd wanted to talk, I would've talked. But you hid behind a script and made the AD arrange your pickups."

He turns to stare off into the dark of the backyard, frowning. After a few long moments, he shoves his hair out of his face and blows out a breath. "Fair enough. I'm sorry if I was rude then. I was going through a shitty time."

He swivels his gaze back to me, and I suddenly remember the moment when he said goodbye two years ago. The intensity of it. "It's fine. You weren't there to entertain me."

"In any case," he says, in a voice so low and growly I'm not sure if I want to get closer to hear better or run far, far away, "I would never use you to try to 'gin up my career.' First off, I quit that career. Second, I may be an asshole, but I'm not that big of an asshole."

Before I can apologize for insulting him, he continues. "Anyway, I have more incentive to keep it a secret. Brothers Werner just sent down a Morality Memo, forbidding"—he pauses to make air quotes—"'fraternization between employees.'"

"What does that mean, exactly?"

"Fraternization?"

"I'm pretty sure I know what the *word* means. No screwing around with the boss." Which makes me wonder how Helen O'Neill and my friend Sully are dealing with it. She's not his direct superior anymore, but they do work together. "My question is, what would that mean for our fake relationship?"

"They don't want scandals, is what it means. They don't want anybody associated with their shows in the tabloids. I was given direct orders to—" He breaks off mid-sentence.

"To what?"

He shakes his head. "Nothing."

"Uh-uh. None of that." I cross my arms. "If we're going to do this, we need to be straight with each other."

He mirrors me. "You're the one who asked me to pretend to date you."

"After you said you'd do anything if I'd teach you to drive. And it's pretend to be my fiancé. Not just dating. We have to be planning a wedding."

After a long narrowed-eye glare, he drops his arms. "Fine. But what I'm about to tell you is just between us."

"Guess there's going to be a lot of that."

He steps closer again. "My boss, Max, the new showrunner, has asked me to try and diffuse some of the relationship drama between the cast members."

This, at least, makes sense to me. "There were a couple days at the end of last season when a certain actor wouldn't come out of his trailer for hours. And I heard there was some hair-pulling in the makeup trailer between two actresses."

His brow furrows. "How do you know this?"

"People tell me stuff. But back to our deal. We're agreed that it stays a secret?"

"Yes, and to be extra clear, at the doctor's office, the *fake* part of it is a secret. But outside the doctor's, the *existence* of the fake engagement should be a secret. I may not be an A-lister anymore, but I can't risk any kind of scandal showing up in the entertainment news."

"Agreed."

"We tell no one? No family or friends, right?"

"We tell no one outside of the gynecologist's office," I confirm, and to seal the deal, I hold out my hand for him to shake it.

When his large, warm palm grasps mine, I'm struck with a tiny tingle of disappointment. Which is ridiculous. Like a real relationship could ever work between someone like me and someone like him.

I squeeze his hand hard before releasing it to salute him. "See you bright and early tomorrow."

And then I hightail it to my car before I get any other crazy ideas.

CHAPTER FOUR

LUKE

I'm not sure what's got me more agitated, facing my driving phobia or facing another day like today, where everywhere I turned, people were questioning my right to be there. I could practically hear them thinking, *How did we get saddled with a producing director who's nothing but a washed-up actor?*

If they're not, they should be, because I'm wondering that myself. Even though I'm a member of the DGA and have directed episodes of other one-hour TV dramas, I wormed my way into those jobs—like I did this one—because I knew somebody.

It's not like I'd rather be on the other side of the camera. I was ready to quit acting when the ten-year run of *Our House* ended. I was happy to spend the last two years of high school at a boarding school in Ojai and four years on the east coast studying history in college. What I didn't love was spending summers doing movies, because every role was just another version of my character from *Our House*. The cheeky, no-filter guy. Problem is, that didn't go over as well as a nineteen-year-old as it did when I was ten. And at thirty? Without actual acting training under my belt—something I have no interest in pursuing—no one's buying it.

Least of all me. It may have taken me almost two years to pull the plug on acting, but the moment I finally did, all I felt was relief.

In contrast, I truly love directing. The combination of keeping an eye on the big picture while managing every detail feels like it uses every part of my brain. But I didn't exactly study it in school, either. Ironically, it seems I'm stuck with an acting job after all. Playing the role of the guy in charge.

Meanwhile, pretending to be Dani's fake fiancé is barely a blip on the worry radar. It's a pretty sad state of affairs when a guy is more comfortable pretending at life than he is actually living it.

There's only one person who can talk me down when I'm crawling the anxiety walls, and that's the person who's been through everything with me.

She picks up on the first ring and starts right in. "You don't call, you don't write, what kind of fake boyfriend are you?" Before I can come up with an excuse for avoiding her calls she asks, "How's it all going? How's the job? How's Peanut? Do you love him?"

"I miss you" is all I can manage. Just the sound of her voice has my throat clogged with emotion and has me wishing I were back where I could walk to Kellie's house from my own and lie on her couch to complain.

"Poor little Richie Rich," she says in response, her tone an even mix of sympathy and mockery.

"Yeah, yeah, yeah. I know things could be much worse. It's just—everything's harder than I thought it would be."

"Peanut too?"

I look down at the little guy next to me on the couch, pressed into my side. "We're getting used to each other."

"Chiweenies are the best. I mean, they're not good with little kids, but you don't have to worry about that."

Kellie, an animal lover to the core, is convinced that Peanut is a Dachshund-Chihuahua mix, also known as a Choxie or a Doxihuahua. It seems to fit. His spine is long in proportion to his short legs, while his nose is pointy. His ears seem like a combo of both breeds, not quite erect but not fully floppy either. In fact, half the time he's got one up and one down, which my assistants love to document with Polaroids.

While I've never had a pet—as a kid or an adult—Kellie and her partner Janette have a houseful of them, all rescues of one kind or another. They're on boards of a few animal rights groups, including the one that rescued Peanut from truly disgusting conditions. His previous owner apparently collected everything from magazines to dogs and cats.

By the time I got him, he was physically healthier, but still wary of the outdoors and strangers. I don't know why Kellie thinks we'll be good for each other, but what was I going to say? *I don't want to provide a home for this poor creature in need?*

When I don't say more, she adds, "You have to give him time. He doesn't know how to be a dog."

"It's not like I know how to be a dog owner."

"You'll figure it out together."

"Hopefully. I had to beg to get housing that would allow me to have a dog. But he likes going to the office. My two PAs make a big fuss over him."

"The breed is very adaptable. All you have to do is give him lots of love, and he'll be your loyal buddy."

"I could use someone on my side. Seriously, Kel, I don't know what I was thinking taking on this job."

"Why? Did something happen?"

"I don't know what the fuck I'm doing. And I think the rest of the crew knows it."

"Oh, Loo." The nickname is as ridiculous for a thirty-year-old man as it was for a ten-year-old boy, but she's earned the use of it. "Nobody knows what they're doing except the guys running the equipment. You know the old saying: directing is like sex, you can only learn by doing it. And besides, you pervert, you hung around watching other guys do it for years."

She's kidding with the pervert thing, but I'm sure many would agree on the label, if they believe everything they read about me and my sex life. Especially when I've been caught "cheating" on my "girlfriend."

"Yeah, but *producing* director," I grumble. "People keep pointing out that the show never had one before."

"So why does it need one now?"

"*Lawson's Reach* has had its share of drama, both on and off the set. You've heard about the revolving door of showrunners, but there's also been infighting among the top-of-show cast."

"Yikes. Sounds like you're stepping into a hornet's nest."

"Yeah. According to Max, he needs to know what's happening on the ground. It's my job to sniff out any shenani-gans, do damage control, and keep him in the loop."

"Shenanigans? Like cast members sleeping together?"

"Yeah, but also power struggles. You know how it is. Who's got the bigger trailer, the swankier rental house, who's higher on the call sheet. I'm sure it's all made worse by the fact that these kids went from nobodies to stars in a matter of months. They shot the first thirteen episodes before anything hit the air. But for the back nine, they're suddenly on the cover of every magazine from *Vanity Fair* to *Teen Beat*."

"Well, that's something you know a little bit about. Maybe you could be a mentor to them."

"Yeah, maybe." Doing this job is going to be like trying to hold Jell-O in my hands, but just saying this stuff out loud to my best friend makes it feel less impossible.

Barking on her end of the line is followed by a human

voice. "Hang on, Luke," she says, before engaging in a muffled conversation.

I take the time to get up and grab myself a beer from the refrigerator. It's not stocked like it would be if I were one of the show's stars, but Dani took me on a quick grocery run during our lunch break today so I could pick up some basics.

Peanut follows me into the kitchen, and I check his water and give him a treat, which he takes to his dog bed to enjoy. By the time Kellie returns to the conversation, I'm settled back onto the sofa with my feet on the coffee table.

"Sorry about that," she says. "What else is going on?"

I should probably tell her about the trade Dani and I are planning to make, but I don't want to get into the driving thing right now. "You don't think I have enough on my plate?"

"I think you have the perfect number of things on your plate. A job that'll challenge you in ways that you'll like, and a dog to talk to when you're buggin' out."

"You mean when I can't get you on the phone?"

"Exactly."

"Thanks for listening to my whiny bullshit."

"Anytime, brother."

"Love you, Kel."

"Love you, Loo."

After I hang up, I notice that Peanut has found his way next to my side again. Talking with Kellie always makes me feel more like a real boy and less like Pinocchio who can't escape the circus, but even our relationship is a fucked-up one. Maybe having a dog who needs me as much as I need him is a good thing.

The next morning, I start to get into the back with Peanut like I normally would, but then think better of it. If I'm going to try driving, I should practice riding in the front first. Dani seems surprised but not perturbed by the request, so I try another one.

"How come you don't play music in the car?"

She shrugs. "I only do it when a client asks, and you never asked."

Listening to music is one of the tools I use to calm my fears, so I ask. "Can we put something on?"

"Of course," she answers, her tone brisk and professional, as she opens the console between the two front seats and pulls out a CD organizer. "There's a little bit of everything in there, from classical to hip-hop. No country western, though."

I flip through quickly and pull out one she's labeled 1997 Mix, curious what she would've been playing if I'd asked two years ago. The Verve's "Bittersweet Symphony" blasts through the speakers, and Dani quickly turns down the volume before dropping her planner in my lap and putting the car in reverse. When she puts her arm across the back of my seat and twists her upper body so that she can see out the back window as we back down the driveway, it's my intention to immerse myself in all the little things she's doing to operate the vehicle, to put myself in that seat in my imagination as a first step toward driving again, but I can't quite get past studying *her*.

If she were interested, I'd hook her up with my agent. She's kind of like a mix between Winona Ryder and that girl who plays Jackie in *That '70s Show*—Mila Kunis, I think her name is. Probably too guarded to get into acting without a great deal of work to process whatever it is she hides behind that mask, but I can picture her splashed across the front of a fashion magazine. Her long limbs and slim frame are perfect for the runway.

And she's got the bone structure: straight nose, full mouth, and fashionably unfussy brows. Eyes that reveal so little, when you actually catch a flash of humor or softening of empathy, you feel like you've won the lottery.

"Get what you needed?"

Those eyes lasered at me would make a lesser man shrink away, but I've seen worse. "Just studying your technique."

"Here. You can take notes." She grabs a notebook from an organizer attached to the dash and tosses it in my lap before shifting the car into drive. "But it's the schedule I need you to look over. I'm pretty sure I've got all your appointments on there. Please confirm, so I can schedule a doctor's appointment as well as slot in your driving lessons."

When I open the datebook, I have to laugh. "I guess you liked the colored Post-it Notes."

It's customary to tip your driver at the end of the job, as well as give them a bottle of wine or other token gift, but I didn't want to give Dani something generic. The woman had barely cracked a smile for the six weeks she'd ferried me all over town, and I was determined to get some kind of reaction from her.

I was pretty sure I'd scored with the sticky notes, but it's nice to see she actually uses them. Glancing over at her now, I'm rewarded with what looks like a blush, as well as a repeat of the genuine smile I got when she opened that parting gift. It's fleeting, however, just like the last time. At the next stoplight, she's all business as she taps the planner in my lap.

"*All* the greens are you. Dark greens are for the show, light greens are proposed driving lessons."

"How come you wrote Lukas on all these?"

She darts an exasperated glance at me. "Because that's your name?"

"But I told you that my friends call me Luke."

Her brow furrows slightly, so I ask, "Are we not friends?"

"I'll call you Luke if you want me to." She shrugs, but I swear I see a crack in her stoic facade, which feels like a win somehow.

"I want you to call me Luke."

"Now that we have that decided," she says, back to business again, "If you know of any other commitments, please add them so I can make that appointment and we can get this over with."

I pull out my Filofax to do as instructed, but even as I flick through the sticky notes and compare the dates and times to the crossed-out changes in my own messy planner, I'm thinking of ways to breach those walls of hers again.

And then I've got it. Making sure that her eyes are on the road, I sneak a sticky note from her stash and write her a note before closing the planner and setting it on the console between our seats. "Everything seems to be in here, but don't forget, I'm directing the first episode, and for that week and a half, I'll be lucky to find time to breathe."

"Oh, that reminds me. I saw Nate Fowler from Carolina Casting yesterday, and he asked if I knew when you'd be available for producer callbacks for a bunch of day player roles. I told him today at eleven. Don't worry, it's confirmed with your PA."

"Then I guess that's what's happening." I close my planner. "You just tell me where to be and what to do when I get there."

"Smart man." Her tone is gruff, but I catch what looks like a satisfied grin on her face.

By the time she parks the car in front of the production offices, both her expression and tone are free of any emotion. I'm out of the car when she adds, "All your morning meetings are at the studio, so I'll be back at two for the driving lesson. If I can get an appointment with a doctor, we'll do that afterward."

CHAPTER FIVE

DANI

Lukas—I mean, Luke—looks a little worse for wear when I pick him up at two, like he needs to sit on the beach with a beer instead of get behind the wheel of a car. I get that making a movie is stressful, no matter which side of the camera you're on. Usually, I don't mind hearing the people I drive complain or express their worries. But he and I never had that relationship. He ignored me, and I did my best to avoid blurting out that I was obsessed with him as a teenager.

If I'm being honest, I may have been less friendly than I normally would be, to keep myself from saying something stupid like *I practiced kissing with a photo of you from* Teen Beat.

To the point that my lips were regularly ink-stained in eighth grade.

Anyway, now we have things to get done, like learning to drive and pretending to be in love, and I'm only an expert in the former. Thankful that's first on the agenda, I stop him when he goes for the passenger side door.

"Uh-uh, mister. You're driving. Despite what your note said."

After I dropped him off this morning, I opened my

planner to find a sticky note with the message, in what I assume is his handwriting, saying, *Good luck with the driving practice today. I hear that guy's a jerk and an idiot. But if anyone can do it, you can.*

Instead of the cheeky grin I expect, he looks like he's ready to bolt. "Oh, no. I can't just… drive. On… streets. I need to be somewhere safe. Like, away from other cars and stuff."

When he asked for driving lessons, I assumed he meant that he needed a refresher, someone to remind him of the laws so he wouldn't fail a test. "Are you saying you don't know how to drive at all?"

"It's… complicated." In the space between two words, his expression shifts from fear to irritation to something like resignation. "But trust me. I can't just hop in your car and drive somewhere."

I learned how to drive a tractor when I was fourteen, on my great-grandparents' strawberry farms north of Wallington. But most kids' first experience is in the high school parking lot, so that's where I take him. Football and marching band practice won't start up for another couple weeks, so there's plenty of open space to work with. Still, when I park the car but leave the engine running, Luke's still looking pretty worried.

Whatever he's worried about, the only way out is through. "Time to switch seats."

But when I circle to the passenger side, he hasn't moved. Instead, he's lost somewhere deep inside his own head again. "Lukas. I mean, Luke. Time's a-wastin'. Let's go."

He shudders slightly, and then scrubs hands over his face. "Yeah, right. Let's do this."

Once he's in the driver's seat, he grips the steering wheel like it can't be trusted. His Adam's apple jerks, and his jaw clenches so tightly that a vein throbs in his temple.

When he doesn't move his hands or his feet, I begin to give him directions, speaking like I'm talking to a spooked horse. "Okay, first thing you do is put your right foot on the brake, then you shift into drive, then you move your foot over to the gas and gradually depress it."

"I know what to do, Dani," he snaps. "I'm not an imbecile."

I can't suppress the enormous sigh that heaves out of my chest. "I have no idea what you know and don't know, Luke. Maybe you should enlighten me, so I know what to teach you."

His forehead drops onto the steering wheel, his eyes squeezed tight. Just when I'm wondering if this is as far as we're going to get, he sits up abruptly, shifts into gear, and pulls out of the parking space. There's a sheen of sweat on his forehead, and he's still hanging on to the wheel like it might run away, but he does all the things in the right order. When he gets to the end of the row of empty spaces, he stops the car and looks both ways as if we aren't the only car in the entire lot. Then he steers out of the lane and into the next one.

He weaves up and down every single aisle of the empty lot, breath shallow, leaning forward in his seat. If he wants to tell me what makes him act this way, I'm all ears. Otherwise, I guess I'll just sit here and let him do what he needs to do.

Eventually, he returns to the space where we'd started, puts the car in park, and sits back, breathing hard, looking a little green around the gills. When he turns to face me, what I see in his eyes makes my heart squeeze in sympathy: shame.

I don't want him to know I saw it, so I jump out of the car. "Good enough for today. Let's get this gyno appointment over with."

LUKE

Driving practice was somehow as horrible as I imagined it would be and not as bad as it could've been. I'm sure I looked like a total freak as the car crawled around an empty parking lot, but I didn't pass out, so I guess that's a win.

I don't know what Dani thought was going on in my head, but her silence and her steady presence got me through it. I hated the look of pity I caught on her face after I parked the car, but I guess I deserve it. Not too many full-grown men are afraid to drive a car.

After Dani takes the wheel again, I ask if I can turn the stereo on, but music isn't going to be enough to shift my mental gears. Casting about for something else to focus on, I remember an idea I'd had in the middle of the night. "Hey, want to try something that'll make us seem more like a couple?"

She coughs, like saliva went down the wrong pipe.

"Don't worry," I add. "I'm not suggesting anything physical."

She clears her throat before asking, "What *are* you suggesting?"

"There's this game the AD used to play with the kid actors on *Our House*. It's called Two Truths and a Lie."

She shoots me a quick eyebrow raise. "And this would be helpful how?"

"He said it would help us figure out how to make something that wasn't true believable."

"Sounds like a dangerous thing to teach a kid."

I can't help but smile, thinking about the pranks I got away with on that set. I was lucky the show was so successful, or I'm sure I'd have been fired twelve times over. But then I really think about what she's saying. There's got to be a reason she doesn't want kids. A big enough reason that she's gone to all this trouble and spent so much money. So, I throw her a bone. "Yeah, in my experience, most kids are little shits."

She doesn't pile on. Instead, she seems to really consider the statement. "I don't know about that, but I guess it'd be good for a parent to know which of their kids was a talented liar. I should share it with my sisters. Three of them have a handful of kids that are, well, handfuls."

Appreciating this rare release of detail, I add, "My point is, I think for us it could be a good way to get to know each other—our backstories, in case we need to sell the relationship—but also for us to practice lying about what's going on between us."

"Okay. How do you play?"

"It's pretty simple. You tell me three things, two of them true and one not true. I do the same. Then we each try to guess what the other person is lying about."

"What does the winner get?"

"I think we used to play for an extra visit to craft service, but If you need more motivation we could—"

She cuts me off with an impatient wave. "Actually, forget it. I've got plenty of motivation."

"Okay, then. Do you want to start, or me?"

"Does it have to be, like, a big momentous thing?"

"For our purposes, it's more about being comfortable with each other. I suppose it can be mundane stuff."

She bites her lip for a moment and then asks, "Can you go first? I'm still not exactly clear on how it should go."

"Sure, no problem. But give me a minute to think of the three things."

"Good point. I'll do the same. But don't take too long— we're only about five minutes away from the doctor's office."

When I've got my two truths and lie straight in my mind, I ask if she's ready. At her nod, I begin. "Number one: I have four best guy friends that I've known since high school. Number two: my mother is my agent. And number three: I get along better with my sister than my brother."

"Because of the competition?" she asks.

"Uh, what do you mean?"

"You get along better with your sister because you and your brother are so often pitted against each other?"

I snort. "You're not supposed to psychoanalyze me, you're supposed to guess which is the lie."

She rolls her eyes. "Well, that was easy, duh. Your mom is your manager, not your agent."

"You know that?"

"It's in all the fan magazines," she says, a blush coloring her cheeks.

Wagging a finger at her, I say, "You can't trust anything in those. Except the fact that my mother is my manager." I cross my arms and lean back in my seat, a familiar feeling of uncertainty gnawing at me. "Was my delivery that bad?"

She shakes her head. "No, you just chose poorly. Anyone who follows your career knows all that stuff."

She follows my career? Interesting. "Okay, your turn."

"Hang on." After turning into a lot, she parks the car and turns off the engine. "Okay. Number one, I have four best friends that I've known since first grade. Two, I am twice as old as my youngest sibling. And three, I learned to drive when I was fourteen."

Her delivery is impressive. Direct, simple, and very difficult to read. But when I think through it again, I note that she emphasized the numbers in each statement, so I have a feeling she's lying slightly about one of them. If her mom had Dani in her late teens, she could easily have had the last fourteen years later. Sounds hellish to me, but maybe that's exactly why Dani doesn't want kids.

As for the other statements, learning to drive at fourteen is illegal, but we are in the south. When I comb through her delivery of her number one, though, I've got it.

"You *do* have four best friends, but you haven't known them since first grade."

Her jaw drops. "How did you guess?"

"First off, you emphasized the numbers in every sentence,

so that tipped me off. Then I went through the things that could be true, which was basically everything. But then I remembered that you hesitated slightly before saying 'first grade.'"

Eyes wide, she shakes her head slowly. "Jeez. That was harder than I thought."

"There's a reason people go to acting school."

When she slumps into her seat, almost literally deflating, I add, "Don't worry. We can keep practicing. And like I said, we only have to convince this one woman."

"Man. The doctor's a man."

As if she just remembered where we are and why, she sits up straight, her hands fisted in her lap and her face pale. We need to get into character, and she needs to relax, so I say, "Give me your hand."

Her jaw ticks with tension as she mutters, "We don't have to pretend until we get inside."

"Just give me your hand, woman."

"Why?"

"You're obviously nervous, so I'm going to show you a pressure point to massage that'll help ease your nerves."

She rolls her eyes but sticks out her hand. "Could you be more California, right now?"

Not taking the bait, I shift to face her and use both thumbs to smooth open her palm before gently pinching the webbing between her thumb and forefinger. "This is called the union valley."

When I apply pressure, she yelps. "Ow. That hurts."

"Because you're anxious. Close your eyes and take some deep breaths."

She huffs out a tiny breath but closes her eyes.

"Breath in on four, then out on six."

She literally growls at me.

"Humor me?"

As I count out the breathing pattern for her, her nostrils

flare on the inhales and her lips purse on the exhales. Forcing my attention away from that tempting mouth, I press into the webbing of her hand. When she tenses, I remind her to breathe. Massaging this spot is one of the things that helped me when I was afraid to even get into a car after the accident.

Too bad I can't do it while actually driving.

After a bit, I let her direct her own breathing, and I ask if I can touch her on the shoulder. She nods, her eyes still closed, and I squeeze the other anxiety pressure point, the shoulder well. When she winces with pain, I remind her to keep breathing.

I keep an eye on the time, breathing along with her, and when the hand on my watch ticks to two minutes before our appointment, I release her shoulder. "Time to go."

Her eyelids flutter open, and the expression of simple gratitude on her face feels like a gift. "How'd you know how to do that?"

"I've faced down a few fears of my own. However"—I wag a finger back and forth—"be careful with those points. Both of them can induce labor if a person is pregnant."

"If all goes well inside, I won't ever have to worry about that."

With that, she hops out of the car, and I have to jog to catch up with her. "I'm going to take your hand, okay?"

Her stride slows, and she looks like she's going to argue, but then she nods. "Right. Showtime."

"Don't forget. You have to pretend to at least like me."

"I'll keep that in mind," she shoots back, but the expression on her face shifts from amusement back to gratitude. "Listen, I really do appreciate you—"

I squeeze her hand, interrupting her. "Don't thank me until the curtain comes down."

A half hour later, after we've listened to the sixty-something doctor drone on about every detail of the tubal ligation procedure, he turns to me. "Once you're married, and you're still quite sure that you don't plan to have children, we can schedule the appointment."

I look over at Dani, wondering why the guy is talking to me.

"But we're sure now," she says.

I place a hand on her upper back and give it a fiancé-like rub before turning to face him, letting a bit of challenge enter my tone. "We're both sure."

"I don't understand why you'd want to go against God's will," the man persists. "Why don't you want to be parents?"

"Why didn't *you* become a dentist?" Dani asks him, less angry than I would be. "I simply have no interest in it."

"Which should be reason enough," I can't help but add.

Dani presses her knee to mine, and I shut up. She's right. No need to over-argue.

Instead of acknowledging her point, the doctor continues to focus solely on me. "You do understand that the tubal ligation is irreversible, while a vasectomy is. Have you talked to your urologist about that option?"

"I have." I may not be the best actor in the world, but I do have some practice at improvising. "And I'm considering that, but this is what Dani wants, and I fully support her."

He spares a fleeting glance at the woman whose choice he and I are discussing before addressing me. Again. "You may fax or mail in a copy of your marriage certificate, and then we'll put you on the schedule."

"But we're still, you know, in the planning stages," Dani argues. "It could be months."

"And we'll be here when you're ready," he says. "Now if you'll excuse me, I need to move on to my next patient."

It takes everything in me to bite back where I'd like to tell him to shove our marriage certificate. I don't want this guy's hands on any woman, let alone one I care about. Instead, I grind out, "Thanks for the information," and drag Dani out of the office.

My head's about to explode as Dani writes out a check for more than a hundred dollars to pay for this dick's so-called expertise. The minute we exit the building, I let it out. "I can't believe you let that asshole talk to you like that. Aren't there any female doctors you could go to?"

Her mouth presses into a thin line. "My regular gyno is a woman, but she knows that I'm not in a committed relationship, as do the other doctors I've visited. I figured going to a new one would be safer."

"Well, we're not going back to that guy."

"Wallington isn't LA, Luke."

"There's got to be one that won't treat you like... like you're my property or something. I don't want that guy touching you."

She raises a brow. "Do you really think that's your choice?"

I scrub both hands over my face. "Sorry. You're right. That guy... I'm sorry. Men are jerks."

This gets a laugh out of her. "Thank you for the global apology. And I have to admit that you're right. He doesn't look like the kind of guy that keeps up on the latest research."

Back at the car, she starts the engine and turns up the AC, but doesn't put it in gear. "Listen, Luke. You don't have to go through that again. It sounds like it won't work for us to pretend that we're going to get married."

When I open my mouth to argue, she adds, "And don't worry. I'll still help you with the driving. If you're sure that's what you want."

It's not what I want, but it's what I need. To work through my fears. And I'll owe Dani big if she helps me do that. "What do they say? In for a penny, in for a pound? Let's get married."

"Uh…" Her jaw literally drops. "I don't think anyone says that who doesn't live in England."

"Whatever. How much time do we have before I have to be somewhere?"

"Well, you've got the design team meeting in forty-five minutes."

"Let's go get the marriage license. Knock that out, and we can get hitched before the conference call with the west coast at the end of the day."

"But… don't you want to think about this first?"

"What, you don't think you could stand to be married to me for six months?"

Her cheeks flush almost instantly, even as she makes a scoffing sound. "It would be a trial, believe me. And it'd be a year. You have to wait a full year for a divorce after you file."

"Weird. It's six months in California. Anyway, maybe we could get it annulled or something."

"Even so, it seems like a lot."

"For you to get a medical procedure that affects you and you alone? I still can't believe you don't have a say over your own damn body." I don't care why she wants this procedure. It doesn't matter. She should get to make the choice.

"Believe me, I've been mad about it for years. But what can I do? Can't perform the surgery myself." She blows out a breath. "It's only a year till I'm thirty, though. One doctor said she might agree to do it for a single woman if she's thirty."

I stew in righteous indignation on her behalf for a few moments before saying, "Well, whether it's six months or a year, I'm happy to marry you. For the principle of the thing."

"I don't know." I can practically see her patching the walls that I'd begun to chip away at earlier. "If we're actually married, it'll be a lot harder to keep it a secret."

"We'd have to be careful when we actually go through the ceremony, but it's not like we're going to put our wedding photos in the paper. And we'd still only have to act married at a doctor's office."

"But you're Lukas Keith. If the fact that you're married gets out, that's news."

"Nobody cares about me anymore."

"Have you forgotten about the last time you were here?" When she smiles, I'm relieved to see it, even if it's at my expense. "When you went running on the beach and fans chased you until you agreed to give them your autograph?"

I can't help the shudder that runs through me. "I still have nightmares about that. Signing bare skin is weird."

"Poor little famous actor," she intones, just like Kellie would.

"I don't know why people think that's a good idea." I shake my head. "Anyway, that was the only time I got mobbed here. And since I quit acting, fewer people are interested in hearing about me."

Her brow furrows. "But what about Kellie?"

Ah, Kellie. My other fake girlfriend. What does it say about me that I'm so popular in this regard? That I'm incapable of a real relationship?

"It won't be a problem" is what I say out loud.

"Are you sure? I mean, if you need to have, like, conjugal visits with her—"

I have to act quickly to stifle a laugh. I wish I could tell Dani the truth about Kellie and me, but it wouldn't be right to do so without my other fake girlfriend's permission.

"Believe me, it'll be fine."

CHAPTER SIX

DANI

Friday's surprises churn through my thoughts, as well as my dreams, all weekend. It appears that Luke does know how to drive, but is afraid to do it for some reason, which means that we'll need a different approach. Something akin to exposure therapy is what I'm thinking. Little bites of driving here and there so that he can have positive experiences without getting overwhelmed.

That's the easy surprise to deal with.

Learning that I have to be actually married to get the tubal is much more problematic. Luke may think that it's no big deal, but it *is* a big deal. Not because I have some ideal wedding in mind. It just seems way too complicated and way too risky.

I've put off deciding what to do about that.

When I take Luke grocery shopping on Saturday, he seems preoccupied, and when I ask if he needs other transportation over the weekend, he says he'll be holed up working at his apartment. We get in two short drives in empty parking lots before and after errands, and he seems slightly less panicky each time, which supports my theory.

Monday morning, after driving Luke to work, I get some work done in the little cubicle set aside for me in the *Lawson's Reach* production offices. It's the biggest project I have right now, and it's nice to be able to use their office machines. There's a fax in my mailbox from the show's LA-based locations manager with new settings we need to find, so I add them to my spreadsheet. The exterior for a new family of characters is my main priority at the moment, however. So far, every option I've run up the flagpole has been shot down for one reason or another.

Flipping through the notebook I keep of homeowners who've filled out an interest form, I get an idea. The producers didn't request a waterfront location, probably because they want a contrast from the lead character's home, so I hadn't even checked that section of the notebook. But there's a place I vaguely remember that might work.

"Yes," I say to myself when I find the listing. Sleek and modern, it's nothing like Lawson's house with its white clapboard exterior and sprawling wraparound porch. Crossing my fingers, I chant as I dial the number, "Please be home, please be home."

Score. The guy's not only home, he's interested, and I make an appointment for twenty minutes from now. My luck continues when I find Luke in his office. "Wanna go for a ride?"

He looks at his watch, but before he can check his planner, I tell him, "We'll be back for your next meeting."

Without even asking where we're going, he gets up and precedes me through the door, telling the PA that he'll be back.

I explain the nature of our errand as I back out of my parking spot and steer the car toward the waterfront home. "I found a place that I think will work for the Petrie family characters, but we need to sign off on it quick. Production back in

LA wants someone higher up the chain to take a look. I figure you'll do."

"Sounds good."

"Also, this place is at the end of a long, straight road, so perfect for your next step."

"Next step?"

"Well, I've been thinking about your situation with driving. It reminds me of this actress I drove a few years ago, who had to overcome a dog phobia for a role. Her therapist used exposure therapy to help her overcome the fear. First, she imagined a dog, while doing some relaxation exercises, then looked at pictures of dogs, then watched dogs from a safe distance… it took some time, but now she even has a dog."

"I have done some work with a therapist. Cognitive Behavioral Therapy."

"Right. That's what she called it." I glance over quickly. Since he doesn't seem to be freaking out, I add, "I was thinking we could try something similar with your driving. You did okay in the parking lot, so next would be driving on a street, but one that's straight, with little traffic."

I glance over again, and it looks like he's struggling to swallow. "You okay?"

"I… I don't know if I'm ready for that."

"Okay, well, maybe you just imagine doing it for now."

LUKE

After touring the house she's found, I agree that the modern mini mansion is indeed perfect as a stand-in for the home of the new family that's joining the storyline, even though it's on the water like the one we use for Lawson's family house. Instead of a lawn sloping down to the water's edge and a dock, the angular steel and glass structure is nestled in a dense forest on the three sides not facing the intracoastal. The floor-to-ceiling windows front and back could be a challenge for lighting and sound with all the reflective surfaces, but the natural light may offset those issues.

Additionally, a neighbor has an empty field we can use, and the grocery store at the intersection with the main road has a lot we can use for crew parking.

The owner's primary residence is in Connecticut, plus he's going through a divorce and would appreciate the income. I told Dani I was good with her choice after the walkthrough, so she assures the guy that if we get the final okay from the west coast, she'll get contracts to him by the end of the week.

Walking back to the car, I say, "Nice job. That place ticks all the boxes."

Just as I'm wondering what a place like that goes for around here, Dani takes my hand and presses the car keys into my palm. When I tense up, she closes her fingers over mine. "Wax on, wax off, Luke."

I lift my eyes to meet hers, which, unbelievably, hold no judgment. "Why have you never asked what I'm so afraid of?"

"Probably for the same reason you haven't asked why I don't want kids."

I take in a deep breath, nodding, and then step away from her, telling myself that it's a quiet country road, not a super-highway. There isn't another car in sight.

And I'll be with Dani. Not a bunch of party-ready guys.

Putting one foot in front of the other, I get myself to the vehicle and into the driver's seat.

"Do you want music?" Dani asks, her voice soft.

"Sure. Maybe something from before 1996?" That way I won't be surprised by the song that was playing when the accident happened.

She pulls a CD and changes it out for the one already in the player. As Stone Temple Pilots' "Interstate Symphony" begins to play, I recognize the irony of the title as I focus on my breath as I adjust the mirrors. My hand's shaky as I slide the key into the ignition, but when the engine turns over, I'm able to shift into drive.

"You don't have to drive all the way to the main road. You can pull over to the side whenever you need to," she reassures me.

I can't quite get words out to answer her because it takes everything in me to press the accelerator. We crawl out of the gravel driveway, and when I stop the car before turning onto the actual road, Dani reminds me to breathe.

In and out, in and out. My body knows how to operate the vehicle. The accident wasn't due to poor driving. It was a fluke, a freaky thing.

Which could, theoretically, happen again. Anytime. Anywhere.

Not helping.

Somehow sensing that I need it, Dani whispers, "You've got this."

Nodding, glad there's no one else around, I accelerate like a grandma, but I do get the car moving.

Five miles per hour, ten, fifteen.

It's a straight shot to the busy road that runs north to south, parallel to the coast. There are no other cars around to worry about, but the minute the car goes over fifteen miles per hour, I suddenly get so dizzy it feels like I might pass out.

Before I can say that I don't think I can go further, Dani places a hand over mine on the steering wheel. "Slow down. You can pull over here."

After shakily maneuvering to the side of the road, I put the car in park. Flopping back into the driver's seat, I realize I must've been leaning forward like a little old man the entire time. But I'm grateful. Grateful to at least be taking steps toward the independence that being able to drive again will mean.

I turn to face Dani, to thank her. When I take in her expression full of compassion rather than pity, I wish she'd let me help her in return.

DANI

After we switch seats again and I begin to drive back to production, I turn down the volume on the stereo. "Could you tell me what exactly happens when you get behind the wheel? You don't have to tell me why you have the, uh, feelings you're feeling, but I think it'd be good for me to know, like, if I need to intervene."

He doesn't say anything for a long time. When he does, his voice—thready and higher-pitched—is almost unrecognizable. "My heart races, my palms get clammy, all the moisture leaves my mouth and turns into sweat. I get so tense that my muscles twitch."

"Do you get dizzy? Feel like you might pass out?"

"Sometimes."

Whoa. His body's reactions to driving are a carbon copy of my reactions to having sex.

Which makes me wonder: could that shrink be right? That it's not the fact that I'm afraid of getting pregnant that makes it impossible for me to enjoy intercourse? I'm technically not a virgin, but I've had a penis inside me only a handful of times, and the last time was so long ago I don't even remember the guy's name.

And it's not because of lack of desire. I want to do it, but no matter how hot and heavy things get, the minute a penis gets near my vagina, I have a hard time even staying in the room.

"Dani?"

"Yeah?"

"I said, do you not feel comfortable being in the car with me when I'm driving?"

"No, no, not at all." *Shit.* Not only have I been completely on autopilot as I operate the car, but I was so zoned out that I had no idea he was talking to me. "No, I was just thinking about—nothing, it doesn't matter."

"If it's something that might help, I want to hear it. Even if it's out there."

A weird little laugh barks out of me. "Ha-ha. Oh, no. That's not—forget it."

"Come on, Dani. I just told you that I'm so afraid of driving that I might pass out. It can't be worse than that."

"Oh yes, it can."

Catching a glimpse of his face out of the corner of my eye as he shifts in his seat to face me, I'm surprised by the level of anger in his expression. "You don't think it's embarrassing that a thirty-year-old man practically pisses himself when he gets behind the wheel of a car? Something any teenager can do?"

"Well, I assume you have a good reason."

"And I assume you have a good reason for not wanting to have kids."

My face heats, and I wish like hell I wasn't driving so I could hide it from him.

He shifts again, and the town car suddenly feels like it's the size of a Geo Metro. "Dani? Are you saying you have a similar fight-or-flight response when you think about having kids?"

There's something about his direct attention that makes me powerless to resist answering him. "Um, not exactly. Well, yes, but it's more, uh…"

"More when you're potentially making a kid?" he asks, in a voice as demanding as those eyes of his.

"Yeah," I say, my own voice now as unrecognizable as the

hoot of laughter that explodes from my mouth. "Ha-ha. Maybe I need exposure therapy too."

Before he can say anything, I add, "I'm kidding. You know I'm kidding, right?"

He doesn't answer that question. Instead, he asks, "Two Truths and a Lie?"

"Now?"

"Yeah. About why we're doing this. What we're afraid of. Me with the car, you with having kids."

"But I said you didn't have to go through with marrying me, so you don't really need to know why I don't want kids."

For a moment, it seems like he's hurt by my rejection, but then he shrugs it off.

"I'd like to tell you what happened to me, but I'm not supposed to talk about it. For legal reasons. But I figure if you guess…"

When he trails off, I get it. If I guess, he didn't exactly tell me. "Sneaky. Well, okay. Two Truths and a Lie. For your thing. We don't have to do mine."

"I'd still like to," he says. "In case you change your mind."

There's no way I'm sharing my sex issues with a man who's been one of *People*'s Sexiest Men Alive, but I am curious about the seeds of his driving phobia. "Whenever you're ready then."

He pushes his hair out of his face, a gesture I've noticed him do when he's trying to decide something. "You know what? I'm just going to tell you. You're not going to call *US* magazine or anything, which is the point of not talking about it."

He clears his throat and shifts in his seat, as if telling the story isn't easy. "Three years ago, I was driving friends to dinner in the usual crazy LA traffic. Meaning, five lanes going seventy miles an hour. We're on the far left when this wheel— tire and axle and all—comes flying over the median. Every-thing goes into slo-mo as this thing rotates through the air. I remember checking the rearview, the side mirrors. There was nowhere to go. I couldn't get out of its path. It slammed right into us, cratering the hood and smashing the windshield."

"What the fuck?"

When I glance over at him, he's staring straight ahead like he's watching it happen all over again, his face pale, his breathing shallow. "They said we were lucky because there wasn't a chain reaction. Still, I couldn't see a fucking thing because the windshield was this net of cracks, and the wheel was half in the car. I lowered the window and somehow the car got over to the side."

"Was everyone okay?"

"No one was fatally injured, but—"

When he breaks off and seems to struggle, I reach for his hand and press the spot he showed me, between the thumb and forefinger.

He closes his eyes tight. "One of my friends got hit with the axle. It sliced open his face from his nose to his ear."

"Was he… okay?" I whisper, my heart squeezing in pain for him and his friend.

He swallows audibly a few times before answering. "He survived, but his career didn't. He'd shot a pilot that had just gotten picked up. We were actually headed out to celebrate. He got plastic surgery, but it wasn't enough to save that job. And then he kind of spiraled out. We all did our best to help him, but he lost his mojo, I guess. When it came time for a settlement from the other guy's insurance, I had the idea that we get as much money as we could in exchange for our silence, and then give it all to him."

"What's he doing now?" I ask softly, as we pull into a parking spot.

"He actually works with my mom. He's a good manager." He turns to face me, and his pale-blue eyes are shiny. "But he was an amazing actor."

"Was everyone else okay?"

"Yeah, just bruises and whiplash. Tiny shards of glass they had to pull out of our skin."

"But you lost the ability to drive."

"I tried to drive soon after it happened, but I couldn't. I've talked to therapists, and now I have coping techniques I use when someone else is driving, but to this day, I avoid the highway, even as a passenger."

"What a freaky thing to happen."

"Apparently it isn't. All it takes is an overloaded aging vehicle hitting a big pothole." He gestures around the interior of the town car. "These things are weapons. Rolling death traps."

"And yet we've created a world where we're dependent on them. Unless you want to move to a little village somewhere and raise goats," I add, doing my best to bring a little levity to the moment.

"I'm in. Let's do that."

When he smiles at this idea, I'm ready to take off with him. Until he says, "Your turn."

"Oh. No. I mean, look, we're here. Back at the office."

"Are you really saying that you're not going to tell me your reasons?"

I point at his planner. "Yep, because you have an afternoon full of meetings."

"That I do." He narrows his eyes briefly before opening the car door and then pauses before getting out. "Thank you."

"For what?"

"For listening. And for putting up with my crap."

I wave that down. "Eh, everybody's got some form of crap. It's what makes life interesting."

CHAPTER SEVEN

LUKE

Despite the fact that I've got back-to-back meetings all day, I can't stop thinking about what happened in the car yesterday. Making progress on my driving was good. Getting behind Dani's walls felt even better. But learning that she's ashamed of something to do with her sex life, makes me sad. Then there's guilt, because I'm not holding up my end of our bargain.

Most ridiculous of all. I feel hurt, like I've been jilted.

How lame can I be? Ditched by yet another fake girlfriend.

At least she now knows that I'm not just a spoiled brat lucky enough to have a driver for most of his life.

Speaking of spoiled brats, the lead actors are back in town, and per Max's instructions, meeting with them is at the top of my to-do list. Realizing that I have an appointment set up with number one on the call sheet in a few minutes, I do my best to shake it all off and hustle back to my office.

Even though I haven't yet met the actor playing the title role, photos of Leif Nilsson cover the hallways outside my office, so I know that the guy's looks are as Nordic as his name. Tall, broad shoulders, cleft chin, blond hair styled a bit like mine.

The girls love him for his puppy dog eyes and bashful smile; the guys want to be him. Between the show's smart dialogue and its angsty and sexy plot lines, he's set up for success. I just have to keep him from getting derailed by the actor's worst enemy: his own ego.

I'm a few minutes late getting back to the office, but he's even later for the appointment. How he handles it will tell me whether his tardiness is a power move or not.

I extend my hand when my PA shows him into my office. "Hey, Leif, thanks for coming in." His grip is strong, but not like he's trying to intimidate me.

"It's pronounced 'layf' actually," he says, a trace of arrogance coloring his words. "Rhymes with 'safe.'"

My gut tells me to go for low status with this guy, so I shove my hands in my pockets and tip my head to the side, so as to take up less space. "I had a buddy in school who pronounced it the other way. He always said, 'Life is a beautiful thing,' and we never quite knew if he was talking about himself."

"Yeah, that's the typical American pronunciation, and I don't correct journalists when they say it that way, but maybe I should."

I'd been planning to run this meeting from the other side of my large desk, but propping him up seems to open him up, so I gesture toward the small seating area instead. As we get settled, I consider his quandary seriously. "That's a tough call. You hate to get on the wrong side of an entertainment writer. But maybe it's something we can add to the press materials."

His look of gratitude is encouraging. "Yeah, that'd be cool."

"That's what I'm here for," I say, my hands open, but not spread too wide. "To grease the wheels, keep this show on the road, generally be of service."

He nods slowly. "We didn't have a producer on the ground for the first season, so I wasn't sure."

"In addition to overseeing creative continuity, as well as being a resource for the directors coming in for one or two episodes, Max thought I might be someone you and your fellow actors could lean on." Elbows on knees, I round my shoulders. "Since I know a little bit about insta-fame myself."

He tips his head to the side, studying me. "You're an actor too?"

No need to play low on this one; he's gutted me. Either he's too young to have watched *Our House* or I'm truly no longer recognizable as Lukas Keith. Either way, it's official: I'm washed up.

Doing my best to sweep my own bruised ego under the rug, I shrug. "I was a series regular on a show from the age of six to fourteen."

His brow furrows. "In America?"

I can't contain my laugh. "Yes, in the United States."

He's obviously trying hard to place me, so I let him off the hook. "You might be too young to have seen it. *Our House*?"

He leans forward, as if to study me. "Whoa. I'd never have recognized you. I mean, you didn't have a beard or glasses…"

I jump in before he can add wrinkles, a receding hairline, and sagging skin. Instead, I run a hand over the beard that's slowly coming in. "Yeah. This is my producer look."

"You look great, just not like Joey."

I pray he won't say it, but of course he does.

Throwing his hands in the air, he cries, "I'm outta here," squeaky voice and all. Laughing, he shakes his head. "Man, that line is classic."

That's one word for it. It's one thing to have a well-known catchphrase. It's another to have it repeated back to you in your preadolescent voice.

"My point is, back in the day *Our House* was a surprise hit too. Nobody knew who any of us were, then seemingly overnight, *everyone* knew who we were. Some of the cast really struggled with it. I was lucky—my mom had been in the business, and she's an excellent manager."

Leif's mouth twists as he looks off to the side. "Yeah, it's been a little wild. I mean, it's weird seeing yourself on billboards."

"Dealing with the hype can be brutal. Or a buzz kill, depending." I leave both doors open, hoping he'll walk through one of them.

He sits forward, nodding. "Yeah, like, who gets written up and who doesn't. I mean, the show's called *Lawson's Reach*, and I play Lawson, so it makes sense that I'm the one who gets interviewed the most."

"But it's really an ensemble show, wouldn't you say?"

He rests his forearms on his thighs. "Can I be honest with you?"

Score.

"Hang on." I pointedly close the door before returning to my seat. "I'm here for you, man. For all the actors. But for me to be able to show up for you to the suits back in LA, it'll help if I know what's going on."

Sitting on the couch adjacent to him instead of the chair across from him, I continue. "I know if there had been someone I could've talked to about bunk that was going down—not when I was little, I was clueless then—but later, you know. When I was a teenager." *Just like you* is my subtext, even though he and the rest of the cast playing teens are in their early twenties.

"Well, if you're serious…"

When he hesitates, I go hands up. "As a heart attack."

"The thing is, from the scripts we were getting at the end of last season, I'm not sure where the show is going anymore."

At least we're truly on the same page about this. "I get it. More important, the network agrees. That's why they hired

Max. He started young, like me, so he's been in the business a long time for his age. He's in the sweet spot between having enough experience to run the writers' room, while still having enough of a connection to our audience."

Before he gets the idea that this'll be all Kumbaya, I add, "But for him to shape the show, give it an arc that'll keep viewers invested, we have to shoot the scenes we get. No more sending them back with edits from the cast."

"But I've been playing Lawson for over a year now. I know him better than anybody."

"I get it, I do, believe me. But it's not a one-person show. You're not the writer, and you're not paying for it."

He stiffens, almost like I've slapped him, so I literally make myself smaller, leaning forward and resting my forearms on my knees. "You have ownership for the character, and that's awesome. But I'll tell you something Hasselhoff told me when he did a guest spot on our show. Dave said, 'The consummate actor is the guy who gets that it's not only about him, or his character. Every production, whether it's TV or film or theater, has a bazillion moving parts. Your job is to do the best you can with yours.'"

"David Hasselhoff said that?"

"He's a wise man."

I may have resorted to name-dropping, and I definitely cleaned up Dave's language, but my words seem to have landed. Before he can come up with something else to complain about, I stand and open the door. "This is always open to you. You need anything, you come to me first. I'm not saying I'll give it to you, but I'll listen."

When he stands, I get another firm handshake with a side of dazzling smile, and I let out a silent sigh of relief.

On the way out the door, he pauses to ask, "What would you think about starting a kickball league? You know, like the one your brother runs in Hollywood?"

DANI

After I drop Luke back at the office, I swing by my house to grab a late lunch. Just as I'm pulling into my driveway, my neighbor Ida waves at me from her porch next door. She's got mobility issues, so I walk over to see if she needs anything.

"How are you, Dani-girl?" The older woman uses my aunt's nickname for me, lifting a gnarled hand to shade her eyes from the late afternoon sun. "Are you having a good summer?"

I step to the side until I'm acting as her shade, and she relaxes back into her rocker. "Trying to stay cool," I answer.

"And working long hours, I see."

"Keeping busy, for sure."

"That's the best way to keep out of trouble." She leans forward slightly and puts a hand on my arm. "I wanted to make sure you'd heard about Charles Worth. He had a stroke a few days ago."

"Oh, no. Was it serious?"

"Well, he'll be in the hospital, or some sort of facility, I don't rightly remember, for some time. Lorna will be shuttling back and forth, so I thought we should get some meals together for them."

"That's a good idea. I'll start up the phone tree if you'll keep the schedule."

"That would be lovely, dear." She sits back in her seat and then looks past me toward my house. "It looks like you've got visitors, so I won't keep you."

"You let me know if you need any help," I say, as I check out the unfamiliar car parking in front of my place. "I'll check in with you this weekend."

By the time I get to my front door, my cousin Aimee has beat me to it and is peering at my neighbor's house. "Why were you talking to that old black lady?"

"What do you need help with, Aimee?" Ignoring her stupid question, I unlock the door and glance pointedly at her car, where some young punk sits in the passenger seat smoking a cigarette. "He's gonna have to quit that if you're pregnant."

After blowing him a kiss, she tails me inside. "Yeah, well, that's the thing, Danielle. I was hoping you could help me avoid that."

"Avoid getting pregnant?"

When I turn around to face her, she's biting her lip and blushing, but nodding. "Everybody in the family says you're the one to ask."

"I'll always help with that. Do you need me to make an appointment for you?"

She sticks her hands in the back pockets of her cutoffs and rolls her feet so she's standing mostly on the outsides of her jelly shoes, making her look like a little kid.

"How old are you again?" I ask as I continue on to the kitchen. "Sorry, I need to grab some food. I missed lunch."

"Sixteen last month."

"And this is something you want, right? That guy out there isn't pressuring you or anything?"

"No way. And I'm not a virgin. I've done it before. But I don't want to have to worry about it. I love him, but I want to finish high school and then go to school to be a lab assistant or something. I want a good job."

"Well, good for you." I've got the Planned Parenthood number memorized, so I grab the phone from the wall, intending to make an appointment for her while I make a sandwich. "Any times not good for you?"

"Actually, I have an appointment." She glances at the clock. "It's in, like, fifteen minutes."

"What are you doing here, then?"

She swallows, her blush deepening. "I'm kinda skeeved

out about it. I don't know what they're going to do to me there."

"You'll let a boy stick his penis in you, but you're afraid to let a trained doctor check you out?"

She shrugs. "I don't like doctors. They make me feel sick."

If it were up to me, people wouldn't get hit with hormones until they're mature enough to deal with the consequences. Which, for some of us, would be never.

"Will you go with me, Danielle? Please?"

"What about Wonder Boy out there?"

"He'll go, but you know what's going to happen, and you know what all to say to them."

My eyes roam the contents of the fridge I've held open for the last few moments. Nothing in there to grab and go, so I check the clock over the stove and give up. "Fine. I'll follow y'all there."

She claps her hands together and actually jumps up and down. "Thank you, thank you! You're the best, Danielle."

I stay with my cousin all the way through the appointment, even after the doctor explains that as long as she doesn't have any pain or other concerns, she won't need a pelvic exam until she needs her first Pap smear at twenty-one. My stomach's grumbling by the time the doctor writes her a prescription for birth control pills, but one of the nurses catches me before I make it out the door.

She motions for me to follow her into an exam room and then closes the door behind her. "Are you still looking for someone to do a tubal?"

A huff of irritation precedes my answer. "Oh, yeah. So far, no one will do it unless I'm hitched."

"Well," she says, lowering her voice. "One of the practices in town just hired a new doctor. She's going to be working here one shift a week, so we met her yesterday. She's young, female, and is obviously very progressive."

I get the woman's name and office number and thank the nurse profusely.

"You're always bringing us patients," she says with a grin, "so I'm happy to help."

On the drive back to my office, I consider what this news means. I'd pretty much convinced myself that marrying Luke was a no-go. I mean, what if we went through with it and the doctors still said no? After grabbing a snack from Randy's craft service and checking messages, I spend the next couple of hours driving all over town doing locations errands: following up with homeowners, picking up and applying for permits, and delivering address details to the show's ADs so they can create maps for the first week of production.

As I drive, I turn over the pros and cons in my head.

Pro: I could finally get this procedure done and then be free to have a normal sex life.

Con: Actually getting married to a TV star would mean a higher chance of a leak, which might put our jobs in danger.

Pro: If we're married, then the Morality Memo wouldn't apply.

Con: If my friends found out I'd been lying to them, they'd be really mad.

Pro: I'd get something in return for the driving practice, which is cutting into my work time.

Con: If the news gets in the tabloids, everyone from my family to the local news would be all up in my business.

By the time I get a page from Luke letting me know that he's ready for a ride home, I've pretty much convinced myself that, while the pros and cons are even, it's still too risky to actually get married to Lukas Keith.

But as I walk through the door to his office, it hits me. I wouldn't be marrying *Lukas Keith*; I'd be marrying Luke Zelazny.

"Why do you want to do this?" I ask.

He looks up from his desk and takes off a pair of glasses.

"Also, are those prescription or, like, a fashion statement?"

He shakes his head like he can't quite keep up. "Uh, do what? And, yes, they're prescription. Sometimes I can't be bothered with my contacts."

"Huh."

"And what was it I want to do?"

I check over my shoulder and then close his office door behind me. "Marry me."

He sits back in his chair and looks off to the side as if he's really considering the question. "Well, you're really helping me with the driving thing. I've tried before and couldn't get past turning the key. You don't judge me, and I feel calm. I want to help you in return."

Before I can remind him that he is paying me for my time, he adds, "And I'm still so pissed off that you don't get to make this choice for yourself. We can't change the doctor's opinion, but we can change your circumstances."

He makes a good point, but it still feels risky to me. "Are you not worried about it somehow getting out? I mean, it's one thing for you to pretend to be my fiancé for a couple of doctor's visits, but to get a marriage license, go through a civil ceremony—it seems like there are so many opportunities for someone to leak the news that Lukas Keith got married to someone that wasn't Kellie Kingston."

"I'm telling you, no one cares about me anymore. When I met with the kid who plays Lawson today, the guy didn't even recognize me."

"Seriously?"

"Seriously." He sighs, like he's still trying to let go of it. "Anyway, lucky for you, I have two identities. You won't be marrying Lukas Keith."

"About that. I'm wondering if you'd consider a whole new look." Sitting on the chair by his desk, I sweep a hand up and down. "I mean, the glasses are a start. You could wear them all the time. Keep growing that beard."

"And maybe Luke"—I pause and do my best to not mangle the pronunciation—"Zelazny, producing director, should have a different look anyway. So people forget that you were Lukas Keith, the Dennis the Menace of family TV."

He rubs the stubble on the side of his face. It's unfair that whatever he does with his looks, he'll still be sexy as sin. "Good point."

"You know the other thing that'd really change your look?"

"What's that?"

"If you cut your hair."

His hand spears through his hair, almost reflexively. "Cut my hair?"

"Yeah, that flop in your face look is for the Brads and the Leos. The kids. You want to be taken seriously, go for more, I don't know, George Clooney in *ER*."

He touches his hair again, muttering, "My mother'd kill me."

I'm not touching that one, so I stay mum. Instead, I ask if he's ready to go. He grabs his things, tells his PAs to go home, picks up Peanut, and follows me down the hall and to the car without a word.

But as I pull out of the lot, he turns down the Mighty, Mighty Bosstones singing about never knocking on wood and says, "I can't do it myself."

"Fair enough. I know someone who can do it." *If I can get her to leave the house, that is.*

He's quiet for a bit, and then he clears his throat. "One more thing, though. We should go over the parameters."

"What do you mean, parameters? With your hair?"

"No, I mean, we should've done this before the first doctor visit. We should agree on how and where it's okay to be touched."

Just the idea of Luke touching me has all the blood leaving my brain and rushing south. I risk a glance his way and am horrified to find him smirking at me.

He holds up a hand. "Don't worry. I'm not going to do anything that'd have the other patients at the doctor's office yelling 'Get a room.'"

I try to find enough saliva to get words out of my mouth. "What exactly *are* you talking about then?"

"For me," he says, like this is a conversation he has all the time, "you should probably avoid my waist if you don't want me squawking like a chicken. I'm super ticklish there."

"Good to know." I do my best to return his smirk, but the idea of touching still has me squirming in my seat.

"What about you?" he asks. "Any place I should avoid, other than the, you know, typical erogenous zones?"

Erogenous zones. Those words set me off like a pinball machine. Doing my best to focus all my brain cells on driving, I don't touch this question until we're safely parked in front of his rental.

But when I turn to face him and those eyes point at me, pupils so big you can barely see the blue, I can't. No way can I be this close to him and calmly say words like "erogenous" and "touch." Even "tickle."

So I ask, "Doesn't Peanut need to pee?"

Peanut barks, obviously agreeing with me, so I get my hiney out of the car lickety-split and maintain a safe distance from Mr. Sex Talk.

He must know he's having an effect on me because he's got this pleased little grin on his face. "I can touch you... wherever?"

I shove my hands in my back pockets in an attempt to be all casual. "Sure. Whatever."

"Okay if I kiss you? On the cheek, maybe the forehead? You know, an affectionate kiss?"

Great. All I want now is to feel those lips on my skin. My

cheek. My forehead. My fucking mouth. But I shrug again like it's no biggie. "Sure, but we still only need to convince the doctor. It's not like we're putting on a show for the whole world."

We stare at each other for a long moment during which I cannot stop thinking about kissing him. I'm not sure who moves, but somehow, we get closer to each other. And I'm pretty sure he's staring at my lips. Is he thinking the same thing?

"Arf, arf, arf, arf, ARF!"

Peanut lets loose, and I practically jump out of my skin. By the time I land on my feet, Luke is picking up the dog, shushing him, and I use the opportunity to escape to my car. "See you tomorrow at eight? We can work out the rest of the details then."

And then I turn tail and run.

It's almost ten by the time I get home, so when I pick up the phone, my great-aunt's voice echoes in my head. *It's rude to call after nine o'clock in the evening, Danielle.*

It may be rude and it's definitely risky, but I punch in the number anyway.

I know it by heart because I've done this once a month for the past year. After the first couple of times, I learned to only call midday, when her husband is less likely to be home. We talk, but she never really says anything. I know she's unhappy, but she's either too stubborn or deluded to admit it. I'm pretty sure it's my fault she ran straight into that asshole's arms, so I keep calling. To let her know I'm here in case she ever comes to her senses and leaves him.

Tonight, *he* answers. Even the man's voice makes my skin crawl. He's polite when I pretend to be a cousin of a rich girl we all grew up with, adopting the snooty coastal drawl that forgets there's a letter *R*, falling all over myself with self-effacing apologies for my idiocy as I claim to need the address of a made-up "fundraisah that's happening *tomorrah*, which ah can't *possibly* mi-yuhss."

There's a long pause before he tells me that of course he'll get Whitney so she can help me out. I'm kept waiting for some time, and when she finally picks up the phone, her voice is uncharacteristically soft and tentative. I hate that he's done this to her. But I keep my own tone free from any emotion.

"Who is this, again?" she asks when I don't immediately reply.

"He-ey, Whitney," I begin, still pretending to be this mythical cousin. Hardy could be hovering next to her for all I know. He could be listening on another extension. "I was hoping you could help me out."

There's a beat of silence before she asks, "Did you say it was for sea turtle rescue?"

"Uh-huh, that's it," I say, my voice cracking with strain as it tries to keep up the unnaturally high pitch.

"Right. I've got that with my outfit for the event. Hang on while I get it."

As I wait for her to return, I'm so unsettled by the fact that I have to lie in order to talk to a girl I've known since kindergarten, I find myself opening and shutting kitchen cabinets, looking for I don't know what. When Skye bumps me from behind, I sink down to the floor and put an arm around her, needing someone to hang on to.

"Okay, let me see if I can remember what I was going to wear." Whit's voice in my ear is unnaturally high-pitched too. I hear a door close on her end, and then she clears her throat. "What do you want, Dani? And why are you calling so late? Didn't your momma teach you better than that?"

"I'm sorry, Whit," I say, matching her urgent whisper. I've got to assume that Hardy's not listening in since she used my real name. "But I've got a hair emergency, and I need your help."

"You didn't bleach it again, did you?" she asks, her voice appropriately horror-stricken. That bad move in high school took almost a year to recover from.

"No, no. It's not me. I need to help a friend change his look so he can—" I break off, not sure how to explain the situation without giving it away. "He wants to hide in plain sight, if you know what I mean."

"What did he do?" There's a conspiratorial note in her tone that sounds like the old Whit, which makes me unreasonably happy.

"He didn't do anything wrong, he's just..." As I trail off, I realize that I can use his celebrity as an excuse. "The guy I'm driving right now was a child actor, but now he's in town as a producing director on *Lawson's Reach*, and he wants to be taken seriously, so I suggested changing his look."

"Lukas Keith?"

"How'd you know?"

"A girl I played tennis with told me she saw him at the grocery store. And I remember that you were sweet on him when you drove him last time he was in town."

"I was not."

"Mm-hmm."

"Whatever. I'm doing this because I don't want to have to deal with his celebrity crap myself."

That is the truest thing I've said so far.

"Oh, hey, honey," Whitney's voice goes high and breathy again. "I'm almost done. I just forgot where I put that address."

Her voice gets muffled, like either she or Hardy has covered the mouthpiece.

"He's gone," she whispers. "But I don't have much time."

"Okay," I answer, wondering for the millionth time what

is up in that household. "Could you come to the studio and cut his hair sometime this week?"

I'd like to make an appointment with the doctor as soon as possible, but if we're doing the cloak and dagger thing, I should wait until he's fully disguised.

"I'm sorry, Dan, but I can't get away this week."

"Not even for an hour? It won't take long."

She hesitates for a beat or two before answering, "I'm sorry. I can't. But you can do it. His hairline's been receding, so he should go really short anyway."

"I don't know how to do hair, Whit."

"Dani, you shaved your little brothers' hair at least twice a year when they were in grade school. Every time there was a lice outbreak, remember?"

I'd forgotten about that. Probably blocked it out, more likely. I shudder as I remember. Getting that close to a head potentially crawling with lice really skeeved me out.

"Trust me, Dan. You can do it. You do everything you put your mind to."

Before I can beg her one more time to help me out, suddenly needing to see her in person, she says brightly, "I'll see you tomorrow at the Henderson's. Bye now!"

All I'm left with is the dial tone in my ear.

CHAPTER EIGHT

LUKE

Dani sneaks in another driving practice on the way to wherever I'm getting my hair cut, so my eyes are blurry as I stare out the window and do my best to get myself under control while the Barenaked Ladies go on about how it's all been done before.

They may be right, and changing my hair isn't as terrifying as getting behind the wheel, but it's no small thing. My agent has been pushing for me to cut it for some time now, lining up a series of my headshots to bolster her argument. Airbrushing can do a lot, but it can't fix everything.

You have to face facts, Lukas, she'd said, over a year ago. *Your hairline is receding. It happens. And keeping it long just calls attention to it.*

My mother feels differently. Like me, she's attached to my old look. I mean, when fan magazines devote entire paragraphs to describing "thick chestnut waves run through with gold" blah, blah, blah, you start to think that shit is important.

I should've done it the minute I told my mother I was quitting acting. And Dani's right that a more serious look could give me more authority.

I still don't want to.

Before I know it, we're pulling into the driveway of a charming bungalow. There are a lot of Craftsman-style homes in Los Angeles—in fact, my family lived in one before we got famous—but I didn't know they existed in Wallington. I look up and down the street full of houses just like it, in various states of repair. No commercial signs, though. "Does this person cut hair in their home?"

She avoids my gaze as she exits the car. "Uh, yeah."

"Can I bring Peanut in?"

"Yes, but there's another dog here. We should introduce them out back."

Instead of knocking on the front door, she gestures for me to follow her around the side. When she opens a gate, I follow, wondering if she's going to let the homeowner know that we're here.

Instead, she points at Peanut. "Unclip his leash but hold him in your arms."

I admire the backyard while she disappears inside. It's a real haven. The fenced-in space goes deeper than I'd imagined, and everywhere you look the green is sprinkled with pops of color. It smells heavenly. Honeysuckle or jasmine, maybe.

As I take in the scented air, I try to convince myself that it's better to do this at someone's home instead of at a barber shop or salon. Not only will we avoid the risk of someone recognizing me, but if he or she cuts my hair on the back deck, I'll have all this natural beauty to distract me.

"Ready?" Dani calls from behind the screen door.

"For what?"

"For me to bring the dog out."

"I don't know what I'm supposed to do, but I'm holding him like you said."

After opening the door and giving the "heel" command, Dani appears on the back deck with a dog that's shaped kind of like a German shepherd but is smaller and buff-colored all over. She tells the dog to lie down and stay. It obeys, even as it lifts its nose to sniff in our direction.

"Good girl, Skye," Dani says, her attention tracking back and forth between the dogs. "Two pointy-nosed blondes," she observes.

"That's about all they have in common. What kind of dog is that?"

"Skye's a Carolina Dog."

"Is that a breed or where she's from?"

"You can still find wild ones in South Carolina, but it's a recognized breed." She tips her head to the side to study Peanut. "Do you know what he is?"

"A Chiweenie."

She snorts out a laugh, and Skye whines. "Sorry, girl. What the hell is a Chiweenie?"

"Dachshund-Chihuahua mix."

"Probably not good with little kids then, huh?" she says. "Little scrappy dogs can be ankle-biters."

"You think they'll be okay together?"

"Skye will be fine. Come closer but keep holding Peanut. We should chat for a few minutes. Let them get bored."

No one else seems to be coming to join us on the porch, and Skye looks at Dani like she hung the moon. "Is this your house, Dani?"

She meets my gaze, her expression guarded. "Yep."

"Is a stylist meeting us here?" I'm unable to keep the challenge out of my tone. Call me vain, but when your entire career has depended on what you look like, it's not easy to let just anyone at your hair.

Instead of answering my question, she tips her head to the side as her gaze narrows. "Is your hair clean?"

"It's not dirty. I took a shower today."

"I mean, is there gel or mousse or whatever in it?"

I'm tempted to say that my hair styles itself perfectly

without intervention, just to get her goat, but I don't. "Yes. There is product in it."

She shifts her attention to the dogs. "Okay, put Peanut down."

After reminding the big dog to stay, she mirrors my squat as I set Peanut on the ground.

"Hey, Peanut, this is Skye," Dani says, her voice pitched high and soft.

Peanut seems completely unfazed by the fact that Skye is ten times bigger than he is and could probably eat him for lunch. He just trots up to her rear end and sniffs. Skye checks his butt out, too, but remains lying down.

After what seems like a very thorough smell-fest, Dani says, "Okay, Skye. Go play."

Skye pops up, and Peanut stiffens, tail up. I'm worried for a moment, but then Skye takes off into the yard and Peanut follows, chasing her. They change leads a few times, but for the most part, Skye races around trees and under bushes with Peanut hot on her tail.

"That's right, Skye, show him your circuit," Dani calls. "That dog can run for days. She loves it when another dog will chase."

After watching them for another moment or two, Dani says, "Follow me."

Inside, she grabs a towel from a hall closet and points at a door. "There's a nozzle thingy in the shower so you don't have to get your body wet. Wash your hair, towel it dry, and then meet me back on the deck."

"Does this mean that you are cutting my hair?"

"Yes, Luke, that's what it means. If you don't like the result, you can go to a barber next time, but my friend isn't available."

I open my mouth to protest, but her stubborn chin and single raised brow make it clear she's not going to back down.

Fighting the impulse to flee, telling myself, *it's just a haircut*, I take the towel.

I repeat this mantra as I turn on the water and adjust the temperature.

But as I remove my button-down shirt, a voice that sounds an awful lot like my mother's echoes inside my skull. *It's your signature look, Luke.* As I do the awkward lean over the edge of the tub to get the hair wet without soaking the rest of my body, I remember how women tell me they have to hold themselves back from running their fingers through it. Or pushing the one recalcitrant curl out of my eyes.

Sometimes they don't stop themselves. They just do it.

Of course, I concede as I work the shampoo in, the distance that curl has to travel to cover my eyes keeps getting longer. Its texture these days is more horse's mane than spaniel's ears.

None of the hairs are gray. Yet. But the color's fading. Maybe it'll be good to get rid of it instead of watching it curl up and die.

"Are you coming or what?" Dani yells from the other side of the door.

Facing myself in the mirror, running a hand through the curls one last time, I turn off the bathroom light, and force myself to face their executioner.

DANI

When Lukas finally walks through the screen door to meet me on the back deck, he's looking almost as disturbed as he did when I tried to hand him the car keys back at the studio. His shoulders creep up to his ears when I set the clippers on the rail of the back deck, and when I pick up the scissors, he actually flinches.

"Do you know what you're doing with those things?" he asks, his tone clipped.

"I'm not going to cut your ear off, if that's what you're worried about." I gesture at the barstool I dragged outside and offer him a dry towel. "Here, put this around your shoulders."

He takes the towel but doesn't take a seat, so I ask, "Are you Samson or something?"

"Huh?"

"Like in the Bible? The guy who loses his superpowers if he gets a haircut?"

This gets a smile out of him, and then he shakes his head and slides his butt onto the stool. "I'm sorry I'm being such a jackass. I guess I am a little worried about it. I've never had short hair. I know it's stupid and vain, but it feels like I'm really kicking Lukas Keith to the curb by cutting it off."

Instead of beginning to snip away, I move into his line of sight and lean against the railing. "Are you sure you want to do this? We don't have to."

He presses his lips together for a couple of beats, and then shakes his head, like he's shaking off excess water. In fact, a couple of droplets land on my bare arms. "No. This is good. Maybe it'll convince my mother that I really am done with acting."

When I start to move behind him again, he reaches out a hand to stop me. "Don't make me look too bad. Please."

As if that could even happen.

I'm tempted to tell him the lice story, but I do need the guy to relax. I don't really want to be thinking about picking nits off my brothers' scalps, either. So, as I run a comb through his hair, I begin to tell him about my other experience cutting hair. The one I'd buried so deep I'd forgotten about them until I dug the clippers out from under the bathroom sink.

"This place was my great-aunt Gracie's house," I begin,

gesturing to the house and yard. "I moved in here to help her out when she was in treatment for breast cancer. She had a full head of hair at the time, long and black like mine, though hers was streaked with silver. It was beautiful. When it started falling out, she sent me to the beauty supply store for supplies, so I could cut it off and then shave her head."

I let that sink in for a moment. When I ask, "You okay to go on?" he takes in a deep breath and releases it before nodding.

When I pick up the scissors and move in close to begin snipping away the curls, I need a little distraction to keep myself from inhaling his intoxicating scent, full of pheromones likely to tango with my hormones and give them bad ideas. Since he's got a good view of the backyard, I tell him about its history.

"You've probably heard how big azaleas are in Wallington."

"Uh, yeah. There's a festival, right?"

"Yep. Parties and parades and princesses. And the azaleas *are* gorgeous. But only in the spring. Unless you have those ones that also flower in the fall, but my aunt always said that was cheating."

Smiling at the memory of her in this garden, I start with the lantanas, currently in bloom, and give him the lowdown on the various bushes and bulbs and vines that make up the landscaping, from the hydrangeas and gardenias to the irises and camellias. "She wanted to have blooms all year round, so during her recovery, we planted."

My aunt never got to fully appreciate her vision. She lived for another five years before the cancer came back, but now, after more than a decade of growth, it's finally the paradise she described as we got our hands dirty.

"It is beautiful," Lukas murmurs. "So different from most gardens in California."

Mother Nature seems to have worked her magic on him.

When I move to his side, I can see that he's lost the pinched look around his eyes and jaw. Unfortunately, he tenses up again when I pick up the clippers.

"Almost done," I reassure him.

I don't want him flinching when I run the clippers, so I place my palm on the top of his skull to steady us both. But when the towel slips from his shoulders, revealing smooth golden skin covering taut pecs and lats, barely contained by the slim-fitting tank he's wearing, I'm the one who's a little unsteady.

I whip the towel off completely, turning to shake off the clumps of hair, and then drape it over him again. "Can you hold this closed in front? I don't want the little hairs to get under your shirt."

Once he's covered, I flip the on switch. "I'm going to give you a buzz cut like all the military guys around here have."

"A buzz cut?" he asks, his voice going way up in pitch.

"It'll be great. You'll fit right in." Before he can argue, I add, "Do you want to hide in plain sight or not?"

He nods but looks so forlorn that I can't leave it there. Against my better judgment, I add, "And you've got a well-shaped skull. It'll be hot, don't worry."

"Danielle Goodwin," he says, his tone making it clear that I blew right past assuaging his fears and went straight to massaging his ego. "Did you say you think I'm hot?"

"Uh, no. That is not what I said. My comment was purely in regard to the latest hairstyle trends."

My sarcastic response to his cocky assumption comes easy. What's difficult is facing the reality. In my experience, when you act as a chauffeur, it doesn't take long for the most attractive person to reveal the ugly underside that spoils the pretty facade. With Lukas Keith, I have the opposite problem. I assumed he was going to be an egotistical asshole, because, well, *duh*. Child star. Rolling in money. Perfectly symmetrical features, except for this little crook in one eyebrow that somehow ties it all up in a red bow.

Which brings us back to the present, where his unrelenting sexiness just keeps bashing away at my carefully constructed walls of Not Interested, built with bricks of indifference stuck together with irritation. I need a distraction from his physical perfection, especially now that I need to get even closer. Literally closer, in order to finish this buzz cut, and figuratively closer, in order to pretend to be married to him.

Without the benefit of actually having sex with him.

No, no, no, Danielle. No thinking about sex.

Dialing my mind back in time to childhood, when we were both obnoxious little brats, the words *I'm outta here* echo in my mind, in a squeaky little-boy voice the world knows well.

After telling him—gruffly, mind you—to close his eyes and keep his chin up, I ask, "How did they come up with your catchphrase on *Our House*?"

His eyes flutter open. "I'm outta here?"

"Did you have any other catchphrases?" When he shoots me a *don't be a smart-ass* look, I remind him to keep his eyes closed. "Unless tiny hairs scratching at your eyeballs rocks your boat, I mean—"

Hands up and lips pressed together, I tell myself to stop wandering into the dangerous territory called What Rocks Luke's Boat until he closes his eyes as instructed and begins to tell the story.

"Actually, it was one of those things that just happened. It was the third episode. Joey was set up to be a catalyst from the beginning, to push buttons and stir up trouble. Sometimes on purpose, but mostly by accident. It was so long ago, I can't remember the exact setup, but I remember the moment it happened like it's got its own storage container in my brain."

"Maybe because you've seen it," I suggest as I run the

blade over his skull. "That show has been playing in the pre-dinner rerun slot for years."

He shudders, and I have to jump away to avoid nicking him. "Be still, dammit. Unless you want to lose an ear."

He blows out a breath. "Sorry. Just the thought of watching that show… Ugh." He shudders again.

"Got it out of your system?" I ask, holding the clippers well out of the way.

He opens one eye and shoots me a sheepish half grin. "I think so."

Damn, his face is expressive. I'm suddenly curious about why he quit acting, but I also want to hear the rest of this story. I also want to nuzzle my nose into the crook behind his ear, but that dog won't hunt, girl.

"Okay, I promise, I'm good now."

Hovering, clippers running, I prompt him to continue his story.

"Right, right. So, whatever Joey had done or said created some chaotic argument. We were shooting in front of a live audience, and I knew that I was supposed to sneak out of the room, but everyone was so loud, I couldn't hear my exit cue. I looked around until I found the AD in charge of me—who happened to be standing right next to a live camera—shrugged, and improvised with, 'I'm outta here.' Suddenly, the crowd erupted in laughter."

His smile turns almost wistful. Naturally, this too is a good look on him. "It was like the TV gods wanted it to happen."

"What do you mean?"

"Well, I wasn't being covered by the boom, so what I said shouldn't have been recorded. However, I *was* standing right in front of one of the set mics, so the crowd heard it, and the sound mixer had it." He sighs. "I still can't believe they kept it in."

"Why not? It's such a thing. I mean, they used it in that

Raid commercial. It's in a rap song. It was even on *Saturday Night Live*, for heaven's sake."

"It wasn't the line itself that was a big deal. It was that I looked at the camera and broke the fourth wall. Like I was talking directly to the people at home."

"But they did that on *Fresh Prince* and *Saved by the Bell*."

"Yeah, it's nothing new. I mean, Shakespeare's full of asides to the audience, but we were the first on prime time."

"Seems to have paid off."

"Yeah, well, a lot of factors made the show a hit. As cheesy as it seems now."

It's good that his stories make it clear how he lives in a whole other stratosphere, even as his warm, real, physical presence wakes up parts of me that I can't be listening to until well after I've had the tubal.

As if they know I need the distraction, Peanut and Skye suddenly leap up from the deck, where they'd been lazing in the sun, and scramble for the bushes, barking their heads off.

"What the hell?" Lukas jerks, his eyes popping open, and I just manage to avoid shaving a weird dent in his hair.

"Squirrel, probably." I clamp a firm hand on his shoulder. "Almost done. I really need you to hold still for this last part."

Aiming every ounce of focus I've got at the skull in front of me, I go over my work until I'm satisfied that the length is uniform. But when I step back, and he removes the towel revealing those broad shoulders and perfectly defined arms and chest, it's suddenly clear.

I fucked this up big-time.

This man will never disappear into a crowd.

The close-shorn hair in combination with the close-cut beard emphasizes his rugged square jaw. And those eyes. Ice blue flecked with gold, framed by mahogany-brown brows and lashes, they're the only thing you see now that curls aren't flopping over his forehead.

Two years ago, I worked hard to build up an immunity to

Lukas Keith's charms. Spent the hours driving him reminding myself that he's in love with someone else, behaving professionally, and generally letting myself be annoyed by the way he floated through the world on a magic carpet of privilege blissfully unaware of mere mortals.

But this version of him, the Luke Zelazny who's terrified to drive, who is nervous about his new job, and who looks like a fucking Greek god… I have no defenses built up.

And now I'm supposed to marry him?

I guess it's a good thing he's the 'I'm outta here' guy, or I'd be tempted to ask him to stick around.

LUKE

"That bad, huh?"

Dani's frown could mean all manner of things. That I look like crap, that I said something to stir up her disapproval, that she's regretting asking me to fake marry her. Any or all of which are likely true.

But I need to learn to drive, and she wants this procedure, so it's time to go on the offensive. "It's probably a good thing if you made me look like Gomer Pyle. I need to be undercover."

She mumbles something as she turns away to pack up the scissors and clippers.

"Sorry, I didn't get that."

"I *said*," she says, now overly loud, "you should definitely wear your glasses. And keep growing that beard."

Scratching under my chin, still getting used to the feel of the beard, I acknowledge that she's probably right, even though I'm pretty sure she's deflecting for some reason.

Well, two can play that game, and I actually have something I need help with.

"Hey, I've been meaning to ask you. I met with the leads

over the past few days, hoping to get off on the right foot with them and head off any dramas."

She doesn't stop packing up her haircutting supplies, but her smirk is back. "How'd that go?"

"Well, I didn't get a straight answer on who's sleeping with who—"

"Oh, well, I can tell you that. I did a little recon in the makeup and hair trailers." She begins to tick off the list on her fingers. "Last fall it was the Lawson guy and some older guest star who was around for a few episodes. He got pissed when they ended her storyline. This spring it was the guy playing Parker and the girl playing Charlie. There may have been an actual fistfight between him and the Lawson kid. What's his real name? Leaf, Life?"

I raise a finger and adopt a snooty voice. "I learned from the man himself that 'Layf' is the correct Scandinavian pronunciation."

"Isn't he from, like, New Jersey?"

This gets a snort out of me. "Uh-huh."

"Well, if it's your job to keep the peace, good luck."

"Actually, Leif had a good idea. My brother started this kickball game back in LA, and—"

"Kickball?" She tips her head to the side. "Like you play in elementary school?"

"Exactly. Kind of as an ironic goof, but also as a way that a bunch of people who have no athletic skills could blow off steam."

"Why not softball?"

"Even that requires a certain level of skill and equipment. With kickball, it's easier for it to be co-ed. You can't really get hurt, and all you need is a field and the red ball."

"Would this be just for the cast?"

"No, no. Even in LA, the group of people who play do all sorts of things in the industry. Above and below the line. Producers and writers along with gaffers and best boys. And everybody's in a different place in their career. Some still waiting for a break, some doing steady work, some washed up, like me."

"Pfft. You're hardly washed up. You're only, like—how old are you?"

I try to run a hand through my hair but end up awkwardly patting my now prickly skull instead. "It's considered impolite to ask an actor his age."

"Yeah, but if I'm going to be your wife, I should know."

I raise a brow and take a chance, meeting her eyes. "I have to admit, I kind of like the sound of that."

"Yeah, well, don't get used to it." Grabbing the broom she'd brought out earlier, she busies herself with sweeping up the remains of my curls. "Anyway, I know exactly the guy to help you get this started. My buddy Sully is the boom guy on *Lawson's Reach*. He's the nicest guy you'll ever meet and can get anybody to do anything."

"Someone you have a thing for?"

A shudder runs through her. "Ugh. No. I've known him since we ran around naked at the beach."

"Excuse me?"

"Not like last week, you idiot," she says, laughing at what must be a ridiculous expression on my face. "When we were four years old. Anyway, he's with Helen."

"O'Neill?"

"The same."

"Interesting."

"What do you mean?"

"It's hard to imagine her being with anybody. She seems so… self-contained." Kind of like Dani herself.

"Well, they are madly in love," she says, sweeping with a bit too much ferocity.

I can't help wondering if, despite her denial, she's jealous of Helen and this guy. "So, you'll put me in touch with him?

Sully? I'd love to be able to announce it at the first read-through on Friday."

"Sure, I'll see if I can get him on the phone now."

Fifteen minutes later, Sully's promised to find us a playing field and help spread the word to the show's crew. When I return to the porch, I find Dani still holding the broom, staring off into the backyard. As soon as she hears me, a professional smile replaces the uncharacteristically vulnerable look on her face.

"Good news?" she asks, in a chipper tone as fake as her smile.

"He's in," I say, clapping my hands together. "And I am too. Whaddaya say we get married? Like, tomorrow."

CHAPTER NINE

DANI

Things are ramping up for *Lawson's Reach*. Luke's got meetings galore today and the first read-through of the season is tomorrow. But when I tried one last time to let him off the hook, he insisted that we squeeze in a wedding as soon as possible.

There's a teeny, tiny corner of my heart that doesn't want to do this. That doesn't want to treat marriage like a convenient thing two people do in service of some other goal. But I don't think I'll ever be in a place to fall in love if I'm so worried about getting pregnant that I can't have intercourse, so I've spent the morning convincing myself that marrying Lukas Keith will be a silly story I tell the man I someday find to share my life with.

If that man even exists.

Midday, I swing by craft service for snacks, page Luke with the code we established for "meet me at the car," and then we head downtown.

The minute I park, Luke jumps out of the car. "So where do we go? Time's a-wastin'."

"First we visit the Register of Deeds to get the license."

Luke pulls a CD from his bag. "May I?"

"Uh, sure."

I have to snort when I realize what it is, and Luke has me laughing out loud as he dances along to Elton John's version of "Chapel of Love."

The tune in my head ends with a record scratch when we walk into the county government building and I see one of my cousins working the front desk. Turning around so fast that I almost plow into Luke, I grab him by the arm and steer him back out the door before she sees us. "We'll have to come back another day."

"What? Why? What's the problem?"

"The problem is," I hiss, "my cousin is guarding the gate."

"So? She doesn't need to know what we're doing here. I mean, we could be checking on a *deed* at the Register of Deeds. Something to do with the show."

"Oh. Yeah. Right. Good point." When he heads for the door, I call, "But I don't know if she'll believe me."

"You did a fine acting job when we played Two Truths and a Lie."

"Yeah, but the stakes were low. If anyone in my family suspects that I'm marrying Lukas Keith... well, let the leeching begin."

He grimaces. "One, ick. And two, I'll do the talking if you want me to."

When I still don't move, he adds, "Remember, you're not *marrying* Lukas Keith. You're *working* with Luke Zelazny, and we're here on a work errand."

I wipe my hands on my khakis. "I guess we'll find out if your disguise works, because I'm pretty sure my cousin has seen every episode of *Our House*."

"Hasn't everybody?" he mutters. Before I can figure out why that makes him irritated rather than proud, he's opening the door and ushering me inside. "After you."

The minute she sees us, my cousin starts in. "Well, Danielle Goodwin, it's been a dog's age since I saw you."

"Hey, Regina." I don't know if it's because I work with people from all over the country on a regular basis or what, but I'm pretty sure she sounds way more country than I do. We're about the same age, but like my other cousins and sisters, she got married right out of high school and started churning out the kids.

"What can I do you for?" she asks.

When I just stand there, mouth gaping like a stuffed fish, Luke jumps in. "We'd appreciate it if you'd direct us to the Register of Deeds office."

Regina's smile when she checks out Luke is positively feral. As she looks him up and down, obviously enjoying the view, it seems she's completely unaware that she's talking to the guy whose picture she had plastered all over her walls in junior high. "I sure can, it's right down that hall." She breaks off, her eyes widening. "Oh. My. God. Are y'all gettin' married?" Her face falls as fast as her pitch rises. "Damn. And nobody told me?"

"Don't get your panties in a twist, girl," I say, employing the snarky attitude she'd expect. "Why the hell would you think that?"

"Because that's what most people do at that office if they're not a Realtor." Naturally, she pronounces it "reel-luh-ter." Suppressing an eye roll, I keep talking. "Lord a mercy. You'd think getting married was the be-all and end-all."

She shakes her head slowly, even lets out a pitying cluck or two. "Honey, when you finally find a man, you'll get it, and then you'll want a family too." She picks up a gilt frame from her desk. "Did you see the photo we had done after Riley's graduation from elementary school?"

I take it and do my best to say all the things you're supposed to about how she's so pretty and they grow up so fast. Then I hand it back and clear my throat.

"We're here on business for the filming of *Lawson's Reach*," Luke says, perhaps sensing that I've run out of steam.

"But the permit office is in the city government building," Regina says. "You of all people should know that, Danielle."

"What do you mean, Regina?" I ask, unable to keep defensiveness out of my voice.

"I bet she's proud of the work you do in Wallington's film industry, which I'm sure brings all kinds of added value to the city. In any case, ma'am, we're here to do research on a property the show is considering for *purchase*. Thus, the need to check out the *deed*." Luke gives that magic spot on my shoulder a squeeze before steering me in the direction Regina had pointed. "Nice to meet you, ma'am, and thanks for your help."

"Regina. Regina Taylor." When he just waves instead of giving her his own name, she calls, "Y'all have a nice day now, ya hear?"

The disgruntled look on Regina's face when he calls her "ma'am" instead of "miss" has me grinning for hours, despite the fact that I have to wait around for the next break between Luke's meetings to put the license to work. Still, when he hops into the car with a jaunty, "To the courthouse, James," I can't quite believe this is happening.

My research pays off. The magistrate only performs weddings two days a week with limited hours, but I've slotted us in a half hour before they close.

"And your witnesses?" the clerk asks after we hand over the license. "You need two."

"Can someone who works here do it?" Luke asks. "We can pay them for their time."

The woman purses her lips in disapproval, but before she

can say no, a woman says, "We're here to get married too. We can be your witnesses."

A couple sitting on a bench waves when we turn to face them. "That'd be great, thank you," Luke says.

We wait in silence as the couple and their friends go into the magistrate's office. When they emerge, obviously over the moon with happiness, I get up. "Are you sure y'all don't want to just go on and celebrate? I'm sure we can find someone to stand up for us."

"Nah, we're happy to do it. It'll be like a double wedding." The man's grinning from ear to ear, and I feel a little guilty, like we're pulling one over on them too.

Luckily, the ceremony is as short and sweet as you'd imagine. When the magistrate asks if we have rings, I begin to shake my head, but Luke produces two wedding rings from his pocket. It's no small effort to squelch my surprise.

As he slides one ring onto my finger and offers the other to me to slide onto his, I'm equally unprepared for the look on his face, which looks a hell of a lot like tenderness.

It's replaced quickly by that "in for a penny, in for a pound" expression. When he crooks his crooked brow at me and looks pointedly at my lips, I answer with a what-the-hell shrug.

The kiss I expect? A brief, ceremonial meeting of lips.

The one I get? Circuit-breaking.

All formulated thought abandons ship and my body leaps into the breach with unrecognizable enthusiasm. One hand grasps the back of his neck, two breasts squish themselves against a broad chest, and two lips and a tongue open to welcome him like a prodigal son.

A throat clearing from the officiant brings me crashing down to earth, and I step back so fast I trip on my own two feet.

Luke saves me from falling on my ass, one hand on my elbow, the other around my waist. It takes every bit of discipline I've got to keep my hands and my mouth to myself. I use the remaining brain cells to rearrange my face into something resembling normal.

"Thank you for your service" is what I think I say to the man and the couple that stepped in as witnesses.

As Luke closes the door behind us, he whispers, "Nice acting job. You totally sold that."

Disappointment howls behind my breastbone. He was *acting*. It's not like he hasn't had practice pretending at passion. Those Hallmark movies he was in? He can't have been in love with all of those actresses.

"You okay?" he asks once we're outside.

"Of course. Why wouldn't I be?" My thumb worries at the unfamiliar ring on my finger, and I jump on the change of subject. "Hey, where'd you get the rings?"

"Props department. Told them I needed them for a prank."

A prank. Because this is all pretend, Danielle.

He holds the driver's side door open for me, something he's never done before. "I'm sorry if that wasn't what you imagined. For your wedding day."

For a nanosecond, I fall for the concern in his tone and his eyes, but getting into real feelings feels real dangerous at the moment. I force a scoff of a laugh. "Come on, Luke. You really think Danielle Goodwin has a dream wedding?"

He narrows his eyes at me briefly but then shoots me a grin. "Yeah, I guess that's about as likely as Luke Zelazny fantasizing about his."

There's a moment where some sort of energy passes between us, like the moment in a musical before the lovers break into song, when the spotlight hits and the rest of the world disappears. I have no idea how long we stand there, him on one side of the car door, me on the other.

"Are y'all comin' or goin' from that parking spot?"

The spell broken, I call, "Oh, we're going" as I quickly fold myself into the driver's seat.

LUKE

After the wedding, we head back to the office. I've got a conference call scheduled with the suits back in LA for which I sincerely hope Helen O'Neill will bring her A-game, because I'm still a little shaken. As much as I tried to convince Dani that getting married wasn't a big deal, it seems like it was.

Because, *that kiss.*

It's not like I stole my sister's Barbie and Ken dolls to act out dream weddings when I was little. I mean, I stole them, but it was primarily to use them as crash test dummies with my Tonka trucks.

Pretty ironic, considering.

I gave up on ever finding true love a long time ago. I figured you get one of those in a lifetime, and Kellie was mine. No one else could possibly get me the way she does; no one else could accept me and my many flaws. No one's even known me long enough to actually know the real me.

Whoever that guy is.

But she's, as they say, just not into me. Because Kellie's dream wedding—one that may be a pipe dream the way things are in this country—involves two Barbies, no Ken.

So, when Dani asked for my help, it seemed like a no-brainer.

Until that kiss. The kiss—an impulse I obviously should not have acted on—that opened Pandora's box.

I mean, I'm no saint, and the woman is hot as hell. I appreciated her looks the day she picked me up at the airport two years ago, but I shut that down the minute I got into her car. One, it's gross to hit on a woman when her job is to spend time alone in a car with you, oftentimes late at night. Two, I was not in a good headspace. I hadn't yet let myself imagine a life after acting, even though I hated everything about the never-ending lineup of treacly movies where I played some version of myself. Where I couldn't even land the role of the romantic lead. Oh, no. I was always the player who was the lead's best friend. The guy who didn't get why his friend would want to settle down with one girl when there were so many other fish in the sea.

I can't even count the number of times I've had to utter some version of that exact quote. Multiple takes in multiple movies.

Anyway, two years ago, "Loolie" was happening. Which meant I couldn't even be that player I played in real life whenever things were officially off with Kellie. That is, dating girls I could actually have sex with. Kellie keeps trying to get me to commit to someone, but how would I know that the person was falling in love with the real me, if I don't know who the hell I am? If I'm not sure where the fantasy ends and reality begins?

That kiss, though. It wasn't the kind of hot kiss you'd see in an R-rated movie. Nor would it have had an orchestra swelling with joy in the background like in a G-rated family film.

It just felt. I felt. I felt and fell. Like nothing else in the world existed except for the millimeters of skin in contact with hers, while a slideshow played in the back of my mind.

Little moments where I made Dani smile. Or frown. Or roll her eyes.

And now, I'm greedy for more. More kissing, more making her feel. She's so contained—not shut down, exactly, but definitely closed off—that every reaction I can get from her feels like a huge win.

Do I want these things because it's a challenge?

I have to admit, ever since she joked about needing exposure therapy for sex, the idea's been tickling the back of my mind.

Or my balls. I mean, who wouldn't want to be the guy who makes sex good for a woman? That's like the Olympics of lovemaking. And if she thinks she's just going to walk into some bar and pick up some stranger after she has that procedure? No way.

I know, even as her fake husband, that I can't tell her what to do. But I could try to convince her to practice with me. Even the thought of it has me itching for more.

"We're here," the woman in question announces, breaking into my thoughts.

"Where?" I ask, looking around.

"Back at work," she says before shifting in her seat to study me. "Are you sure you're okay with all this? You've been frowning for the past fifteen minutes."

"I'm sorry. I was, uh, thinking. About… stuff."

"Well, if you're worried about the clock ticking down before you can file for divorce, don't. Getting in to see the new doc in town is at the top of my to-do list."

Scrubbing a hand over my face in an effort to shift gears, I remember something I can safely talk to her about. "It's not that. In fact, I was thinking that since we're married, you may as well use my insurance. I hate that you're having to pay for everything out of pocket."

"But—"

"No buts. It's no big deal. I'll keep it on the down-low. Probably have to mail in a copy of the marriage certificate or something."

"Well, if you're sure. It would save me a couple thousand dollars."

"I'm sure. It's ridiculous that it's not free. I mean, all birth control should be free. It's like Puritans started this country or something."

"Or something." She cracks a smile, which has a silly shiver of glee dancing in my belly.

"Tell me, wife. What am I doing now?"

There's a hint of something new in her expression when I call her "wife," something secretly pleased that I like seeing a hell of a lot more than I'd ever imagined.

Unfortunately, opening her planner to flip up overlapping sticky notes, she's all back to business as she mutters, "I can't believe you've been here two weeks already. Tomorrow's the last day of pre-production."

Contemplating next week's schedule has me frowning again. Just the directing part of my job will be sixteen-hour days. I'll have to squeeze producer-hat duties like casting sessions, location visits, and planning meetings into lunch breaks and crew moves. As I'm wondering how the hell I'm going to get myself from point A to point B when my driver's services will no longer be covered, Dani interrupts my thoughts.

"How about this? Since you're not quite ready to drive, if your insurance covers the tubal, I'll keep driving you. We'll tell people that you're paying me directly."

"But will that really cover it? I'm happy to actually pay you."

"Pay your wife for giving you a ride? That seems weird."

"Yeah, but you're not—"

She holds up a hand to interrupt me. "Really your wife. Don't worry, I won't forget." A pained look creases her brow. Not a reaction I like seeing.

"I was going to say that it's not a fair trade. I'm going to pay you. We'll have to figure out the division of assets once this is all over, anyway."

Her eyes widen. "Luke. I'm not taking money from the marriage. I would never…"

"I know that's not what this is about. Regardless, I'm

going to take you up on your offer. You're right. I'm not ready to do it on my own. I'm sorry."

She places a hand on my forearm and squeezes it, removing it so quickly that I'd think I imagined the gesture if her warmth didn't linger. "It's okay. I can tell you're doing the best you can."

After I get out of the car, I watch as she backs out of the parking space, following her progress until her taillights disappear. Even when I turn to head back to my office, back to the grind, I can't shake the feeling that this woman is going to turn my world upside down.

DANI

When I find Luke behind his desk at the end of his day, he's unusually chipper. I'm tempted to say, *Guess married life agrees with you*, but I stop myself just in time. The memory of that kiss may have been playing on repeat in my head all day, but he's probably forgotten it by now.

"Good day at the office?" I ask instead.

"Exceptionally good. I'm actually kind of excited about next week." After grabbing his computer bag, he asks, "I'm also starving. Want to grab dinner on the way home?"

Despite all the reasons why it's probably a bad idea, I want to say yes. Part of me would like to go all in with playing the role of this gorgeous man's wife. Luckily, I have a dog to keep me from leaping before looking. "I have to get home, sorry. Skye's there, and she needs her dinner."

"Duh. I've got a dog to take care of too." He does a playful *I could've had a V-8* forehead slap before ushering me out the door. Once in the larger production office, he calls Peanut, clips on her leash, and sends his PA home.

"Have you eaten, though?" he asks as he watches Peanut do his business on a bush outside.

"Uh, no. Not since breakfast. It's been a busy day."

He shoots me a half smile. Not his usually cheeky grin, but one that's almost bashful. "I kind of feel like we should mark it somehow. Even if it was, you know, fake."

I start to protest, but then my stomach makes a god-awful grumbling noise.

"See, you agree. You're just too stubborn to admit it."

As he settles the dog in the back seat, he continues. "What if we did takeout? The dogs can play while we eat on your back deck. Please, Dani. I'm honestly so sick of the two restaurants I can walk to from my place."

This is a bad idea echoes in the back of my mind, even as I say, "Sure. Why not?"

We swing by a new little gourmet shop I've been meaning to check out, and Luke goes crazy putting things in the shopping basket: cheese, salami, olives, crackers, even a bottle of champagne. Back at my place, once we've got the dogs fed, he asks for a serving tray and then shoos me outside. After setting glasses and cutlery on a table nestled between two Adirondack chairs, I turn on the string of fairy lights hanging overhead and light citronella candles to keep the mosquitos at bay.

It looks quite romantic, but the moment Luke steps outside, my trusty belly spoils the mood with a truly unfeminine and unattractive growl.

"Sounds like someone needs to eat," he announces, setting a beautifully arranged charcuterie plate on the table.

"Impressive. You get Martha Stewart to swing by and put that together?" I ask before shoving a piece of salami in my mouth.

"Not this time," he says, making me choke on said salami.

After I reassure him that I'm okay, he lifts a finger in the air. "The champagne! Be right back." Reappearing with the bottle and popping the cork, he pours me a healthy swig of wine, which I use to get the salami the rest of the way down.

"What do you mean, not this time?" I manage. "Actually, forget it. I don't need to know about how you pal around with famous people until I've got more food in my stomach."

Luke isn't exactly a name-dropper, but he does seem to know a lot of celebrities. Cooking show hosts, basketball players, politicians, you name it. I guess when your entire family is influential in Hollywood, you can't just hang out with regular people.

Like me.

Which is why you need to keep your feet on the ground here, girl. This marriage is not going to evolve into anything. And even if it did, you'd never survive in his crowd. Better to keep things clear and simple.

"I did want to ask you—" he begins.

At the same time, I say, "Oh, I do have news."

"News?" he asks, switching gears. "Good news?"

"I think so," I say, talking with my mouth full. Always a good way to turn a guy off. "I got a doctor's appointment for Saturday."

"This Saturday?"

It's hard to tell in the dim light, but I swear a look of disappointment crosses his face. But when he leans forward to grab his glass and raise it in a toast, his smile seems relieved. "I hope it works out this time."

After we clink glasses, I cover my own weird disappointment with a large swallow of the fizzy stuff. This was the point, Danielle, remember? Get the tubal so I can have sex like a normal person. Casual sex, dating sex, sex that might lead to a relationship. With someone local and appropriate. Not with a frickin' celebrity who actually lives thousands of miles away.

Needing distraction, I focus on the dogs, who have abandoned chasing each other around the backyard. Instead, they look like they're barking without making sound. Standing, I squint into the near darkness. "Look at them."

Luke joins me at the rail. "What the hell?"

"I think they're trying to catch fireflies," I whisper, a little undone by the sight of them launching their bodies into the air with abandon.

Why can't sex be like that?

"Why can't sex be like chasing fireflies?" Luke asks, turning to face me, bringing his pheromones and his wicked grin way too close for comfort.

Whoops. I said that out loud.

After a long moment, during which I try to pretend that I don't know what he's talking about, he leans his forearms on the deck and turns his attention to the dogs again. But just when I think he's let me off the hook, he says, "I don't know if I'd want snapping jaws with sharp teeth anywhere near my junk."

Groaning, I scrub my hands over my face, grab my glass, and pour myself more champagne. "I meant..."

What the hell *did* I mean?

"You meant?" he prods when I don't continue.

Closing my eyes, I whisper, "I meant, why can't sex be silly and fun like that?"

He doesn't answer, so I'm sure he thinks I'm a complete wacko. Digging through my brain for another topic of conversation, I remember he had something to ask me. "What were you going to ask me about?"

"Ironically enough," he begins before taking a sip of his own champagne, "I can't stop thinking about what you said the other day. About exposure therapy. For sex."

My heart somehow manages to exit my rib cage and land in my throat, which is probably a good thing, because while I can't say, *Yes, totally awesome idea,* I don't want to say no. Instead, I take another sip of champagne.

"See," he continues softly, "I have a feeling that your body's reaction to having intercourse is a lot like my body's reaction to driving a car. Like, no matter how many times I tell myself that it's very unlikely that another auto part is going to land on my car and maim my friend, my instincts override the arguments. Similarly, you know, logically, that you'll be protected by birth control, but your body is convinced that you won't be, so it takes over."

He keeps his eyes on the dogs, as if he knows that I can't face him and talk about this. Sex. Sexy talk. Sexy ideas that have a life of their own.

"So, maybe the solution is the same," he says in the same low-pitched gravelly voice that has me edging closer even though I should stay far, far away. "I'm not saying you shouldn't get your tubes tied, but I also think that won't magically solve the problem. Like, how is your body going to know the difference?"

"Because *I'll* know," I argue, despite the fact that the psychiatrist pretty much said the same thing.

"But isn't there still the slightest chance you could get pregnant? Nothing is a hundred percent."

"But it is the most foolproof." My own voice seems to be rising in pitch, even as I fight to stay calm in the face of what he's saying, so I take another sip of champagne.

"I'm not convinced your body will agree."

"So, what? I join a nunnery?"

"No, you do what I'm doing."

"Oh, right. Excuse me, I'll just go check the Yellow Pages for Sex Doctor."

"I wouldn't be surprised if you could find someone. Well, maybe not in Wallington, but definitely in a bigger city. Anyway, I was thinking that we could do it. You and me."

"You? And me? *Do* it?"

"Well, we are married."

"But I can't have sex."

"I think your idea of sex is very limited," he says.

I spell it out for him. "I. Can't. Have. Intercourse. I'm not exaggerating. The last time I tried, I actually threw up on the guy."

I've never shared this detail with anyone. Not even the shrink. But Luke obviously needs a reality check here.

But instead of running for the hills, he turns those intense fucking eyes on me, making my knees weak to the point that my ass drops into my chair, while he keeps on talking.

"Intercourse is not what I'm talking about. I'm talking all the other forms of sexual intimacy."

I raise my glass in a sarcastic toast. "Yeah, yeah, yeah. You go down on me, I suck you off, bing, bam, boom. That does nothing for me. It just feels like a prelude to something that's not going to happen, and everyone ends up disappointed."

"Okay. So those are off the table too."

"Are you nuts? You want to walk around in a state of sexual frustration all the time?"

"Sweetheart, give me a little credit," he says, his attitude unbelievably ho-hum. Like he's suggesting we join a couples' tennis league or something. "One, if absolutely necessary, I can take care of myself. Two, I'm thirty, not eighteen. I have some self-control. Plus, I have a demanding job that requires my attention most of my waking hours."

"Even if that could work—and I'm not sure what exactly you're suggesting—what about, you know, feelings?"

"Didn't we have a whole sexual revolution that made it possible for two consenting adults to enjoy each other's bodies without getting entangled in other ways?"

A large pang of totally unwarranted disappointment hits me right behind the breastbone but "I guess" is all I can say in response.

"I mean, I like you, Dani. I have a lot of respect for you. I wouldn't be here if I didn't. But, honestly, I'm not the kind of guy you marry for real."

"I never said I wanted to marry you for real," I say,

sounding like a ten-year-old in a schoolyard. "Or anyone else. I simply want to be able to have sex. And enjoy it."

"Exactly. Let's use the time we have together before the tubal to work up to that."

I flop back into the chair and stare at the sky. "I don't get what you get out of this."

"Well, first off, I feel bad that it's taking so much of your time and energy to get me through my own phobia, so I'd like to help you in return. But honestly, I think it could be fun. And I have to admit I'd be a little bit pleased if I'm the one who can make sex good for you."

His grin is a little *too* pleased. Meanwhile, my heart's ricocheting between my throat, my belly, and the place between my legs. Could he be right? That getting the tubal won't make enough of a difference on its own? And that easing my way up to it could be *fun*?

I mean, now that the guy knows about the throwing up, I've pretty much surrendered my pride. I also get the sense that he's good at keeping secrets. I can't see him sharing this as some sort of conquering hero story with his bros. But even if he did, if it works, what do I care?

I blow out a long breath before dipping my toe into the pool he's created between us. "So, if we were to do it, how exactly would it work?"

"I'm thinking we make it a game. We could use Two Truths and a Lie."

"What do you mean?"

"Each night, we play a round. If you guess right, you get a prize."

"Wh-what kind of prize?" I whisper, my voice thready.

"If I guess correctly, I get to touch you anywhere I want, using any body part I want."

"B-b-but—" I sputter.

"But no, uh, penetrations further than, like, half an inch. Does that feel doable?"

My hands instinctively fly up to hide my face. Doable? His damn voice is so fucking sexy, pitched soft and low like that, *I'm* feeling doable. Bring on the penetrations. Maybe everything that's happened previously was a fluke.

The sweat suddenly soaking my pits and crotch serves as an ugly reminder: *whoa there, girl. You are not at all doable.*

He's gone silent, and eventually curiosity has me peeking through my fingers. Even in the dim light, the glint in his eyes wakes up my nipples, which stiffen against the fabric of my bra, almost painfully needy.

Fuckers.

The remaining fluid in my body—whatever didn't just release as perspiration—must race to my vagina, because my throat's suddenly so dry I can barely speak. Unfortunately, that doesn't stop me from whispering, "And what if you guess wrong? In the game?"

He hesitates for a moment before answering, "Then the other person gets a touch wherever they want."

"Any subject in particular? For the Two Truths and a Lie?"

"Any subject you want. No holds barred."

I can't believe I'm actually considering this, but consider I do. Will I have more control if I win and take my prize? But what if I do something that turns him off, and he decides to chuck the whole idea altogether? Better to let him make the first physical move, which means, "I'll go first."

"Okay by me."

The look in his eyes when I say okay is entirely new to me. Never before seen in real life or on the small screen. This is raw, fierce, with something to prove.

Question is, do I give him a lowball, or make him work for it?

The subject matter can't be sexy stuff. That feels way too loaded.

"Don't want to rush you, but we do have to work tomorrow. And I'd love to get in early so I can pull together a proposal for kickball before the read-through."

"Aha! The topic is sports." Sitting up quickly makes me a little dizzy, so I relax back into the seat in order to concentrate on keeping things straight in my head. "Number one: I was the kind of kid that always got picked last for teams in elementary school."

"Okay."

"Number two: I was captain of the cross-country team in high school."

"Mm-hmm."

"And number three: in junior high, I got knocked out cold during a game of dodgeball when a ball hit me in the face and my head hit the brick wall."

"Yikes," he says, before tucking his hands behind his head and leaning back in his chair, putting perfect biceps on display. Not too big, not too small. Not too hairy, not bare either. Not so cut that his veins are sticking out, but nicely defined.

"You're getting better," he says.

"Wanna hint?" Weird. My words are a little slurred.

He shakes his head definitively. "Nope, no hints." After a beat, he turns to face me again. "Number two."

"What? How'd you guess?"

"Number three definitely happened to you or someone you know, but my gut says it was you. I almost went with the first one, because you seem so naturally athletic, but then I remembered that little kids can be shits and not pick you for all kinds of reasons. Also, you lifted the word 'captain' a hair, which made me think that you were on the team, but you weren't the captain."

"Damn." I should probably shut up, so he can do whatever he's going to do to me, but my mouth keeps going. "That's right. I got knocked out. I didn't get picked because my clothes came from Goodwill, and I couldn't be captain because I missed too many practices."

I don't tell him why because I'm not here for a pity party.

And then I remember what happens next.

"Time for my prize."

All breath has left my body, so I just nod in response.

Without another word, he stands to lean one hand on the arm of my chair. Hovering close, slowly threading the fingertips of his right hand from the base of my skull up the back of my head, his thumb gently tips my head to the side. After several long strangely delightful moments where all I feel is the caress of warm breath on the space he exposed on my neck, his lips drag along my neck until he finds the center of the ridge. The place he squeezed before our first doctor's appointment. His mouth opens, his tongue lands, his teeth scrape the skin, and every single bit of me contracts as he slowly sucks on my neck.

I have no idea how long this goes on—it could be seconds, it could be an hour—but I can't think about anything beyond his teeth poised to break through my skin, the heat of his body near and yet not near enough to mine, the pressure of his fingers against my skull. All I know is, the moment he moves away, my entire left side feels bereft, cold, abandoned.

Jumping up from the chair, I sway a little on my feet.

"You okay?" he asks, taking my elbow to steady me.

His expression shifts from pleased to concerned, but what I have to say is probably going to change it to pissed.

"Uh... I think I'm drunk."

LUKE

If it were any woman other than this one, I'd suspect her of pretending to be wasted or getting drunk on purpose. Like, hey, we're stuck together, so let's make the best of it.

But she's too professional, too responsible, and despite the heat in that kiss after the wedding ceremony, way too skittish about sex to go for that kind of setup. On top of all that, she looks miserable. Most likely, she drank too much, too fast because she's freaked out after getting married.

"I'm so sorry. I really didn' mean"—she breaks off, rubbing her hands over her face—"I can make some coffee. Sober up enough to get you home."

But when she tries to walk into the house, she weaves so off course I have to lunge to keep her from walking into the doorframe. "Did you eat at all today before now?"

"I…" Tipping her head up, she stares at the sky like the answers might be there. "I dunno."

"Let's you some water. And maybe you should eat some more." When she turns to face me, her expression is still so wounded that I add, "And don't worry about driving me home. We'll figure something out."

I steer her into the kitchen and get her settled at the counter before bringing in the food. She picks at the remains of my charcuterie arrangement as I grab a couple glasses and fill them with water. I'd noticed the day she cut my hair that, while the house seems to only have one bathroom, it looks like there might be three bedrooms. There must be an extra bed where I can crash.

I wait until she drains the glass before asking, but when I do, she squeezes her eyes shut. "Ughhh. Tina and George."

It takes some doing, because Dani keeps getting lost in her own story, but I eventually get the gist of the situation. "So, they're your roommates, they're really a couple, but they're afraid of going public because of the Morality Memo, so they've rented both bedrooms" is the conclusion I eventually come to.

"Oh shit," she says, interrupting me. "*We* could lose our jobs."

"No, no. We're fine because we're married."

She gasps and then whisper-shouts, "I forgot!"

It's a struggle to keep a straight face, especially when she cups both hands over her mouth in the shape of a megaphone to yell, "Did you hear that world? We're married!"

"You're married?" a female voice asks.

We both spin to face the front of the house, and I have to grab ahold of Dani to keep her from falling over.

"To each other?" a petite, curvy woman with a lot of hair asks from the doorway. The big guy next to her turns beet-red, almost like he's envisioning us going at it on the kitchen counter or something.

Dani throws her hands in the air. "Isn't it crazy?"

But then she claps her hands over her mouth and turns to face me. I get a glimpse at the look of horror on her face before she clonks her forehead into my sternum. Staggering backward, I put both arms around her to steady her.

"I'm sorry," I whisper to the couple over her shoulder. "She had a little too much to drink."

"Well, it's a lot to celebrate," the woman says. "And what a surprise."

"It's a long story" is the best I can come up with.

Dani is saying something to my chest, but I can't quite understand what.

"You're her roommates, I take it?"

The woman steps forward, her hand out. "Yes, sorry. I'm Tina, and this is George."

I do my best to shake her hand while keeping Dani upright. "I'm Luke Zelazny."

George pales. "Luke Zelazny, the producing director on *Lawson's Reach*?"

"That's me," I confirm, unsure if I should let them know that I know their situation or not.

"Guess we'll be seeing a lot of you then," George says after a long pause. "We're writers on the show. Our next episode shoots next week."

"Right. I'm directing it."

"Great! That's... awesome," Tina says, neither her tone nor her forced smile matching her words.

I'm about to put them both out of their misery and promise to keep their secret if they'll keep ours, but a moan from Dani and barking in the backyard remind me that I've got more pressing concerns.

"Do you think you could let the dogs in? The little one is my dog, Peanut. I should get this girl to bed."

Before I can do so, however, Tina says, "We are not a couple, by the way. Just writing partners."

"Yep," George says. "We only work together. We don't sleep together. Separate bedrooms and all. Those two right down the hall," he adds.

"Got it," I manage as Dani slumps in my arms.

As I practically carry Dani to the bedroom that I'm pretty sure is hers, I sort through the mess we've created. The actual couple will sleep in separate beds, so I don't narc on them to my boss. Meanwhile, I can't sleep on the couch, or the real couple will suspect that our marriage is a sham.

Looks like I'll be sharing a bed with my sexy, intoxicated, fake wife.

CHAPTER TEN

DANI

This is the best dream ever. And it has to be a dream because this has never happened to me before. Because the thing is, when you freak out about having intercourse, the guy never stays for the night.

Like I'm sick and it might be contagious.

But in this dream, the easy rise and fall of a chest under my cheek soothes my usual morning anxiety. Firm muscles wrapped in soft skin make such a safe cocoon that my to-do list fades to the back of my mind. A body tangled with mine to the point that it's hard to tell where he ends and I begin, makes me feel less alone.

The musky scent enveloping me even has desire stirring deep inside.

The dream is so much better than I could imagine. So much better than what I've read in books or heard about from friends. Even though, obviously, I am imagining it. Because there's no way this is really Luke Zelazny lying next to me.

In my bed.

Except, maybe it is.

My *husband*, Luke Zelazny.

Bits and pieces of the previous day float through my mind. The kiss at the wedding. The romantic picnic on the back deck. The dogs chasing fireflies in the backyard. Me being too drunk to drive. The dull pain between my brows. My roommates returning.

Oh, shit.

"Good morning, sunshine," the all-too-real man next to me says. Easing his arms out from under me, he stretches in the bed, revealing ridiculously cut abs and a happy trail leading—thankfully or disappointingly, I'm not quite sure— to a pair of boxer shorts. Scrambling up to sitting and pulling the sheet over my own body, I peek underneath to discover my parts covered by sleep shorts and a tank... which I vaguely remember putting on after stumbling into the bathroom. As well as Luke coaching me through brushing my teeth.

When he turns on his side to face me, propping his head on his hand, I make myself ask, "Wh-what happened exactly?" Even though I'm pretty sure I just remembered it all.

His smile is wicked, waking my nipples all the way up, and sending a shivery little feeling to my lower belly.

"Did we... have sex?" I whisper.

A look of horror crosses his face. Great. Sex with me is *that* unappealing.

"Are you serious?" he asks, his expression shifting to hurt. "Having sex with a girl who's drunk is date rape."

"Oh. Yeah. Sorry. You're right."

"You really don't remember anything? I didn't think you'd blacked out."

I cover my face with my palms. "I remember a bunch of stuff, but I'm hoping that some of it is wrong."

"Like the fact that your roommates heard you yell that we're married?"

I peek through my fingers. "I really did that?"

He nods, and weirdly, he looks like he's holding back a laugh.

"Why aren't you mad?"

He shrugs. "I don't know. I mean, it's done. Why get mad about it?"

The Cheshire cat grin he's got going on is really freaking me out. Jumping up to grab my robe from behind my closet door, needing to both separate from this way-too-sexy man and unscramble my thoughts, I pledge, "Don't worry. I'll figure out a way to walk it back."

Scooching across the bed and swinging his perfect body closer to me, he grabs my hand. "Seriously, Dan, I don't mind. Maybe it's for the best."

Shoving aside the little zizzle wrought by the way he shortened my name, I whisper-screech, "How can it be for the best? This will turn both our worlds upside down. I mean, what about you and Kellie? And the… paparazzi or whatever? Not to mention my family coming around looking for money and attention and who knows what all."

He shrugs. "We keep it quiet. We tell people on a need-to-know basis, and we let them know that we don't want attention. Since we're married, we can't get in trouble with the morality police at the studio."

He's still holding my hand, which makes it difficult for me to concentrate. "I don't understand how you can be so calm about this."

Rubbing a thumb across my knuckles with what feels like real tenderness, he leans in to catch my eye. "Honey, my life has been one circus after another. This is just another sideshow."

LUKE

I honestly don't know why I'm not more freaked out.

Maybe it's because of my long history with Kellie, or maybe I'm compartmentalizing because today is the first day I'll be stepping up as producing director in front of a large group.

But honestly, I think it's because I loved waking up next to Danielle, even though I couldn't act on the desire she stirs in me. Lying down next to her without touching her the night before had been easy. She'd been so silly and helpless, so unlike the I-don't-need-anything-from-anybody woman I'm used to, that all my focus was on making sure she was comfortable. But this morning, drifting to consciousness with her silky hair under my chin, with her beachy scent enveloping us both, I had the oddest feeling.

Like I was finally home.

The feeling has fueled me all morning. We actually woke up pretty early, a couple hours before I needed to be at the office. Bright-eyed and bushy-tailed, I somehow talked Dani into dropping me back at my place so I could go for a run before she drove me to work. Since she was obviously a bit hungover, I offered to trade dogs. Skye could run with me, and Peanut could lounge with her while she got ready for the day.

The grateful look I got in return was one I'd like to see again and again.

Maybe even with her naked body splayed in front of me post-orgasm.

However, this is not a thought I should be having while sitting at the head of a long table filled with actors, crew, and the two writers who keep shooting me worried looks. If not for the damn memo, they'd have nothing to worry about. Their words leap off the page, and their storyline maintains the will-they-won't-they tension between the main characters without getting bogged down in it.

Meanwhile, the cast seems relaxed and in good spirits, nary a dirty nor flirty look shared between the lot of them.

The new additions are, predictably nervous, but that's something I can deal with.

When we get to the union-mandated break, I stretch, happier than I've been in recent memory. But when I head outside to get a breath of fresh air and a very large man steps into my path, I go on high alert. Noting the absence of an ID tag, required by security on the lot, I stand tall and thread a challenge into my tone. "Can I help you?"

Either ignoring or missing my threat, he sticks out his hand. "You're Luke, right?"

Instead of answering, I point at his chest. "How did you get in here?"

He looks down at his chest. "Oh, shit. Forgot my ID again."

The man's disarming smile along with his easygoing drawl brings me back to reality. *Calm down, Luke.* This is North Carolina. No journalist is going to sneak onto the lot and accost you about whatever scandal you've found yourself in. Like marrying a woman you barely know.

"Anyway," he continues, apparently unaffected by my paranoia, "I'm Sully Calloway. We talked about kickball last night?"

"Right. Of course. Good to meet you in person."

"Yeah, man. It's an awesome idea." He rubs his hands together like he'd play right now if we could. "I did a little calling around this morning, and I've got a field reserved for Sunday mornings at ten. Figured that's early enough that it won't get too hot; it'll be quiet 'cause the locals are at church, and the tourists'll be getting in their last hours at the beach. And Randy's all in. He's gonna bring his van and sell coffee and pastries and all."

"You did all that this morning?"

"Yeah. It was easy."

"Wow. Thanks. This could be just what this show needs. Are we talking about this Sunday? Like two days from now?"

He shrugs. "Yeah, if you want. Field's a little bit off the beaten path, but I could work up a map and make copies."

I check my watch. Time to get back into the read-through. Hooking a thumb at the stage door, I ask, "Could you get the maps back here in the next hour? Then I could make the announcement at the end of the read-through."

"No problem."

As I leave the sunshine for the dim light of the sound-stage, I'm eager to get back at it. This day just couldn't get any better.

Unfortunately, after I deliver the invitation to the cast and crew chiefs, encouraging them to spread the news to everyone in their departments, Helen bustles up to me, a not-so-pleased expression on her face.

"Can we discuss this *idea* of yours," she hisses, "in my office?"

I'm outta here echoing in my head, because it would be so nice to disappear, I turn down the offer of a ride in her golf cart and follow her on the bike I use to get around the large complex. After trailing her down the rabbit warren of hall-ways the leads to the production office, the feeling that I've been summoned to the principal's office intensifies when she points at the chair across from her desk.

Instead of sitting, I pause in the doorway. "Can you just spit it out, Helen? I've got meetings to get to."

"So do I." She punctuates her sentence by dropping a legal pad on her desk. "And now you've added to my already endless to-do list."

"I'm sorry, I really don't know what's going on here."

She doesn't sit either. Instead, she grabs the back of her office chair like she wants to throw it at me. "Did it occur to you to clear it with anyone before you set up some sort of sports league? Do you have any idea what kind of insurance problems this is going to cause?"

"No, but—"

"Did you?"

"Uh, no. I didn't. It didn't occur to me to."

She just nods, and her message is clear. *You didn't because you don't know what the fuck you're doing.*

She's right. But I'm here, and I'm doing the best I can. Still, I don't want to make work for anyone. "I apologize. It was a hasty action. I will take care of whatever issues this raises with insurance or—"

"Agents, managers, unions." Straightening, she ticks the list off on her fingers. "We are not paying people for this. This cannot be some kind of PR op."

"No, no." I wave my hands in the air, hoping to dispel her spiral of worries. "That's not the idea at all. And if you want me to distance it from the show completely, I'm happy to do that."

She narrows her eyes at me but doesn't speak.

"My brother started a regular kickball game back in LA. It's a super low-key networking-slash-blow-off-steam thing. I guess Leif knows about it because he asked me if we could do something like that here."

I check over my shoulder to make sure we're still alone and then step further into her office, lowering my voice. "One of the things I was tasked to do here is get ahead of any competitiveness and other... entanglements between the cast members, so it seemed like a good idea to say yes to Leif's request. When I asked Dani what she thought, she called her friend Sully Calloway—he's the boom guy on the show?"

I drop the guy's name as if I don't know perfectly well what their relationship is, which I'll allow is a little mean. When Helen's face pinks up, I know I've hit her where it counts.

"I am well aware of who he is."

"Well, he jumped on it. Signed us up for a field with the rec department. But it can just be a bunch of friends getting together. No pressure to participate at all."

"Hey, boss." The man himself appears in the doorway as if on cue. When he catches sight of me, he waves. "Oh, hey, Luke. I've got the extra maps if you want 'em. Or I can put 'em up on the bulletin board outside."

"You're in on this crazy plan?" Helen asks him. "You of all people should be careful about getting hurt."

He leans against the doorframe. "O'Neill. What did I say about that?"

She mutters something that sounds like *I can't wrap you in Bubble Wrap.*

"I'm cleared to do whatever physical activity I want from the doctor." Turning to me, he explains, "I was in a boating accident last summer and broke my leg pretty bad. Couldn't boom for a while. But my *girlfriend* here is a little overprotective."

I turn back to Helen, suppressing a smirk. "What do you say, Helen? I really think it could be good for morale. Make us all feel like a team, you know?"

"Oh, and Vi said she'd umpire. She'll keep everybody in line." Sully turns to me. "Violet Davenport is the local casting director, and she's pregnant so she won't be able to play."

"Sounds great," I say.

Helen keeps me and Sully waiting for a long moment before pulling out her desk chair and taking a seat. "Fine, whatever. But check in with Max and insurance sometime today and get the all-clear. And don't expect me to participate. I'm too old for that kind of crap."

CHAPTER ELEVEN

DANI

Saturday morning, after I take Skye for a run—so much more appealing when one doesn't have a hangover—I stop by Deluxe and pick up a coffee and Danish for Luke. He doesn't look like he eats sweets, but I feel like I'm monopolizing a heck of a lot of his time lately, so I figure a treat is in order.

When I pull up in front of the garage under his apartment, he's playing fetch with Peanut. Rolling down the window, I call, "I don't think you can bring him to the doctor's office."

"Yeah, that's why I'm getting him worn out now. I figure he'll be okay alone in the apartment for an hour or so."

He shades his eyes with his hand as he takes in the car. "You returned the town car?"

"Yep. You have to slum it in my Bronco from now on."

"Eh, more my speed anyway. Be right back out," he adds, scooping up the dog and jogging up the stairs to his apartment.

After he slides into the passenger seat, I hand him the coffee and pastry bag. He takes both, setting the bag on his lap. "Wow, thanks. Anything in it?"

"Two sugars, no cream, right?"

"How'd you know?" He tips his head to the side. "Oh, right, I forgot. You know everything. Usually kind of terrifying, but in this case appreciated. Oooh, Danish. I'm so glad I'm not an actor anymore."

"Was it really that big of a bummer? Being an actor?"

He seems to think about it as he takes a sip of the coffee. "I mean, if I were really passionate about the craft, like my brother is, it'd all be worth it. Counting calories, skin care, not eating foods that stain your teeth"—he waggles the blueberry Danish—"but for me, the costs eventually outweighed the benefits."

When we stop at a light, he offers me a bite of the pastry before shoving the remainder in his mouth, moaning appreciatively. I'm wondering if I could get him to make that sound with fewer clothes on, when the car behind us beeps its horn politely, as one does in the South. Dragging my attention back to vehicle operation, I wave in the rearview mirror before pulling into the intersection.

Moments later, we're at the new doctor's practice. We don't have to wait long, thankfully, and since I'm here for a consult instead of an exam, we're whisked directly to her office, skipping the usual weigh-in and blood pressure check.

Dr. Jane Burrows seems very young, which I decide is a good thing. If she were going to deliver my baby, I might want someone with more experience, but for my purposes, eager for new patients and open-minded is what I'm hoping for.

"What can I help you with today?" she pauses to glance at the file on the desk in front of her, "Ms. Goodwin and Mr. Zuh-uh—"

"Zelazny," Luke says, when she stumbles on the pronunciation. "Dani kept her own last name when we got married. In fact, I've thought about adopting hers. Easier to pronounce."

The doctor winks at him. "You can say that again."

"Anyway," I say, suddenly not so happy that the doctor is

young. And also quite attractive. "I'd like to make an appointment to get my tubes tied."

"Oh yes, I saw that." She taps the file a few times before opening a file drawer. After searching for a moment or two, she slides a stack of pamphlets across the desk.

Not to Luke, but to me. Solid start.

"I've actually done a bunch of research. It's something I've wanted for a long time." I point at the file. "You should have a letter in there from a psychiatrist."

Her manner lacks judgment, but Dr. Burrows still asks every question all the other doctors have. Have I tried other forms of birth control, how long have I known I don't want to bear children, do I understand that this isn't a reversible procedure, yadda, yadda, yadda?

Only after I've answered them all, calmly, does she turn to Luke. "And Mr., uh—"

"You can call me Luke," he says, beaming his most charming grin at her.

"Thank you," she says, blushing. Does she think my husband is flirting with her?

"Do you have anything to add, Luke?"

He shrugs. "It's her body, her choice, obviously. But I don't want children either, so I'm totally on board."

"Well, then." She stacks the papers with all my information and places them in the file. "You can make an appointment with the receptionist on your way out."

"Really?" I ask, heart pounding with surprise and about twelve other feelings. "Just like that?"

"You've obviously thought this through and weighed the consequences carefully. We'll need to have you in for some pre-op bloodwork and an ultrasound."

"Great, so I'll make that appointment and the one for the tubal, too?"

"Yes, any time after the thirty-day waiting period," she says, standing and rounding her desk.

We stand, too, but my mind trips over her last words. "What thirty-day waiting period?"

She pauses and turns back to face us, her hand on the door. "I'm sorry, I figured you knew about that. Some states, including North Carolina, have a waiting period between the date a patient elects sterilization and the date of the procedure."

"But I've been waiting for, like, years," I say, hating how whiny my voice sounds, but unable to control it. "Why do I have to wait longer?"

She winces slightly. "I'm sorry, but it's a pretty strict law. And for good reason. Far too many women were sterilized against their will in this country in the name of eugenics. Including right here in North Carolina. The law is there to protect women."

I feel like someone gave me a shot of horse tranquilizer. Luke saves me from collapsing by putting an arm around me and hugging me into his side. "Thanks for your time, doctor. I guess we'll see you in a month."

I'm still in shock as he follows the nurse's directions to the checkout window, so it takes me a minute to realize that this affects him too. Stopping our progress halfway down the hall, I whisper, "Luke. It's too much. You don't have to go through with this. Or maybe you can go ahead and start the divorce proceedings before the surgery."

He lowers his head until I meet his gaze and speaks softly but firmly. "Dan, I'll say it again. I'm fine with this. One more month doesn't make a difference to me. And besides, this'll give the insurance company time to get their ducks in a row."

When I open my mouth to protest, he holds up a finger and ticks it back and forth. "No. Big. Deal."

LUKE

On some level, I know that this is gonzo. I mean, despite being in and out of a fake relationship for my entire adult life, this one feels... real. Like, I could actually picture myself building a life with this woman. Which is scary as shit and intriguing in equal measure.

"Ready to go?" Dani asks, once we've finished signing out.

Thankfully, she seems to have recovered a bit from the shock, but I put an arm around her shoulders and give her a comforting squeeze anyway. "What do you say we go grab some breakfast? Maybe get a little driving time in?"

"Sure. I could be up for that." Her arm snakes around my waist, her hand resting on my hip, and it's like puzzle pieces snapping into place.

Until—halfway across the waiting room—she steps away from my side so quickly that I trip over my own feet, having to grab a chair to avoid landing in a pregnant woman's lap.

"I am so sorry, I—" I begin, but before I can finish my apology, Dani's words cut my thought in two.

"Oh, hey, Vi. Hey, Nate. I thought y'all were in California."

I know this couple. Violet Davenport and Nate Fowler, from the local casting office.

"We got back last night. What are y'all up to?" Violet asks, her tone making it clear she knows something's up.

"Oh, you know..." Dani says, making a vague circling gesture with her hand.

Violet lowers her chin to give her the look, and it's clear she will definitely be one of those mothers you can never lie to. "No, Danielle, I don't know. That is why I asked."

"Right. Well. See, I brought one of my cousins in the other day, but she forgot to bring her, um, insurance card, and since Luke and I are out doing errands, because you know, I'm still driving him because, he, well, he needs me to, so we stopped in. For that. That's all."

Eyes narrowed, Violet lets Dani ramble on until she runs out of steam. "That's your story?"

To her credit, Dani lifts her chin. "Yep. And, uh, we gotta go. Time's a-wastin'. Y'all have a good, uh, visit, with the, uh, doctor."

I can't watch her flail any longer, even though I'm loving how her accent deepens with every word, so I open the door, planning to usher Dani out. "See you all next week."

But before we can escape, a voice calls, "Mr. and Mrs. Zelazny? I need y'all to fill out this other form."

Eyes wide, Dani looks at me in panic. I catch a glimpse of Violet out of the corner of my eye, and her jaw is practically on the floor.

Sometimes, the only way out is through, so I put my arm around my wife, and steer her back to the receptionist. After filling out the form, we go for take two of our exit. This time, Violet jumps out of her chair to intercept us, but before she can say anything, a nurse calls her name.

Before following the woman back into the exam area, however, Violet stops to poke Dani in the sternum and give her a stern command. "You need to call me, girl."

CHAPTER TWELVE

DANI

Luke's arm draped protectively across my shoulders is something I could get used to. I never wanted to be a woman who relied on anyone—especially not a man—for anything, but, well, no one's ever offered. For some reason, the way he stepped up to take care of things feels okay. Like he's just pitching in. Not because I can't take care of it myself, but because he's there and why not share the burden if you can?

Not something to get used to, missy. This is a temporary solution to a specific problem.

Still, I can't quite make myself shrug out of the embrace any more than I can forget the feel of his mouth on my neck the other night, and when he suggests grabbing breakfast, I don't say no. Since it's Saturday in the summer, there's no sense in going to the Causeway on Wrightsboro Beach, so we head for Salt Works instead. It's busy, but we manage to snag a couple of seats at the counter.

Once we've ordered, he swivels on his stool to face me. "I think we might need to reevaluate."

Disappointment floods my systems so fast I have to hang on to the counter to remain upright, but I quickly rearrange my face to hide it. "I get it. Like I said, go ahead and do what you need to do to file for divorce. I mean, it's only been a couple days. Maybe we could even get an annulment."

He places a hand over mine, the one currently fiddling with a teaspoon. "Dani, I'm not backing out. But I think we need to make some decisions about who to tell and what to tell them." He looks around the restaurant and then lowers his voice to continue. "Your roommates think our marriage is for real. What are you going to tell Violet?"

I pick at the fraying edge of the plastic menu with my free hand as I do my best to shift gears. "I can't lie to Violet. Not just because she's my best friend, but because she'll see through it."

He leans so close, I can see that his blue eyes have tiny brown freckles in them. "Can you trust her to be discreet?"

"Vi? Yes. I mean, she has to be for her job. But also, she's a good egg. She wants what's best for me." Then I realize that he might be more concerned about his own reputation. "But also, she won't sell the story to some fan magazine. You don't have to worry about that."

He rubs a hand over the dome of his skull, a new gesture that seems to have replaced pushing his hair out of his eyes. "I honestly don't give a shit. There are other people in my life who do, but I'm thinking about you. I know you don't want to deal with the circus of being publicly attached to"—he lowers his voice even further and leans even closer—"that guy Lukas."

I don't care what his real name is or where we are, a hunger that has nothing to do with the pancakes I ordered yawns a gap inside so deep that it takes everything in me to avoid shifting a few inches closer so I can get another taste of those full lips.

"Western omelet and pancakes," the waitress announces as she slides two plates across the counter. "Side of bacon coming right up. Y'all want anything else?"

"Nope. Nada. Nothing for me." Picking up my cutlery and taking a stab at the stack in front of me, I stuff my face before I can blurt out what it is I find myself really wanting, where I want it, and how.

In between bites, I convince Luke that it's best if we keep things between us a secret, apologizing again for mucking things up with my housemates. He keeps saying that it's okay, but if I were him, I'd be pissed, so I don't quite believe him. After breakfast, which he manages to pay for without me even getting a chance at the bill, he begs off driving practice, which makes me more suspicious.

"I need to put in some time with the script, and I probably shouldn't leave Peanut alone for much longer."

To top it all off, on the way to his place, when I ask if he needs a ride to the kickball game the next day, he says he'll ask Sully if he can pick him up instead. "That way we can make sure everything's ready to go before the crowd shows up. At least, I hope there's a crowd."

"Cool, cool. Well, call if you need anything. I've got your call time for Monday."

"Will you come to the game tomorrow?"

It seems like he needs time away from his needy wife, so I pretend I do too. "Not sure. I'll see."

"Okay, well. I'll see you when I see you."

As I back out of his driveway, I try to console myself with the lesson I've just learned.

It's a hell of a lot easier to be okay with being single when you're not married to someone who doesn't want to spend time with you.

On the drive home, I crank up the volume on LEN's "Steal My Sunshine," and psych myself up to call Violet. If I don't, she'll be on my doorstep before the day is over, so the minute

I walk in the door, I go straight to the telephone to face the music that is Violet Davenport.

She doesn't even say hello. She just launches right in, thank you very much, caller ID.

"You got some serious 'splainin' to do, my friend. What the hell is going on? Are you actually married to Lukas whatever his real name is, or pretending to be? And why? Oh, please don't tell me he hasn't dragged you into the soap opera that is his love life with Kellie Kingston."

"Do you actually want answers to any of these questions, or do you just feel the need to yell at me?"

"Yell at you? Believe me, this is not yelling. I am concerned about you. Marrying some guy out of nowhere is not something the Danielle Goodwin I know would ever do." She gasps. "Oh my god. Nothing nefarious is going on, is it? I mean, he's not forcing you or—"

"Jesus, Vi. You gotta get that imagination under control." I'm pretty sure my roommates aren't home, but just in case, I drag the hall phone and its long cord into my bedroom and close the door, like I used to do when I was a teenager. "No one is forcing me to do anything."

"Oh, okay, phew. Sorry, these hormones make me kinda crazy."

"Crazier than usual, you mean?"

"Not crazier than you, apparently."

I slump back onto my bed. "I think you might be right about that."

"All right. I'm calm now," she claims, even though her voice still has an edge of hysteria. "Just tell me."

"It's all a little hard to sort out, actually. One thing kind of led to another—"

"Wait. Facts first. You really are married?"

"Well, yes, technically. Legally, I am Luke Zelazny's wife. For the moment."

When I don't go on, she sputters, "Are you going to tell me why?"

I always thought I'd be able to tell Violet everything. But ever since I found out that she's pregnant, I've felt weird about talking to her about getting my tubes tied. I told her the first couple of times about the doctors who refused to do it, but I kept rejections number three through five to myself.

And if I'm really honest, it's been hard to watch two of my four best friends pair off so happily this past year. Ford's still playing the field like it's his job, and Whitney's stuck in an impulsive marriage that you'd think we'd all learn from, but Sully and Violet are so damn starry-eyed it makes me want to puke sometimes.

I wish I were a bigger person about it, but I don't like losing my friends.

"Dani? Are you okay? Do I need to come over?"

"No, no, sorry. I'm trying to figure out how to explain."

"Well, if it's going to take much longer, you'll have to listen to me eat. Now that I'm past the throwing-up-all-the-time stage of this pregnancy, I'm like a bottomless pit."

"You go ahead and grab something. I can wait."

"Okay, hang on a sec."

There's a muffled conversation that seems to be mostly her yelling things at Nate. I picture her on the couch with her feet up while he runs around getting a snack for her, and I have to squelch the envy again. It's not like I want what she has, but it seems I do want something other than what I've got now.

"I'm back. Nate's making me a smoothie."

"Right."

"I'm here, Dani. I know I'm across town, and I know I've been super busy with Casting Carolina and Nate. I hate that I only see you when we trade off Skye."

It's on the tip of my tongue to say, *it'll only get worse when you have the baby.*

"I'll admit I'm also freaking out a little bit. You know I don't exactly have the best role models for parenting—"

"Sure, you do. Even if your parents dropped the ball, your grandparents picked it right up."

"But you know more than I do about taking care of babies. Hell, Nate knows more than I do. He's great with his niece and nephew."

"Vi, you're awesome with kids. And the baby thing is easy. They just need to eat and poop and sleep and be held."

"Damn. Here I am making it all about me. Again. Ugh, I'm sorry I'm such a shitty friend. No wonder you kept whatever's going on with you to yourself."

Not gonna say she's right, but not gonna say she's wrong.

"But I'm here if you want to tell me now," she adds with a heavy dose of expectation.

I don't know if I'm ready to talk about the confusing feelings I'm having for Luke at the moment, but since the cat's already out of the bag, I may as well give her the 411.

To her credit, she just listens as I fill her in on how I went from being Lukas Keith's driver to Luke Zelazny's wife. She doesn't say a single judgmental word about the tubal. Instead, when I finish, she asks, "And how are you feeling about all this?"

Ugh. *Feelings.*

This is the point where I have to lie to my best friend. Not because I don't trust her, but because I don't even know what the truth is.

"Oh, fine. It's obviously complicated, I mean, secret-wise. And speaking of which, please don't tell anyone. We really only have to keep up the ruse for the doctor."

"And everyone who works in that office, which is like fifty people," she insists. "It's a huge practice, and this is a small town. If y'all are out in public, you're going to run into someone at some point."

"Vi, it's not that big of a deal. We'll get through the next month, I'll get the surgery, and then we'll file for divorce. It'll be over in six months. Or so."

She sighs. "Well, I hope it's worth it."

"Yeah. Me too."

After the call, my feelings—especially the frisky ones—are still in a jumble, but I feel better about my friendship with Vi. She's not my mother after all. She's not her mother, either. She's just another woman having a baby who happens to be one of my closest friends. And who will continue to be for a long time, even if it takes some effort on my part.

But when I head into the kitchen to make a grocery list so I can stock up before what will likely be a busy first week of production, I find the other two people caught up in this web of lies.

"Hi, Dani!" Tina says, way too enthusiastically.

George peers around my shoulder and down the hall. "Where's Luke?"

"Oh." I haven't actually spoken to my roommates since my drunken announcement two days ago, and "He's... at his apartment" is the best I can come up with.

"He isn't moving in with you?" Tina asks, understandably confused.

"Yeah, well, he has a place through the show, and so he's going to, you know..." I trail off, hoping they'll fill in the rest of the sentence for me because I have run out of words. Unfortunately, they just stare at me, heads nodding slowly in unison.

Eventually, Tina breaks the silence. "He's going to what?"

"Use it as an extra office," I blurt. "He's got so much work to do, and he can't always get it done at production because people are always interrupting"—I have no idea if this is true but it seems like it could be so I keep on keepin' on anyway—"so, yeah. He's working."

"But he'll be here for, like, living?" George asks.

"Eating? Sleeping?" Tina adds.

I jump in before she can add anything *else* to the list. "Yeah, yeah, mostly. But like I said, his schedule is crazy, so he might sleep there too. Some. Maybe a lot. We'll have to see how it goes."

Tina's brow furrows. "Oh, no. That's so sad. With you being newlyweds and all."

"Pshaw." I wouldn't usually find myself saying any of these things, including words like "pshaw," so I may as well dive into the deep end of not normal. "You know how it is. Double-income household. Ya gotta be flexible."

There's a long pause, during which I hope they're buying this act. I sure as hell wouldn't. Finally, George clears his throat.

"He didn't say anything about"—he draws a line in the air between himself and Tina—"*us*, did he?"

"No, no." I shake my head. "I don't think he's bothered."

"But does he suspect that we're… you know?" Tina asks.

"Uh. No. I doubt it. He's pretty"—I wave a hand in the air—"clueless. About that stuff."

"Well," Tina says, her voice practically squeaking, "since it's the weekend, I guess he'll be here tonight, so we'll just, you know, sleep in separate rooms again."

I start to protest that it's fine, he probably won't sleep over, but then I realize that him not doing so might raise suspicions. But then again, who are they going to tell that'll get the news of our fake marriage back to the doctor?

I'm about to go ahead and tell them the truth and put us all out of our misery when the phone rings. As I reach for it, George and Tina say that they'll see me later and scoot out the door.

Since I left the hall phone in my bedroom, I hustle back there to answer it.

"I am so sorry to bother you, Dani," Luke says, his voice tight. "But I don't know what to do."

"Ugh. Join the club."

"What's going on? Is everything okay?"

"Other than the fact that I created a major tangle of lies, you mean? Yeah, everything's peachy."

"Was your friend upset?"

"Vi? No, she's fine." I peer down the hall to make sure George and Tina aren't still hanging around and then close my door again just in case. "But my roommates are in a lather. They're wondering why you're not living here, while being all antsy about the fact that you are."

"Well, I sure won't be living at this place anymore. Not as long as I have Peanut."

"What happened? Did he pee on the floor while you were out?"

"Worse. He clawed the hell out of both the front door and the drapes and barked so much that the neighbors called the landlord. When he came over and saw the damage, he said the dog has to go."

This image has my heart squeezing, and I sink onto the end of the bed. "Poor little guy. He must've been really scared."

"He probably hasn't been on his own before. He was always with other animals or people."

"Maybe he needs toys or a crate."

"Unfortunately, the landlord won't give him a second chance. Says he doesn't want the neighbors making a fuss about him renting out the place to quote, unquote, 'movie people.'"

The perfect solution is also one that might make me explode with unrequited sexual desire. Even as my brain says "No, no, no" while my body says "Yes, yes, yes," my big ole mouth opens wide to say, "If you're okay with it, I'm okay with you staying here. You and Peanut, that is. That way, you don't have to worry about him, and we can keep up the ruse for my roommates."

When he doesn't answer immediately, I try to backpedal. "But if that makes you uncomfortable—"

"No, of course not," he says, cutting me off. "I mean, we did fine the other night. It's a big bed. We're adults."

"Maybe just until you figure something else out?"

"Or until they go back to LA," he agrees.

"Which will be at the end of the first episode, I imagine. At least, that's what they told me when I agreed to rent them the rooms."

"Okay, well. If you really don't mind, I guess Peanut and I will get packed up for a couple days. If it doesn't work out, I'll go to the office. Most of the stuff I sent via transpo is there, and the couch is surprisingly comfort—"

"Luke, don't be silly. I'll come pick you up in, like, an hour? I'll get something to make for dinner on the way."

"Or you could wait for me, and we could go shopping together."

"Oh, well. Sure."

"Good. See you in a bit."

"Yep. See you soon."

And I thought asking a famous guy to be my fake husband was a bad idea. Now I've topped it with sleeping with one of the sexiest men on earth without being able to have sex with him. Un-fucking-believable.

Like, literally.

CHAPTER THIRTEEN

LUKE

It's too hot to leave Peanut in the car while we shop, but the ever-resourceful Dani has a better idea than the grocery store, anyway.

"I wish I knew about this place last time I was here," I say when she pulls up in front of a roadside fruit and vegetable stand on steroids. After tucking Peanut into a beach bag that Dani offers up, I follow her under the wooden structure.

After we drift through the rustic tables stacked high with produce, she says, "They've even got local seafood in the coolers over in the corner."

"Do you have a grill basket?"

"Yeah, Sully bought one for me." She narrows her eyes at me. "You getting ideas? I'm no fancy chef."

I tap myself on the temple. "Lucky for you, this guy had to take private lessons from a chef for a role, so he's pretty good in the kitchen."

She holds out the empty grocery basket. "Here, if you're so inspired, let's trade. I'll take the dog; you pick out the food."

Shopping for dinner is so fun, I almost forget about the

awkwardness that awaits us back at Dani's house. But when we walk in the front door, it hits us full in the face.

"Oh my god, Tina, yes!" George's voice reverberates down the hall.

Tina answers with a high-pitched squeal of passion.

"That's it, right there," George continues, panting heavily.

"Yes, yes, yes! George! Don't stop! This is so fucking good," Tina shouts.

I look over at Dani, who has Peanut clutched to her chest, covering his snout to keep him from barking.

"Does this happen often?" I whisper.

The look of horror on her face tells me that's a no.

"Should we make noise?" she asks. "Let them know we're here?"

"I've got an even better idea," I say. "Let's rewrite this entrance. Talk loudly on the way in and then slam the door."

We slip out the door quietly. The commands a first AD would give echo in my head as our eyes meet, preparing for our second take. *Roll sound, speed, marker, aaand… action.*

When I open the door this time, Dani waves me in and yells from the stoop, "Oh, shoot, hon. I left the watermelon in the car."

Grinning like a lunatic, I nod and yell back, "I'll get it on the second trip. My hands are full."

Once inside, I slam the door behind us, and Dani releases a yapping Peanut. This time, there are no sounds from the housemates. I run a hand over my brow with an exaggerated "phew" before following Dani to the kitchen.

But when George and Tina join us moments later, Dani's cheeks turn pink. "Hi, guys! We didn't know you were here!"

Tina's pretty flushed herself and places a hand over an actual heaving bosom. "I'm surprised you didn't hear us."

"Hear you?" Dani squeaks.

"We just got in from the store," I cut in.

Tina seems like the more talkative and emotional of the

two, but George beams as he announces, "We just came up with the best idea for a storyline. And sometimes we get a little excited when that happens."

When I look over at Dani, she's got a hand clamped over her mouth.

Tina narrows her eyes at us briefly before gasping. "Did you think we were having sex?"

Dani nods, literally biting her lip.

"Did we sound like that scene from *When Harry Met Sally*?" George says before smacking both hands to his cheeks *Home Alone* style.

"More like *Basic Instinct*, if you know what I mean," Dani manages before releasing a snort-laugh.

"I mean—" My words ride a ridiculous snort-giggle of my own, and I can't keep myself from pitching my voice high and mimicking what we'd heard. "George! Don't stop!"

"I am totally buggin' here." Tina turns as red as Dani. "This is so embarrassing."

"We were seriously writing," George says, a look of real panic on his face. "Not... you know."

"Having loud, passionate sex?" I can't help but ask.

The four of us gape at each other for a moment, before erupting into laughter again. Each time I think we've got it together, somebody repeats "George! Don't stop!" and we start up again.

"Well," Dani says, once everyone finally calms down. "I don't know about y'all, but now I'm starving."

I point to the grocery bags in the kitchen. "As usual, I got way too much food. You guys are welcome to join us."

An hour and a half later, Tina's making the orgasmic sounds again, but this time it *is* à la *When Harry Met Sally*. "I didn't even think I liked shrimp, but I guess I only ever had it cold and dipped in cocktail sauce."

George, busy peeling the shells off his own shrimp, says, "You couldn't even get this at a *fancy* restaurant in Indiana."

I sit back in my chair and wipe my hands and mouth before taking a sip of my beer. "Yeah, it's a bit messy, but I love this recipe. Got it from the caterer on the movie I did here a couple years ago."

"Old Bay seasoning makes everything good." Dani nods.

"Add fresh corn along with tomatoes and cucumbers picked from the vine in this woman's backyard… what else do you need?"

Tina's eyebrows waggle. "Ice cream for dessert?"

Dani points at her. "My kind of woman."

"Too bad we only went to the produce market."

Dani places a warm hand on my forearm. "Oh, honey. You know my fridge is never not stocked with ice cream."

Once every last shrimp has been peeled and devoured and every ear corn chewed down to its cob, George and Tina insist on cleaning up. Dani turns down a second beer, but I go inside to grab one before joining her back on the deck, where I find her relaxing with her feet up on the railing, Peanut in her lap.

It's only then that I realize that Skye is missing. "Where's your dog?"

"She's at Violet's this weekend."

When I sit down next to her, she doesn't stir or even open her eyes when she says, "That was awesome."

"Kinda fun, too." I hook a thumb toward the kitchen. "Those two are all right."

"Having them here is a mess, but I agree."

Suddenly, all I want to do is snuggle up next to my wife and kiss her on the forehead. Pick her up and carry her inside. Throw her on the bed and watch her laugh. Crawl over her long limbs and slim torso and nuzzle right into the place behind her ear.

I *really* want to know what Danielle looks like when she comes. Even if I can't feel her walls pulsing around my dick, I want to see her let go.

I don't care if it takes the entire next month to get her there.

DANI

Maybe it was the whole "we thought y'all were having loud sex" thing or the amazing food, but the four of us seem to truly enjoy each other's company. Until it's time to go to bed. There's only one bathroom, which probably adds to the awkward, but I have to stifle an eye roll when Tina calls out theatrically, "I'm going to bed now. In my room."

Luke, damn him, calls back, "Sleep well!" before shooting me a smirk.

"You're not nice," I hiss, hightailing it into the bedroom before I start laughing again.

"Never said I was," he says with an odd glint in his eye.

A glint that sends a shivery feeling to my belly.

He changed into a T-shirt and gym shorts while I was in the bathroom, and while he takes his turn, I do the same, determined to be under the covers and on the way to dreamland by the time he gets back.

Or at least pretending to be.

As I crawl into bed, I remember that I almost sold the king-sized bed frame after my aunt passed, especially when I saw the price tag for a new mattress, but now I'm glad I sucked it up and handed over my credit card. Otherwise, I'd be paying for it now. Hopefully, I'll keep my hands to myself this time and not end up cozied up on Luke's shoulder tomorrow morning.

As pleasant as that was, I don't want to muddy the waters in this fake marriage we've got going on.

Although, a very mean voice inside my head whispers, *no one ever actually said you couldn't fool around.*

No. No, no, no. Not going there. You know what'll

happen. You'll try, you'll freeze up, and then it'll be even more awkward. He'll either feel sorry for you or think you're nuttier than he probably already does.

But when the door snicks closed, bare feet pad across the floor, the other side of the bed depresses, and a lamp clicks off, it takes every bit of willpower I've got to keep my eyes closed.

And to stay on my side of the bed.

Just when I think I've convinced him that I'm asleep, he whispers, "Want to play Two Truths and a Lie again?"

Pretend to be asleep, pretend to be asleep, pretend to be asleep.

The bed creaks and the sheets rustle, like he's turning to face me. The air between us crackles with some sort of magnetic energy that rotates my own body to face his, and then words spill out of my mouth. "It's your turn."

"Right," he says, rolling onto his back. "Gimme a sec to remember what I was going to say."

As my eyes grow accustomed to the dim light in my room, his profile comes into focus. I still can't believe how good he looks without all that hair flopping around. The shadows accentuate the shape of his brow and cheekbones, his jaw and chin. All hard angles except for the curves of his long eyelashes and plump lips.

I'm about to reach out and touch that tempting lower lip, but when it separates from its partner, I jerk away.

He turns to face me. "You okay?"

"Yeah," I say, my voice all breathy and high. "I had, uh, one of those somebody walking over my grave moments."

Those lips press together again, and the brow furrows momentarily, but then he seems to let it go. "Okay. Number one: when I was on the show, all I wanted was to be a normal kid. Number two: when I went to boarding school, I ran track, and my specialty was the four hundred. Number three: I've been playing hacky sack since I was twelve because I learned from the crew on *Our House*."

Oh, he's good. He doesn't hesitate between words; no word is emphasized more than another. His delivery is almost a monotone. I think about the content. He's got an athletic build and still runs today, so unless he had a different specialty in track, number two is likely true. I suddenly get a flash of him playing hacky sack with the crew here in Wallington two years ago, so that's true. And then I picture his life as a kid. As glamorous as it seems, I know that life is tough enough for adults. It could be a lot of pressure on a kid, not to mention the fact that he'd miss out on friendships with boys his age.

I can't imagine life without my lifelong friends.

"Number one," I say.

He turns to face me again, his grin wicked. "Nope."

"What?" I can't believe I'm wrong. "Are you lying now so you'll win?"

"Nope. It's number three. I wanted to play with the crew, but the producers wouldn't let me."

"You didn't wish you could go to school and do all the regular kid stuff?"

He shakes his head. "Now I regret it, but at the time I didn't know what I was missing."

The idea of those regrets tugs at my heart so hard, I forget about what happens when I lose. He, on the other hand is already sitting up, rubbing his palms together. "I'm going to move the covers down, okay?"

Exposed to the cooled air and his attention, the nerve endings on my skin wake up instantly. When he lowers his hand to touch the place on my neck that he'd kissed the other night, a tingle reverberates down the length of my body.

Two fingers trail lightly down my neck to my shoulder, dipping into and over the indentations and curves. "I don't know if you heard about this," he says softly, his fingertips never breaking contact with my skin. "But a few years ago,

Sting did some interview and bragged that he and his wife had sex for six, seven hours at a time."

It's impossible to form words while his fingers brush over my skin, but he continues without my input, his low voice as much of a caress as his touch.

"A buddy of mine was obsessed with finding out how to replicate that, and he eventually went up to Northern California—where one finds such things—and did a weeklong workshop in Tantric sex."

His fingers have progressed to my left hand, where he traces up and over my palm and each finger.

"In case you're wondering, I figure this counts as one turn, if I don't break contact," he says, just as I was wondering exactly that.

I'm also wondering what happened at the sex workshop, so I stay silent, hoping he'll get back to that.

"I don't remember everything he said he learned, other than it was mind-blowing, but he always said that after going on an adventure. This one exercise stuck with me, but I've never been in a situation where I really wanted to try it"—he breaks off to shift his body so he can continue his path down my left leg—"until now."

"Okay" is all I've got, because I'm torn between wishing his touch would move to the good parts, wondering what comes next, and feeling self-conscious about the fact that he's doing all the work.

"From what I understand, the key is that one partner only gives, while the other receives. It's important to not have expectations or goals, like getting the other person off. And the receiver has to breathe." His movement pauses, but he doesn't break contact. "Are you breathing?"

I realize that I am indeed holding my breath, so I let it out in a whoosh.

"Good. I think you're supposed to imagine your breath following my touch."

"Like I breath down to my calves? My lungs definitely don't go that far." I may not have been a star science student, and my brain is still muddled by what he's doing, but I know that much.

"Yeah, it's more of an energy thing. And a focus thing. If you start thinking things like, 'I wish I'd had more ice cream,' you use your breath to remind you to pay attention to the touch."

He's at my ankle, and my legs tense up in anticipation of being tickled.

"Relax," he whispers. "Picture your breath relaxing the muscles."

It makes no sense, but I try it anyway. I can kind of imagine my breath like a cloud billowing down the outside of my body, and my muscles do relax as I do so. But when he begins the return journey up my leg, toward my groin, I tense up again.

"Breathe," he whispers.

I keep sending the clouds as he continues, lingering over some areas, changing up the pressure, shifting from drawing lines to curves. At some point, I give up on wondering what he's getting out of this—I mean, it's not like this game was my idea—and let myself receive the... I'm not sure what to call it.

It's not exactly sexual. Sensual, maybe? But at some point, as I get more comfortable with the deep breathing, it's like his touch goes deeper, like it sneaks under the skin and muscle and fat to touch a layer I didn't know existed. Like I've got rivers of sensation running through me that he stirs with his touch. His finger pads swirl lightly over my inner elbow and delicious tingles ride the waves to caress the inside of my rib cage. Connections that don't make sense but feel delicious.

At some point, it's like I can't even distinguish between his real touch and the other sensation because I'm floating. Like I'm not a bunch of parts that don't work when I'm in bed with a man, but a mermaid swimming in a sea of exquisite bliss.

When he breaks contact, I gasp.

Almost like he knows what I need, he tucks the sheet and quilt tightly around me and then lies down next to me.

When I open my eyes to meet his, he looks like he won the lottery. A single finger touches my nose lightly. "Good night, Danielle."

CHAPTER FOURTEEN

LUKE

When I wake up Sunday morning, it takes me a minute to figure out where I am. The last time I woke up in this bed, Dani was snug up against me, completely comfortable using me as pillow and comforter. Until she realized she was doing it, that is.

Today, my only company seems to be a snoring Peanut at my feet. He wasn't in the room when we fell asleep last night, so somebody must've let him in.

Now I've got morning wood thinking about that somebody. And about last night.

What blows my mind? I loved just touching her. I mean, don't get me wrong. I'd love to be buried to the hilt inside her too, but the fact that I gave her so much pleasure with two fingertips makes me feel like a superhero.

Even though I have a giant job to do starting tomorrow, I hope I keep winning at Two Truths and a Lie, because the list of ways I want to pleasure this woman is growing by the minute.

Curious to know more about her, I scan the room, really

taking stock for the first time. Curtains block all but a sliver of bright sunshine, which cuts through the space to reveal a bedroom free of fuss. Framed black-and-white photographs are the only decor. A bureau, bedside tables, and an armchair the only furniture. An oval rag rug is the only source of color, and it's faded.

Simple and spare, like her wardrobe. When Dani was driving me two years ago, I thought her choice of khakis and a black or white polo was a uniform. But she seems to prefer the simple look at home too, swapping out the capris for cutoffs and the polos for faded T-shirts advertising various movies or grip companies or her favorite: Randy's Craft Service.

Shit. Randy. Kickball.

After throwing on a pair of sweats and taking a quick detour to the bathroom, I find her and her roommates out on the back deck.

"There he is," Tina calls.

Shielding my eyes from the sunshine, I have to stifle a yawn. "I slept way later than I wanted to."

"There's more coffee in the kitchen," George says.

"What time do we need to get out of here?"

Dani finally turns to face me, her expression carefully neutral. I really hope that doesn't mean she's uncomfortable with what happened last night. "Weren't you getting a ride with Sully so you could get there early?"

"Dammit, that's right," I groan, running a hand over my beard. "He's picking me up at my apartment."

"Do you need me to take you over there?" I get her subtext: *Are you going to pretend that you're not staying here?* Even as she follows up with, "Did you leave the ball there?"

This is probably a bad idea, one that will get us further tangled in lies, but I say, "Nah, Sully was picking up a couple of balls. I'll call him and get him to pick me up here. Okay if I use the phone?"

"Of course, honey," Dani says, leaning into the endearment. "What's mine is yours and all that."

"Right. Still waking up here," I say, rapping knuckles lightly on my skull. Turning to face Tina and George as I head for the screen door, I ask, "Will I see you all at the game?"

"Oh," George says. "I thought it was for cast and crew."

"You're invited. You're as much a part of the team as I am."

"I'm really bad at sports," Tina says with a grimace.

"That's the thing about kickball. Skill requirements are low. And I'm not letting this get competitive or rough. Strict orders from the bosses on that."

"The network?" Dani asks.

"I'm sure they'd appreciate no one getting hurt, but no, I take my orders from Helen."

She nods. "Smart man."

Her grin is real now, and I have this weird impulse to give her a kiss on the cheek. It'd be in character, but I also want to reassure her, tell her that it'll all be okay. I jog the few steps from the door, brush the curtain of hair from her cheek and brush my lips across her soft skin before whispering, "I'm outta here."

She calls out his phone number as I disappear inside—like she knows that I'd have to go digging through my Filofax for it. The kitchen clock reveals that I need to get my ass in gear, so I dial before I forget the seven digits and then tuck it between my ear and shoulder, the long cord stretching behind me as I search the cabinets for a coffee cup.

Helen answers, which throws me momentarily, until I remember that they're a couple. When I get Sully on the line, I briefly explain that I'm staying at Dani's because of a dog mishap and ask if he can pick me up here instead of the rental.

After a quick shower, I return to the room to find that

Dani's made the bed, leaving a sticky note on my pillow that reads, "Taking Peanut for a walk. - D"

Filing away the cozy feeling this gesture creates for future reference as I dress and slather on sunscreen, I'm on the porch and rarin' to go when Sully pulls up. But the minute my ass hits the seat of his pickup truck, the look he gives me has me worried. "Could you not find any red balls anywhere?"

"No, uh. They're in the back." He hooks a thumb behind him before clearing his throat. "I just need to say something."

"Okay," I answer warily.

When he turns his impressively large upper body to face me, his expression is gravely serious. "I know something's going on with you and Dani. I'm not sure what, but I need to say, don't fuck around with her. She might seem strong, but I don't think she could take getting her heart broken."

My immediate impulse is to deny, deny, deny. To ask where he got this information. And then to argue that of course I'm not going to hurt her, but before I can, I know he's right.

She may project independence, toughness even, but I'd bet there's a hurt little girl behind those walls of hers. And I'm not going to be yet another disappointment for her. "You got it."

He studies me for a long moment before nodding his head sharply. "Let's go play kickball, then."

DANI

Part of me wants stay home and hide from the life that has suddenly become so complicated I don't know which way is up. But another part of me wants to be outside in the sunshine with my friends and not worry about the consequences of my actions. So, when Tina comes to me for help interpreting the directions to the kickball field, I just tell them to follow me.

When we arrive at a few minutes to ten, I have to say I'm surprised at the turnout. Getting a bunch of young people up and at 'em on a Sunday morning is no easy feat. Not only does it look like most of the crew has shown up, but the series' young stars are here in full force as well.

Skye's bark draws my attention to the bleachers, where I'm delighted to see our old friends Lucy and Ben sitting with Violet and Nate. Of course, they'd be invited to the game, because of Ben's recurring role on *Lawson's Reach*, but I didn't know they were back in town.

Thinking that Lucy might have some ideas for dealing with Peanut's issues, I head in their direction. After introducing Peanut to Lucy and Ben's dogs, I finally get a hug from my friends.

"It's good to see you," Lucy says.

"You, too. When did you get into town?"

"A day or two ago," Ben says. "I just wrapped a project in New York."

"Same for me," Lucy adds. "Training a dog for a commercial."

"I'm not called until the second episode," Ben says, "But we came down early to spend some time with my dad and stepmom at the inn."

"How's life?" Lucy asks.

"Life is… you know, same old, same old," I manage. I've known these two for, gosh, almost ten years now, but I'm nowhere near as close to them as I am Ford, Whitney, Vi, and Sully.

Lucy narrows her eyes at me. "Huh. Something seems different."

Deflecting, I pick up Peanut. "I hate to always be asking you these things, but we could use some advice about this little guy."

She tips her head to the side. "We?"

"Whoo boy, it's going to heat up quick out here." I shake my head, hoping the heat I can feel rising in my cheeks can be attributed to the sun that peeking out from behind the clouds. "I'm sure they want to get the game started, so real quick: the guy I'm driving adopted Peanut right before coming east, and the first time he left the dog alone in his apartment, he went nuts. Destroyed curtains and a door."

Lucy nods. "Separation anxiety. There are things you can do, but it requires time and patience. Who's the owner?"

I point out Luke, standing next to Sully with a schoolyard ball on his hip. "This game is his idea. That's why I have Peanut this morning. He's afraid to leave the dog alone."

"Introduce me after the game, and I'll give him some ideas."

As I'm thanking her, Sully yells, "Circle up! Let's get this going."

After Sully and Luke create two teams, Randy announces that he's got drinks and food to fuel the game, and that Luke's footing the bill. This gets a cheer, and after a coin flip decides which side is up first, Vi steps forward.

"I am your self-appointed umpire, since I'm too pregnant to play." Vi was a high school drama teacher before starting her casting business, so she's got the don't-fuck-with-me authority thing down. "Here are the rules, which are all about safety, because you all need to be able to show up to work tomorrow. Bright and early and unbruised. Right, Helen?"

Luke had confided that Helen wasn't happy with the idea of kickball, but she's not only present, she looks ready to play, her short hair tucked into a Mets baseball cap, which she tips in agreement.

"That means," Vi continues, "you can tag someone out by throwing the ball, but you must hit them below the shoulders. If someone is accidentally hit above the shoulders, they are safe. Any egregious aiming at faces, heads, boobs, or groins will result in immediate ejection."

"And no more free food or drinks for the offender!" Randy adds.

"What he said," Vi agrees. "Also, no sliding. And finally, most important: no whining. Umpire rulings are final. Got it?"

A few people call out affirmative answers, but that's not enough for Vi. "I said, got it?"

When she gets a more enthusiastic response, she yells, "Play ball!"

After the game wraps up a few hours later, I wander over to Randy's van to get more water for the dogs.

"You have a good day, Randy?"

"I sure did, hon," he says, his grin wide. "You sure you don't want anything, Danielle?" Randy tips his chin at something behind me. "That guy's paying, after all."

When I turn around, a very sweaty but very happy Luke is jogging our way. For a moment, it looks like he's going to envelop me in a hug, but at the last moment he scoops up Peanut instead. "Hey, so, your friend Lucy gave me a list. Things that I'll need to work on this guy's separation anxiety. Think we could stop by the pet store on the way home?"

A quick glance at Randy tells me his curiosity is piqued by the word "home," so I plaster on a professional smile. "Sure, boss. I'll take you wherever you need to go."

Something like disappointment crosses Luke's face momentarily, but when I tip my head slightly in the direction of the craft service van, he seems to get it. "Thanks, Dani. I'm sorry that you're both having to work on a day off. And don't feel like you have to come every week, Randy."

"Hell, I don't mind working on a Sunday morning for this kind of cash. Gotta make hay while the sun shines."

"Amen to that," Luke says.

As he settles up with Randy, I'm reminded of the fleeting nature of not just my marriage, but this whole way of life.

TV shows and fake relationships have this in common: wrap day is inevitable.

CHAPTER FIFTEEN

LUKE

I'm still riding the high of accomplishment when we get to the pet store. I know that it's a game, a silly kids' game at that, but out on the field this morning, I got a glimpse of a feeling I didn't know I was missing.

I mean, we play for a living. It's hard to remember that when there's so much money on the line, so many moving parts, so many critical opinions. But the best episodes of *Our House* shone because of the joy that was behind the work. Looking back—and having other jobs to compare it to—that's a special sauce that makes a show not just a hit, but beloved.

Until today, I didn't know how much I've longed to be a part of that again. And if my leadership helps get us there, that'd be pretty damn awesome.

When I get happy, I get goofy. And apparently, Danielle Goodwin finds my silliness hilarious, which eggs me on.

As I push a cart with Peanut in the kid seat up and down the aisles, I pretend to be driving the tiny chuck wagon that rolled out of the TV in the old dog food ad, "Hyah, hyah! Dagnabbit, Slim, there's a giant dog chasin' us. Gee up, little ponies!"

When that gets a laugh out of her, I grab a dog toy and make it fly through the air and into the cart, doing the cheesy voiceover from the Mighty Dog ads, "Mighty Dog to the rescue!"

"Puh-lease, Luke," she says, pretending to be stern. "You are out of control."

I can't *not* do Morris the cat, so I adopt his snooty, adenoidal voice. "Who says I need improving?"

After I score a groan and an eye roll, I take the win. "All right, all right. What else do we need here?"

She points to the cart filled with pet accessories. "Did Lucy tell you to get this much stuff? Where are we going to put it all?"

"Some of it's for the office," I protest.

"Let me see that list." After I hand it over, she begins to weed out items from the cart. "Don't think a bat costume is going to help Peanut feel more comfortable being alone."

"How do you know?" I grab it and drape the costume over his back. "Maybe, if he could pretend to be Batman, he wouldn't be so scared."

She ignores me, muttering to herself as she continues to move items to an empty cart nearby. "This is a cat toy. These are to keep guinea pigs' teeth worn down, and this is a bird cage mirror. And none of them have anything to do with separation anxiety."

I push out my lower lip in an exaggerated pout. "Fine. I was just having fun."

"You want to single-handedly prop up our local economy, I don't want to stop you but—"

"Nah, you're right. Let's just get the stuff we're supposed to." I lean close to stage-whisper in Peanut's ear, "Don't worry, buddy, I'll get you the bat costume for Halloween."

Dani rolls her eyes again, but she's smiling when we get to the checkout counter, and I can't help but lean in for a quick kiss on her rounded cheek.

"Y'all are the cutest couple," a woman in line behind us remarks.

Catching her eye, the clerk nods. "Young love. Nothing like it, right?"

"And they're going to have the most beautiful babies too."

Dani blanches, and I put an arm around her to steady us both. When I turn to face the woman, intending to graciously thank her even though she's sticking her nose where it doesn't belong, she gives a little wave. "I'm a nurse in the OBGYN practice y'all visited the other day. Let me tell you, it was the talk of the office, how pretty your children will be."

I have to summon every bit of acting skill to get out of this situation without blowing not only our cover, but my top. I mean, it seems like a major privacy violation for a bunch of medical professionals to be speculating about patients' potential offspring. Still, causing a scene could create a bigger mess.

I thank her for saying so, smile as I swipe my credit card and sign the receipt, and then book it out of there.

"What the hell?" Dani hisses once we're outside.

"Tell me about it."

As she helps the dogs into the back of the car, I unload the cart. "But it's no big deal."

"Are you kidding me?"

She looks so distressed I stop what I'm doing and take her by the upper arms. "Look at it this way. We've obviously sold the people at the doctor's office on this fake marriage, and neither of them said anything about Lukas Keith. Score two-zero for team Goodwin-Zelazny."

Something odd crosses her face, but it's gone before I can discern what. As she crosses to the driver's side door, she asks, "Where to now?"

Feeling slightly less on top of the world, I ask Dani if she'll drop me at the office so I can catch up on messages. "And I promise, I'll leave one of the dog beds and half of the toys there."

"I can take you there," she says as she puts the car in gear. "But I promised to meet my friends at the beach at five, so I'll have to either pick you up before four, or you'll have to find another way home, or… wherever it is you're going."

Her guard is back up, so I redirect. "I didn't think you liked to go to the beach in the summer."

"Only on Sunday evenings, when most of the tourists are heading home. We bring food and drinks and hang out until the sun goes down." She reaches back to give Skye a pat. "But I also need to take this girl on a R-U-N. At the game today, Lucy reminded me that her breed needs more exercise than most, so I want to get back to doing it every day. And I'd much rather do that at the beach in this weather."

Kickball may have involved a sprint or two, but I haven't had a good run over the weekend either. "I don't want to intrude, but I could also use a R-U-N. Could I come along?"

Her shrug is noncommittal, so I walk it back.

"Seriously, if you don't want me to come, I can do something else."

"You're welcome to join us, but I think we have to be, you know, colleagues. Not fake married."

"Can we be friends?"

We've arrived at the stages, and she puts the car in park before answering. When she turns to face me, there's a vulnerability there that reminds me of Sully's warning this morning, so I add, "It would mean a lot to me."

Her gaze narrows briefly, but then she rolls her eyes. "Yes, Luke. We can be friends. Now get out of here. I'll be back at four."

It doesn't take long for me to get lost in work. People on this production communicate via email as well as the phone and fax machine, which triples the number of messages bouncing back and forth. Glenda, the production coordinator, was kind enough to suggest that I assign one of the PAs to triage incoming messages, because many of them are either duplicates or don't require action from me.

Even so, I have a lot to catch up on since I was last in the office Friday evening—which of course is Friday afternoon LA time—so I do my best to address what I can. I'm not sure how I'm going to keep up with all this while spending sixteen hours on a set for eight shooting days, but I do know that it'll require a great deal of caffeine.

The one message I ignore is from Kellie because I'm avoiding telling her about Dani. Just because I've been in and out of a fake relationship with her for the past ten years, does that mean she needs to know everything about my current fake relationship?

I know her PR people would like to be kept in the loop, but there's no way in hell I'm letting them, or mine for that matter, get involved in this.

Whatever *this* is.

Since last night—hell, since we kissed—I haven't really been sure. Every time I think Dani's letting me in, something happens to make the ground shift and the walls go right back up.

I'm probably going to have to do a hell of a lot of spanking it in the shower, but I still can't resist the challenge of helping her address her fears around sex. I mean, I have a hard time resisting any challenge, but there's something about her face, her whole body, really, when she's turned on that has me all-in. There's a fascinating fucking story written in the clench and release of muscles, the ripple of a shudder across flushed skin, the hitch of breath making those luscious breasts rise and fall.

"Ready to go?"

Peanut jumps to his feet, yapping his head off, and I almost fall off the couch at Dani's sudden appearance in my office doorway.

"Shit, you scared the crap out of me," I yelp, quickly covering the bulge in my pants with a script.

"You working or napping?"

"Ugh, a little bit of both."

"You still want to go to the beach?"

Swinging my feet to the floor, careful to keep my lap covered, I scan the piles on the floor and my desk. "I mean, I could stay here all night and never catch up, but a run on the beach might give me a bit more energy for tomorrow."

"Is that the one you're directing?" She points to the script. "Aren't you prepped for that already?"

"Nah, this is the next one. Its director won't be in town until a couple days before shooting starts, so I have to stay on top of any changes."

Refocusing my mind on work instead of the many ways I could get Danielle Goodwin turned on, I turn my body to grab my messenger bag, shove the script and a few more necessities inside, and then snap a leash on the dog to follow my driver/wife/friend out of the building.

The afternoon sun is a cozy blanket after the overly air-conditioned chill of the office. Closing my eyes, I let the vitamin D soak in while she unlocks the car. After I climb in, I notice a bathing suit strap under her tank top. "I've got running shoes and a suit at your house if you don't mind stopping by on the way."

"As long as you just run in. The beach is calling me, and this girl needs to stretch her legs."

Skye barks from the back seat, and I'm not sure whether Dani's talking about herself or the dog, but all I say is "Me too."

An hour later, we're jogging back up the beach, all three of us panting hard from the two-mile run. As we get within sight of the half-moon of chairs arranged in the sand, Dani breathes, "Is that...?" When a man stands and whistles, both woman and dog sprint toward him. The guy meets her halfway, scooping Dani up and swinging her around as Skye circles them both, barking.

It takes everything in me to squelch the desire to go all caveman and roar, *Get your hands off my wife!* As I trudge closer, I repeat *fake marriage, fake marriage* in my head, even as I tally up the points the guy's got on me. He's taller, his muscles more defined, and he's got a perfect tan. But worst of all is that fucking hair. There's no way the blond highlights are real, but the thick locks framing his face and falling past his shoulders are Nature's gift.

The fucker has no idea how lucky he is. Not just with the hair, but to be on the receiving end of a wide-open smile from my girl.

It doesn't matter that I have no right to be jealous of this asshole, whoever he is to Dani. She would've given me a heads-up if her *actual* boyfriend was meeting us at the beach, wouldn't she?

And what are George and Tina going to think?

I need water, but I also need to cool off in more ways than one, so I shuck off my shoes and shirt and drop them by the chair Dani so thoughtfully laid out for me before our run. And then I sprint into the water.

"Whoa, watch out, man!" a voice shouts from atop a surfboard heading straight at my head.

Diving deep, I swim for several moments before coming up for air. When I bob to the surface, another surfer waves at me. "This is a no-swim zone, dude," pointing at the flags and signs onshore marking the area for surfing.

Calling, "My bad," I let the next wave push me back to the beach.

Feeling like a total fart-knocker, I stomp back to the chairs, wishing I could just go home. But like a child, I'm stuck here because I can't drive, and I don't even have a home of my own to go to.

I drink a beer and eat some pretzels and pretend I'm having a good time while watching this group of friends I'm not a part of enjoy what is, admittedly, a gorgeous evening on an almost deserted beach, the sunburnt tourists and their cranky kids having departed. As the sun sets behind us, it paints the wide-open sky over the water in pink and peach watercolors.

If only my wife weren't giggling—*giggling!* I've never seen her giggle—with this Ford guy, I'd be having a good time too.

Ford. What the hell kind of name is that, anyway? Who names their kid after a car?

When Helen announces that she's heading out, I ask if I can catch a ride with her, and tell Dani I'll see her later.

As we drive over the bridge separating the beach from the mainland, Helen asks, "Do you know how to get to your rental? Because I'm still learning my way around here."

This is when I realize my mistake. "Uh, do you know how to get to Dani's house?"

She shoots a raised brow my way. "I do. Sully used to live there."

"Well, that's where I'm staying."

She doesn't say anything as I babble on about Peanut and separation anxiety and how Dani graciously offered a room while I figure things out with the dog. When she pulls up in front of Dani's house, however, she clears her throat pointedly.

"No judgment about whatever's going on between you and Ms. Goodwin, but—and this is from personal experience, mind you—I hope you're not letting feelings for a woman endanger the opportunity you've been granted with this job. The job that came with a damn Morality Memo."

I'd wondered if she got the memo, and now I can't help but ask how she's dealing with it.

She shrugs. "Sully was hired by the sound mixer, not me. But more importantly, that memo was handed down after we joined the crew and long after we began dating."

"You're kind of grandfathered in?"

"You could say that, but more importantly, the point of the memo is: the suits don't want any drama." She lasers a look at me before adding, "And drama seems to follow you, my friend."

I open my mouth to argue, but she flicks a hand at me. "Now get outta here. We both need to be on point tomorrow."

"Good point."

I grab the dog and my towel and exit the car, but before heading into the house, I lean down to meet her gaze through the passenger side window. "Thanks for the advice, boss."

Not that I'm going to listen.

DANI

George, Tina, Ben, and Lucy leave the beach a half hour after Luke goes home with Helen. Why he didn't wait to catch a ride with my roommates or me, I have no idea, but I'm not going to let him spoil my Sunday evening. When Nate takes his board in the water to catch a few more waves, it's just me and Violet and Sully and Ford sitting together.

"Why we live here," Violet says, raising her water bottle to the sea and sky.

Ford mirrors her with his beer. "I've been looking forward to this for weeks. Atlanta in the summertime is awful. Hotter, just as humid, more traffic, no ocean. Why would anyone even live there?"

More steady work is the answer, but no one ruins the moment with the truth.

"Good to have you back," is what I say instead. "Are you here for a while?"

He shrugs. "Till the next gig comes along. Gonna talk to the *Lawson's Reach* mixer about working second unit while I'm home."

Sully nods. "I'll tell him you're back first thing tomorrow."

No one says anything about Whitney, but I'm sure we're all picturing the empty space where her beach chair should be. If she were here, she'd be gossiping and flirting with the guys. Things that used to annoy me, I now miss.

Instead of bringing her up, Violet clears her throat meaningfully. When I meet her gaze, she tips her head at Ford and Sully and widens her eyes. When I mouth "What?" in response, she repeats the action.

"Is Dani supposed to tell me something?" Ford asks.

Violet rolls her eyes and flops back into her beach chair. "I think she should."

"Tell him what?"

"Maybe that you're married?" Sully says.

"You're what?" Ford asks. "What the fuck, Dani?"

"Wait? How do you know?" I ask Sully, before shooting an angry look at Violet.

Violet shrugs. "I'm sorry. He walked in when I was talking to Nate about it."

"Guys. This info is not for, like, public consumption." I look around us pointedly, even though we're practically alone on the beach. "It's also not that big a deal."

"Not that big a deal?" Ford asks. "You've shackled yourself to another person."

I have to laugh. Ford and I are definitely on the same page about the relationship thing. In the year since Whitney got married, I think he's gone out with more girls than in the previous ten years combined.

I quickly explain the exchange of services between Luke and me. "We're just helping each other out."

"Are you living together and… everything?" Ford asks.

Hoping the darkening sky hides the flush now heating my

chest and cheeks, I flick a hand in the air. "He's staying at my house because of his dog, and also because George and Tina found out that we're married but they don't know why, so obviously it would be weird if we didn't live together."

"Jeez, you didn't tell me that," Violet says. "Are you sleeping together?"

"Yeah." I shrug. "No big deal. We're adults."

Sully laughs. "Girl, you are so screwed."

"Whatever." Suddenly needing to move, I hop up and start packing up. "I gotta get home. Early day tomorrow."

To make sure they get it, before I head to the parking lot, I say, "I would appreciate your discretion, though. The guy is still kind of famous."

They promise to keep it to themselves, and I do trust them, but on the drive home I have a sinking feeling that the circle of people who know is getting too large to manage.

When I get home, I hose the dogs off before enjoying a very nice outdoor shower myself. By the time I've put away the beach chairs and picnic remains, the house is quiet. Peanut—who expended a great deal of energy chasing ghost crabs at the beach—collapses into his new bed, and Skye plops onto hers next to him.

In the bedroom, Luke's reading.

"Everything okay?"

"Yup," he says, popping the *P* with gusto.

Something happened at the beach to squelch the light-hearted mood he was in at the pet store. Since I have to sleep next to the guy, I'd like to clear the air. "I call bullshit."

Still hidden behind the paperback, he says, "I don't know what you mean."

"Suit yourself." I grab pajamas and disappear into the bathroom to brush my teeth and change, and then climb into bed, turn off the light on my side, and say, "Good night."

He closes his book and fiddles with his fancy watch, probably setting an alarm, before turning off the other lamp. Then he flops about, getting under the covers, ending up turned away from me, tensioning radiating from him. So much tension in fact, that if I wait, he's eventually going to spill.

"Hope you had fun with your *boyfriend*," he finally spits out.

"My boyfriend?"

"That guy. Chevy, Honda. Whatever his name is."

"Dude. Are you jealous? Of Ford?" When he doesn't respond, I poke him in the side, in the ticklish place he warned me about.

"Stop it!" he squawks, attempting to dodge my hand. "I told you not to do that."

"No, you didn't. You just told me what would happen if I did," I say, ticking my finger back and forth. "I'm going to keep doing it until you admit that you're jealous."

I try to poke him again, but this time he grabs my wrists. "Fine, I'm jealous of Ford who makes you giggle."

"Aww," I say, not letting him off the hook. "But you make me laugh, honeybunch."

"But not giggle."

The pout on his lips actually does make me giggle. "See, there you go. I giggled at you."

"Yeah, but you're laughing at me. Not the same."

This makes me snort laugh. "You're ridiculous."

He lets go of my wrists and flops onto his back. "I know. I know I'm ridiculous."

"Luke. I've known Ford since I was little. Just like Violet and Sully. Even if he wasn't a total player—which he is—I'd never go out with him. It'd be like dating my brother."

Luke turns to face me again. "I'm sorry. I hope I wasn't too rude. I think it was the hair that really got to me."

I'm not getting into this boy's hair issues when we're both tired. "No problem. Let's get some sleep, okay? Big day tomorrow."

"You're right. I'm an idiot, but I'll be an even bigger idiot if I don't show up tomorrow on top of my shit." He rubs both hands over his face, groans, and then turns on his side. "Good night, wife."

Because he's right about work, I brush aside disappointment that he didn't even mention the game. Or the sex experiment. Or whatever it was we did last night. Instead, I tell him good night, and turn in the other direction.

CHAPTER SIXTEEN

DANI

When I wake up Monday morning, both Luke and Skye aren't around, but I find a sticky note on the coffee pot that reads: *Running with Skye, XO, Luke.*

He continues to get up early to run all week, even though he's putting in super-long days. The actor's union requires a full twelve hours of turnaround between the time they leave and are called for the following day, so start times tend to get later over the course of a week. Luke doesn't go in later, however. He uses the morning hours to deal with producer duties. When I pick him up at the end of the day, whether that's eight or nine or ten p.m., he's like a windup toy wound past its limit. He talks in the car; he talks in the kitchen over a beer; he talks next to me in bed, and then he falls asleep.

Like a little kid after a party at Chuck E. Cheese.

When I pick him up at eleven p.m. on Wednesday, he's buzzing with that same energy, even as he apologizes for the late hour.

"You forget, I've done this before," I reassure him. "I know how it works. Your day starts at seven on Monday morning, but that start time inevitably gets later over the week."

He checks his watch and groans. "Tomorrow's crew call isn't until eleven. And we're shooting a split Friday."

A split means shooting half in daylight, half at night. They'll likely be working past midnight. "I might have to charge you overtime," I say, only half joking.

"I hope you'll charge me whatever you'd charge the company. I mean, I'm not exactly holding up my end of the bargain."

"What do you mean?"

"I've passed out in bed before we could fool around all week," he says over a yawn.

"That wasn't exactly part of the bargain. That whole game was your idea. If you don't want to do it, it's totally—"

"I do." He reaches over and places a hand on my thigh. "I really do. My brain's just so full after a day of juggling everything and so many people needing so many things from me, I'm buzzing with this hyper energy."

"In a bad way?"

"What do you mean?"

"Do you not like what you're doing?"

He sits back and stares out the window for a few moments, and I'm ridiculously happy that his hand remains on my leg, where it feels like it belongs.

"I actually love it," he eventually says. "More than I expected I would."

"What do you love about it?"

He turns his whole body in my direction, as far as the seat belt allows. "I was actually thinking about that earlier. It's like, I have the big picture in my head—not only this episode, but the whole season. As we work through each scene and I'm making all these micro decisions, part of me is seeing how each piece fits into the bigger puzzle."

"Ah, so you're that kind of puzzle person."

"I'm—huh?"

"The kind who keeps the picture on the box out for reference."

"I have no idea what you're talking about."

"Did your family not do puzzles growing up?"

He snorts. "Uh, not exactly."

"That's too bad. Even my fucked-up family did puzzles. It's a great time to get kids to talk about shit because you're focused on slotting the pieces in. But our rule was, you only get to look at the picture at the beginning."

"Yeah, I feel like I wouldn't like that. I'd rather do a really hard puzzle but have the whole picture for reference."

"I'll keep that in mind."

"Anyway," he says, sitting back and scrubbing his face with both hands, leaving my poor leg all on its lonesome, "I feel bad that I just unload on you every night. Tell me about your day."

I don't think my days are anywhere near as story-worthy as his, but I do tell him about getting chased by a rooster at a property I was checking out for one of the movies shooting in town next month.

"Sounds like one to cross off the list."

"Yeah, can't have actors being pecked to death."

After I park in the driveway and turn off the car, Luke blurts out, "I still feel like I'm taking advantage of you."

"You haven't even touched me," I say, going for a jokey tone that I can't quite sell. I'm disappointed that he hasn't, even as I've fantasized about how I'd like to touch him. Worse, I've been worried that he changed his mind about the whole thing.

"I've wanted to," he says, as I open my car door. I meet his gaze in the sudden glare of the dome light, and the raw desire in his eyes has my heart rate going from zero to sixty. But then his expression shifts to something almost bashful. "I... run out of steam."

There's too much feeling in this car. I need to bail out with a little white lie. "It's not a big deal, Luke. Let's get inside. We've both got another long day tomorrow."

He releases a breath, like he'd been holding it, waiting for my complaint.

"I swear, it's fine," I say.

He narrows his eyes at me. "If we were playing the game, that'd be your lie."

"Whatever. I'm going inside. You can stay out here if you want."

LUKE

I don't know what actual day of the week it is. All I know is that it's day four of the eight I have to get this episode in the can. And while what I said to Dani last night is the truth, the fact that I love what I'm doing doesn't mean that it isn't a hell of a challenge every moment of every long as hell day.

Is it that I'm so green, or is it human nature? Whatever it is, when Dani dropped me off at today's location—the local university where we shoot the exteriors for the high school—I thought the crew had hit a groove. That we were a team. That I had all the leadership qualities needed to serve this production as both producer and director.

Boy, was I wrong.

The worst thing is, today's debacle was all my fault, brought on by my lack of experience. Last night, when I got a call from PR asking if I could release one of the lead actresses for the morning so she could fly to New York and step in as a last-minute replacement guest on *Good Morning America*, I wanted to impress the suits with my ability to pivot. Also, as a producer, I want the show to get all the free press it can.

As director, I wanted to argue against letting the actress go, but I kept my mouth shut.

As fate would have it, the actress's flight back was

delayed, and by the time she arrived, the skies had opened up. Thunder and lightning and all.

Director me wanted to throw a tantrum and demand a day of second-unit shooting to cover it, but producer me didn't want to blow my budget in the first week. Instead, I put on my producing director hat, called my buddy Max, and let him know we had to move the scene to an indoor location.

None of which kept me or half the crew from getting soaked to the bone in the process.

The end of everyone else's day has me back at the office, my shoes still spongy, shivering from sitting in the air-conditioning in damp clothes, trying to answer email while listening to the director for episode 2.3 on yammer away on speakerphone.

As he goes on and on about other shows he's been working on, I have to stifle a laugh. He's trying to impress me, when I'd happily hand over the reins tomorrow if he were in town.

When Dani appears in my office doorway, backlit like an angel from heaven come to save me, I grab the closest scrap of paper—which happens to be a bright-blue sticky note—write "HELP" in Sharpie, and hold it up.

She bites her lip, probably trying to figure out what she can do to end the call, but the thought of her teeth doing what mine would like to right now sends a pinball of desire ricocheting from my eyes to my dick, lighting up quite a few other spots along the way.

It's suddenly clear that I need to help myself.

"Steve," I say, interrupting the guy mid-sentence, "my driver's waiting for me. See you next week."

Then I drop the receiver into its cradle and raise both hands in victory. "I'm outta here!"

This gets a laugh out of Dani, which revs my engine further. How is it that I've fallen asleep next to this sexy woman without touching her the past three nights?

When we walk in the front door of her house, to find George and Tina still awake and working on a puzzle, I will not be deterred.

Therefore, when Tina says, "Luke, can we talk about the actor playing Lawson's dad? He's been bugging us to write a script with this crazy idea of his," I nod, but instead of getting sucked in, I say, "Yes. Talk to my PA and set something up for tomorrow. Right now, I am going to bed."

"You going to keep working on the puzzle with us, Dani?" George asks. "This baby is challenging."

I give Dani a pointed look, hoping I won't have to pick her up and throw her over my shoulder caveman-style to get her to join me. She bites her lip again, and without thinking, I grab her hand and tug, walking backward, brows raised.

Releasing the plump lower lip that I have all kinds of plans for, her feet follow my lead, and she forces a yawn. "I'm done for tonight. We can go at it again tomorrow."

She catches up to me in two long strides, and I whisper, "What would you think about going at it right now?"

DANI

Ever since I interrupted the phone call in his office, Luke's been looking at me like a starving cat who hasn't had a canary in far too long. When he pulls me to my bedroom, closes the door behind me, and covers my mouth with his own, I can't help myself, and I grab his shirt with both hands and moan as his tongue dives deep, stroking the roof of my mouth. His hands coast up and down my sides, reigniting fires his touch stoked Saturday night. My hands snake up to cup his bearded cheeks, then one palm skates along his jaw, while the other slides to the back of his head.

Even as his muscled chest presses into my cushiony one, my fingertips learn the differences in texture between his beard and his buzz cut. Even as my body heats with desire, I savor the taste of his tongue and lips, layers of coffee and mints and some delicious flavor that is all him.

But when I remember kissing his printed image as a girl, a high-pitched giggle escapes past my lips, and he breaks the kiss, staggering away from me.

"Oh, shit. Are you okay?" he asks, his skin flushed, eyes wild.

Snorting in an attempt to stifle hysterical laughter, I nod, even as a hiccupy laugh escapes past my lips. "I just remembered kissing you."

His brow furrows. "When we got married?"

Clamping my lips together, I shake my head rapidly. *Why did I say anything?*

"That was the only other time we've kissed."

"Mm-hmm," I manage.

Eyes narrowed, he stalks back to me. "Danielle, are you talking about you kissing *me*? Or perhaps an image of me?"

Hands slapping over my face, I groan. "Ugh. How did you know?"

It's his turn to snort. "You wouldn't be the first."

I peek between fingers to try and gauge his feelings on the matter. He does appear to be amused, until he frowns.

"I hope the reality was better than the fantasy."

"Well," I squeak, "not getting ink all over my face is a plus."

"You little minx," he growls before scooping all five foot eleven of me up and tossing me on the bed like I weigh nothing. "You did have a crush on me."

Scrambling back as he crawls over the bed in pursuit, I defend myself. "I couldn't help it. Between *Tiger Beat* and *Teen*, the temptation was relentless."

Grabbing my legs, he pulls them into his lap before resting his hands on my thighs. "Speaking of teenagers and kissing, I had a new idea. Did you ever spend hours making out when you were a teenager?"

I shake my head, wondering how to get him to move those hands. "I didn't, actually. I was too busy taking care of my siblings and then my aunt."

"I didn't either."

"You didn't?"

"Pretty much same as you. When Kellie and I were teenagers, they watched us like hawks, so all we had were stolen kisses. Then I went to a boys' boarding school, and she was working."

"Are you saying that you want to make out like a teenager with me?" I ask, hoping that's where this is going.

"I was planning to talk about it first, but once I got it in my head, I couldn't wait." His head drops on a sigh, and then he slowly raises it to meet my gaze. "I'm sorry I didn't ask permission before kissing you."

I can't stop the grin that takes over my face. "I'm not. It was pretty hot."

"It was?" he asks, like he really means it, before his expression shifts again, to concern. "It didn't freak you out?"

I almost tell him how he makes me feel, like I'm ready to throw my rule book out the window and try having sex with him with only a condom. Because ever since his fingers lit me up by stroking every inch of my skin that *wasn't* in any of my erogenous zones, I can't stop wondering what would happen if he did touch me in those places.

When I don't answer, he adds, "I was just thinking that when you're a teenager, at least at first, sex isn't really the endgame, right? And you don't even expect an orgasm. You're figuring things out, enjoying all the stops along the way."

When I still don't say anything, he starts to move my legs, but I grab his shirt to stop him. "No."

"No?"

"No, I mean, don't go. I mean, yes. To trying that. Making out without the sex agenda. Let's do it."

"Are you sure?"

In answer, I slip my hands behind his head and pull him down until I can brush my lips across his.

"Okay, then," he whispers before meeting me kiss for kiss.

LUKE

From her descriptions of her past experiences with men, I've imagined the names that Dani might've been called.

Tight.

Stuck-up.

Cold.

Frigid.

But none of these words would describe her now. I don't know if the half-baked tantric exercise flipped a switch or what, but I send a thanks to Sting and my buddy Ashton as I welcome kisses so fervent, I need a time-out after just a few moments of making out.

Suspended above her, I take in the flushed skin of her face and chest, the tangle of her hair against the pillow, her lips swollen. She's a siren, calling my name, and I hope I don't drown.

"What's the matter?" she asks.

"Needed a breather," I say. "I thought we were going to go slow."

One side of her mouth quirks up. "Sorry about that."

"Believe me, I enjoyed it, but at this rate, I'm gonna need a shower pronto, if you know what I mean."

Uncertainty replaces the passion I saw seconds ago.

"Not that it's a bad thing," I add.

Her expression shifts to curious. "So how do we slow things down?"

Grateful that she's not shutting me out, I roll onto my side, pulling her by the hip so she's facing me. "Your guess is as good as mine. I've never done this before either."

She bites her lip again, this time more in concentration, but her hand is shaky as she reaches for me. Grabbing it, I kiss the tips of her fingers. "Hey, I mean it. I don't know what I'm doing here. Is that okay with you?"

She nods. And then adds, "Is it okay with *you*?"

Still holding on to her hand, I roll onto my back before placing it on my chest and then covering it with mine. "In tantric sex, I think you're supposed to breathe to relax away from the tension of orgasm, so I'm going to try that when I get too turned on." Turning my head to take her in, I add, "So feel free to test that."

"I'll take that as a challenge." Propping herself up on her elbow, she pulls her hand out from under mine to stroke across my chest and down my belly. Like one of the dogs, I stretch beneath her caresses, and as she teases my waist and thighs, I breathe deep, releasing the buildup of tension.

When it gets to be too much, I blow out a breath and roll her so that she's facing away from me before spooning her, my dick nestled right between her cheeks. Continuing to breathe deeply as I let my hands explore her rounded belly, the swell of her hip, the soft backs of her knees, I whisper, "Wonder if any teenagers ever had this much fun?"

She tenses slightly when I caress her belly, so I remind her to breathe, whispering "Let go," over and over as she begins to undulate into my touch. I haven't gone near her breasts or her sex, but she's obviously finding a deep level of pleasure.

Gradually, I take it down a notch, then two, then three, until I'm just stroking up and down the sides of her arm and hip.

Pressing a light kiss behind her ear, I whisper, "Gonna get ready for bed."

Rolling slowly onto her back, she asks, "Do you still need that shower?"

Pushing up to a sitting position, I think about it. I'm pleasantly turned on but not excruciatingly so. "Nah, I'm good."

Getting up to her knees, she kisses me softly on the mouth. "I'll join you then."

I use the toilet while she lets the dogs out for their final pee, then give her privacy after we've both brushed our teeth. When she returns to the bedroom, she catches sight of my dick before it disappears inside my pajama pants, but she doesn't seem embarrassed. Instead, she holds my heated gaze as she strips off her clothes, before turning to pull on a pair of sleep shorts and a tank top.

It's not that I couldn't guess how beautiful her bare body would be, but I'm still flattened by the renewed rush of desire for her. "Fuck, Dan. Maybe I will need that shower."

Without moving, she whispers, "Would you do me a favor instead?"

"Of course."

"Will you get yourself off in front of me?"

My dick says *hell yes*, but my brain says, "Are you sure that's what you want?"

"If you don't, or if you go and do it in the shower, I'll be imagining it all night long. I want to see it."

Dumbfounded, and even more aroused than before, I can't quite find words.

"I think it'll help me," she adds.

How can I say no to that?

DANI

As the question leaves my mouth, part of me is already planning to pretend I'm joking. The kind of thing I used to do in college when I had no idea how to be in bed with a guy. I'd say something, his face would make it clear it was weird, and I'd walk it back. Like when I suggested to Luke that I could use exposure therapy for sex a few weeks ago. I'd laughed it off, but he took me seriously.

As he does now.

"Do you want me to strip?" he asks softly.

I nod, all in for exposure therapy of the very best kind. Without taking his eyes off mine, he pushes his pj bottoms down and then kicks them away from his ankles, revealing a runner's body, lean and muscular. His penis is obviously ready for this experiment, and he grasps it firmly in one hand.

"Do you want me standing or sitting or lying down?"

My sex clenches as I picture us. Naked, lying next to each other. Touching myself.

"What? What are you thinking?" he asks softly.

I close my eyes, shake my head.

I feel him step closer, feel his warmth press into me before he whispers into my ear, "You don't have to tell me, but whatever you're imagining, I'd love it."

My eyes pop open to search his face, finding the complex expression that's gotten me this far: acceptance colored with curiosity and desire. It's all the permission I need, apparently, because I shuck off my own pajamas.

His eyes follow my inelegant striptease, and the hunger in them gives me the last bit of gumption I need to whisper, "Lie down, facing me."

Skirting opposite sides of the bed, shoving the top sheet and coverlet out of the way, we meet again in its center. My eyes follow his hands as they grip and stroke, while my own hands busy themselves gliding over my own body, covering ground he unearthed with his touch the past week, reawakening the deep pleasure.

"Watching you touch yourself is so fucking sexy," he says, his voice gravelly and urgent, and when I meet his gaze, I know he's speaking the truth.

His back arches slightly, and my gaze drops down again, watching as he adds a flick of his thumb over the glistening head to the long strokes. In response, one of my hands palms a breast. Shoving aside my mother's voice, *If you'd eat a bit more and run a bit less, Dani, your boobs'd be bigger*, I refocus on sensation, mirroring his action by squeezing the soft flesh and flicking a thumb over the hard nipple, gasping at the intensity of the sensation.

"Yes. Do that again," he growls.

I continue to follow his suggestions as well as my body's wishes, alternating between licking my fingers and swirling them over the beaded nipples and pinching them hard. Meanwhile, Luke picks up speed. When he rolls to his back, his torso arching, his hand pumping furiously, his eyes squeezing shut, my fingers drop to my sex, diving between the dark curls to squeeze and pinch the flesh of my mound.

And when his entire body goes rigid, his hand stilling over his cock as the cum spills out onto his belly, I circle my sensitive nub. Sensations that seem like they've been building inside me for weeks come to a head. My eyes close, chasing the feeling. When I hear Luke rustle next to me, I freeze momentarily, but when he begins to stroke my thighs and reminds me to breathe, I imagine him touching me where my fingers are. Circling, I find the swell again, and moments later, I'm at the edge and falling over it.

CHAPTER SEVENTEEN

LUKE

For the remainder of primary photography for episode one, everywhere I turn it feels like someone's questioning my decisions. I know that directing TV is nothing like directing a movie. In the latter, you're the auteur so you have the final say. In the former, you're just another cog in the wheel.

You might think that the producing director title might give me a bit more weight to throw around. Instead, I'm smack in the middle of the push-pull between the crew on the ground and the suits in LA, between the actors in front of me and the showrunner I have to answer to from the end of a telephone line.

The only thing getting me through it? The prospect of getting naked with Dani at night. The minute my pager buzzes with the code that means she's outside, I wrap up whatever I'm doing, scoop up Peanut, and practically run to her car. Once I'm inside, I lean across the console to sneak a kiss behind her ear and whisper, "Teenagers or tantra tonight?"

The past few nights, we've shared some of the most intense sexual experiences I've ever had, even though we haven't actually had intercourse. Watching this woman discover her own sexuality is the honor of a lifetime and a hell of a turn-on. Part of me doesn't ever want to go all the way with her. I'm afraid the buildup will make the deed a disappointment. For her and for me.

And maybe that's the point of all this. That it isn't about the destination, but the journey.

The engine revs, and she shifts the car into reverse. "What about Two Truths and a Lie?"

"We could play on the way home, but I don't want any delays once we close your bedroom door. I need to kiss you right now more than I need coffee in the morning."

"Wow," she says, and I swear that's a blush on her cheek, though it's hard to tell in the dim light. "That's serious."

"Good thing your roommates think we're newlyweds. Otherwise, I'd be stuck doing puzzles or playing pinochle or whatever else they do to pretend that they're just friends."

"You seem extra hyped up today. Does that mean you had a good day or a bad day?"

"I don't want to dump my frustrations on you."

On the surface, Danielle Goodman is fiercely independent. At the same time, it's clear that she cares deeply about her chosen family and watches out for everyone in her orbit, whether they deserve it or not. Obviously, I fall into the latter category, but I suddenly want more than anything to worm my way into the former.

"I'm the one who asked," she says. "And maybe I can give you some perspective, since I've known most of the players longer than you have."

"If you really don't mind, the person I could use the most help with is Helen."

Her brow furrows for a moment. "Helen has been an amazing mentor to me."

"She's nice to you?" I ask, having a hard time picturing the woman speaking a kind word to anyone.

"I didn't say that. I respect her, and she respects me. Anyway, it's not her job to be nice. Being demanding does not mean she's a bitch."

I go hands up. No way am I going there. "I just wish she'd give me a damn break. Or at least stop treating me like the enemy."

"Think about this from her point of view," she says as she checks for traffic before making a turn. "She worked her butt off to keep the train running when they were hiring and firing showrunners this spring."

"Meaning she was getting all kinds of last-minute changes, while no one was really steering the ship."

"Exactly. To completely mix the transpo metaphors, she's used to taking the wheel, and then you show up. Young guy with deep Hollywood connections. You're best friends with the new showrunner. Are you spying on her? Are you two going to pull a power play?"

"All I know is, Max believes in the original concept of the show. Nobody's ever made a show where teenagers really say what they really think about."

"You mean sex?" she asks, and the blush is back.

"Yeah, definitely. Should I or shouldn't I go all the way? But also, all the other worries. What people think of me, who's gossiping about me, am I ever going to fall in love? All wrapped up in a cast that's better-looking and better-dressed than the average pimply kid. It's actually a lot like the show Max and I made together in high school. With girls, but without aliens."

"I'd like to hear about *that* sometime, but"—she puts the car in park and turns off the engine—"we're home."

Home. With a woman that I love talking to and hanging out with as much as I love touching and kissing. If this were a made-for-TV romance, I'd be guaranteed a happy ending with her. But since this is life, I guess I'll just hang on for the ride.

DANI

The moment he closes my bedroom door, Luke's eyes rove over me like I'm a spread at a church picnic and he can't decide what to scoop up first. Things have intensified in the past week. I only had the one little orgasm, which I'm not sure he even noticed, but I don't even care about that anymore. It's like my nerve endings shoot to the surface when I get close to him and all I want is to touch and be touched. Everywhere.

Lifting my chin and adopting some of Helen's bossiness, I say, "Take off your shirt."

His jaw drops slightly as his brows go up.

"C'mon. Move it along. We don't have all night."

"Yes, ma'am." He does his best to hide a grin. "Your wish is my command."

"The pants too." I flick a hand at him.

Almost gleefully, he obeys, and then stands there in his boxers, arms and legs splayed. "What next?"

Surveying the picture-perfect man in front of me, all sculpted muscle and smooth skin, now I'm the one over-whelmed by the feast. Determined not to be cowed by my fears—of not measuring up, of freaking out at the last minute, of what'll happen when this is over—I tell myself to let my fingers do the walking, like the old Yellow Pages ad.

Stepping closer, I start at the top. When I run two fingers over his brow, the furrows relax, and he releases a deep sigh. When I trace the curve of his ear, a shudder runs through his whole body. Down his neck and traps, and his shoulders drop a hair, but as I skim across the curve of his pec, movement draws my focus to the bulge in his shorts. I follow his happy trail south.

When I dip into the waistband of his boxers, he grabs my wrist, breathing, "Dan."

I meet his gaze, to find the blue of his irises almost completely eclipsed by his pupils. The desire and longing I see mirrors my own, and I whisper, "I want to make you come."

"Okay, then." His voice strangled with need, he releases my wrist.

My hands immediately get to work. One dives in to grasp his hard length, the other drags a thumb across his lower lip. Moaning, he nips and laps at my hand until he's sucked my thumb into his mouth. I stroke up and down, marveling at the silky feel of him over the steel of his desire, spreading the wetness at the head until I need to see it.

Dragging my hand from his mouth and down his torso, I shove his boxers down. After pushing him to a seat on the bed, I kneel to caress the skin at the juncture of his hips and thighs with one hand, while the other draws his cock into my mouth.

The moment my lips close over the shaft, a deep moan reverberates through my entire body.

His fingers massage my scalp as my tongue, lips, and hands play and explore. There's no way I can fit the entirety of him in my mouth, but pumping the base and sucking the head has his legs shaking. The feel of him under my lips and palm, the memory of his hands caressing my body along with the urgency in his voice brings a pulse to my own sex and has my nipples straining inside my bra.

When I look up, the rapture on his face has me releasing him from my mouth with a pop, even as I hang on for dear life.

"Any chance you have a condom handy?"

Obviously, this is not what he expected to hear. "But there's still two weeks till your surgery date. Are you sure you'll feel… covered?"

"My body says yes." And I don't want to say no to this aching need.

Standing, he tugs me up to face him before settling both palms on my shoulders. "You set the pace. You need to slow down, you tell me. You need to stop, you tell me. No questions asked. You know I'll hold off or take care of myself, okay?"

"Yep. Just get the rubber."

Saluting me, he gives me a playful "Yes, ma'am."

Instead of making a beeline for his stash, however, he turns in a circle, rubbing the top of his head.

"Please tell me you have condoms."

Instead of answering, he begins talking to himself and gesturing with his hands. "When I moved here from the apartment, I took them out of my dopp kit and put them... where?"

Thinking he might need a little motivation to jog his memory, I take off my shirt and shorts. He's seen me in a running bra and jockey boy shorts, but I found time this week to invest in something that might be a little more inspiring, to me and to him: lingerie.

"You coming or what?"

"I'm working on it, but I—" The moment he catches sight of me, he stops mid-sentence. The hungry look in his eyes as they rove over my body revs me up more. Evidence has shown that he finds me desirable even when I'm not in scraps of lace that push my boobs up and barely cover my hoo-ha. I know it's silly, but even as I handed my credit card to the lady in the bra shop, my confidence went up a notch. Maybe it's because he's made it clear that every step we've taken is my choice, but all I know right now is that I want him inside and out.

"Is that a thong?" he demands.

Hands on hips, I cock a brow at him. "Wouldn't you like to know?"

He juts his chin at me. "Turn around. Let me see."

Crossing my arms over my chest, giving the bra a little help, I singsong, "I will when you show me a condom."

Groaning, muttering something about bossy women, he starts scrabbling through the drawers I cleared for him. When he turns to face me again, he doesn't have condoms, but he does look certain. "The side pocket of my gym bag." Pointing at me as he jogs to the closet, he says, "Do not take those off."

Moments later, he emerges, triumphant, holding up a shiny strip and a small bottle of what looks like lube. "To make sure you're ready. Now, let me see."

I spin slowly, and by the time I finish the circle, he looks like he's having a hard time swallowing. "Have you been wearing these all day?"

"I have."

"C'mere," he growls.

Crawling across the bed to meet him halfway, I kneel to face him. After dropping the supplies, he reaches for me. While one finger trails down a bra strap and over the lace cupping my breast, the other skates over the lace on my hip before cupping my bare ass.

Grasping his skull with both hands, I pull his lips to mine. Between kisses, he whispers, "So fucking sexy."

He said I was to set the pace, but his kisses and caresses are so urgent that they ratchet up my need. I'm a little worried that I could still freak out, but I trust that Luke won't make fun of me or get angry if I do. Besides, this yearning in my core has me impatient to feel him inside me.

Like, *now.*

"Whatever you need to do," I say, panting, "to get ready or whatever, do it, because I'm ready."

He gets this wild look in his eyes, which has my inner walls clenching. When he bites his lip like he can't decide what to do next, I push him onto his back, rip off one of the condoms, and open the wrapper.

"Take off the thong now," he says, his voice gruff.

I stand to do as ordered, watching as he rolls on the condom. As I kneel to straddle him, he squirts a trail of lube up his impressive length. I join him in spreading the goop over every bit of it.

"Use me to spread the lube on you," he whispers.

"Oooh, good idea."

He laughs at my eager tone, but not at me. Instead, he seems to delight in my discovery, as he has every step of the way along my journey to self… whatever. Too much thinking, girl, let's do.

Easing his cock toward my mound, I nestle it between the folds, rubbing up and down, spreading the slickness while leaning into the friction.

"Yesss," he hisses when I gasp at the teasing sensation. "Keep that up, sweetheart, right there."

The friction of my nipples against the bra is suddenly too much, so I release his penis, arch my lower back, and unclasp the bra. Moaning with need when the cool air hits my pebbled nipples, I move his hands from my hips to my breasts.

"Don't forget to breathe," he whispers. "I'm not going anywhere."

His words soothe the ragged edges of my nerves. Remembering how we started this, with just breath and touch, I let go of my impatience, of my fear, of all the pressure to do this the right way—whatever the hell that even means—and do my best to pay attention.

To every little sound he makes, to the colors of his skin, to the textures of the hair on his head, his face, his chest, and his sex. To all the different sensations his touch stirs in me, to the way that sensation builds and flows, reverberates and ricochets inside me.

Every single time I've had sex in the past, I hit get-this-over-with mode within moments of getting naked. Now, as he alternates between caressing and squeezing, flicking and pinching, I want this to go on forever. Something inside me has other ideas, however, and it takes the wheel. Grasping his sheathed cock, I guide it to my entrance. Meeting his questioning gaze, I nod, slowly at first, and then faster as he stretches me right along the edge of pleasure and pain.

"You good, Dan?" he whispers.

So good is what I mean to say, but instead a keening sound erupts from my mouth, a high moan that rides the searing sensation burning through me. I ride the waves, getting closer and closer to the crest, but falling back down every time.

When I start to get frustrated, Luke says, "It's okay, baby. We can stop now."

Shaking my head, I refuse to give up.

"Not everyone has an orgasm this way," he says.

"I'm just so close."

"Can I change the position?"

When I nod, he flips us so he's on top. It's scary for a moment, losing control, but when I see the expression in his eyes, the concern combined with barely holding on desire, I remember to breathe. He hooks one knee over his shoulder, stretching me wider and begins long slow strokes.

"Touch yourself," he whispers. "Touch yourself how you like it."

Sliding a hand between us, I do as he says, finding my clit and circling it with two fingers.

"There you go," he says, before pinching my nipple with his free hand. "Just play."

Arching my back, I circle and press, circle and press, focusing on the sensation of him inside me, the friction. When the shudders begin, he picks up the pace. I'm right on the edge when he groans and seems to break free of whatever bounds he'd placed on himself. His face as he goes over the edge, as he releases inside of me, is the prettiest thing I've ever seen.

"I'm sorry," he pants as he collapses on top of me, his lips next to my ear. "I couldn't hold on any longer."

Wrapping my arms around him, I give him a deep squeeze. "I know."

He pushes up and off me and gives me a quick peck on the cheek. "Be right back."

When he's done, I take my own turn in the bathroom. When I return, he reaches out a hand from the bed and then pulls me in so he's spooning me from behind. After pulling the sheets over us both, he whispers, "Dani, that was… amazing."

I could lie, tell him I came to make him feel better, but he deserves better than that. And so do I. "I didn't have an orgasm."

I feel him take a breath, so before he can apologize, I add, "But I also didn't feel the need to run or vomit."

Snorting with laughter, he says, "You do know how to make a guy feel special."

I reach back to give him a swat. "You know this is a big deal."

Nestling in, his nose behind my ear, he whispers, "I know. Thank you for letting me in. In all the ways."

CHAPTER EIGHTEEN

LUKE

I expected my work schedule to calm down after primary shooting for the first episode wrapped, but the backlog of decisions to be made and meetings to take means that I'm still working stupid-long days. Coming home to a woman discovering sexual pleasure for the first time in her life is an added bonus but taking that journey with her also means less sleep.

In fact, as she drives us home at the end of a day that feels like it should've ended hours ago, I realize I must've nodded off when she asks, "Did you hear what I said?"

"Uh, no. I'm sorry. I think I fell asleep. What was it?"

She hesitates momentarily. "I said, did you want to find your own place now that George and Tina are gone?"

It's a good thing she's driving, because once I've processed her words my heart begins to race, and not because I'm worried about an object being dropped on us from above. "Do you... want me to move out?"

Instead of answering, she bites her lip. For once, it doesn't turn me on.

Arguments for why it doesn't make sense for me to move into my own place scroll through my mind. We haven't had much time to practice driving so I still can't drive myself. Peanut isn't ready to be left on his own. It'd be a waste of money.

All perfectly practical reasons for me to stay. But the uncertain expression I catch on her face when we pass under a streetlight is a punch to the gut. Does she think that what we've been doing between the sheets was part of the role I've been playing for her roommates? Or worse, some sort of obligation for me? Part of the trade?

"Dan," I whisper when she stops the car at a light. "Look at me."

When she does, it's clear that she's thinking all these things. With her walls down, her mask relaxed, her face says it all. Reaching across the console, I caress her cheek with the back of my hand. "What if I don't *want* to go?"

DANI

My hands are so shaky, Luke might be the safer driver in this car, as his question echoes in my ears the rest of the way home.

Home. Does he consider my place his home? Do I want him to?

I truly never thought I'd be in this position. I imagined having a man to share my life with would be a pain in the ass. Roommates are one thing, because you can always close the door and tell them you need to be alone. But when someone shares your bed, you can't do that.

He must sense my turmoil, because he doesn't press for an answer, he rests his palm on my shoulder and runs his thumb lightly over that pressure point he showed me what feels like eons ago. His touch reminds me to breathe, which keeps me calm enough to get us home in one piece.

But once we're in the house—no longer having to

pretend for Tina and George—I go straight to the fridge, pull out a beer, twist off the cap, and drink like I just crossed a desert.

Luke pulls one of the glasses he keeps in the freezer before choosing one of the microbrews that take up space in my fridge. Beer so fancy, you need a church key to open it. Good thing I never removed the Coca Cola bottle opener from the wall, or he'd have to scrabble in the junk drawer every time he wanted a beer.

We drink in silence. I don't know what he wants from me. To beg him to stay so he can keep blowing my mind every night? To say that I want to be his wife for real?

Is that what I want?

I thought I wanted to be left alone, like Aunt Gracie. To create a haven away from other people's needs. But this man snuck in right under my nose.

The real problem, though, is that I fear the shrink might've been right. I mean, I've now had an orgasm next to a man, and I've actually enjoyed intercourse, even though my tubes remain a wide-open highway. So, what has changed? What has made the difference?

It can't be love. I hardly know him, and it's not like I'm doodling hearts all over my notebooks, or worse, writing *Mrs. Luke Zelazny* just to see what it looks like.

Then what is going on here? We're friends with benefits? Who also get along well enough to live together?

Okay. That I can handle. That makes sense.

His glass lands on the kitchen island with a clunk. "I'm sure I can find a place by the end of the week, if that's what you want," he says, his voice heavy. Not only with weariness, though I know the guy must be tired as hell, but with what sounds like disappointment.

Setting down my now empty bottle, I step closer and take his hand. "What if I want you to stay?"

He meets my uncertain gaze with one so fierce I have to

force myself to hold my ground. "I don't want to impose on you."

"I mean"—I take a deep breath, let it out—"I don't hate having you here."

He takes my free hand. Squeezes it. Still holding me prisoner with his eyes. "The dogs do get along."

"And it'd add to my commute to have to drive you somewhere else at night and pick you up in the morning."

"And I'd miss you." He slides our joined hands behind my back to pull me close, and I can feel how much he'd miss me.

My smile matches the one lifting the corners of his mouth. "In bed?"

"Everywhere, Dani," he whispers as he rests his forehead against mine. "I'd miss you everywhere."

After we make the decision to keep living together, Luke moves a few of his things into my house, like expensive pots and pans. Apparently, no Californian can be without a juicer or an industrial blender for smoothies, so those appliances take up residence on the counter. Even though I tell him he can put whatever he wants in my house, he keeps his artwork and fancy bike at his office.

I can't quite tell if he's trying to respect my need for space, or if he's perching lightly so he can say "I'm outta here" at the drop of a hat.

It's possible I'll want to kick him out when I get sick of him, so I haven't pushed to find out.

In the outside world, our relationship is strictly professional. In my home, the sex experiment continues. The man has gone above and beyond to hold up his end of our bargain, from performing the role of fake fiancé to fake husband to sex therapy guide. I mean, it's clear he's getting some benefits, but that doesn't mean I'm going to slack off.

So, a few days after the episode he directed wraps, I manage to get Luke driving again, and it's not long before he's able to drive on a road with other cars without breaking out in a sweat. He's still being overly cautious, to the point that I'm afraid he's going to get pulled over for driving too slowly. Today, it's my plan to get him to drive from the stages to the current location. As an experiment, I try distracting him with conversation.

"You know," I begin, "you said that you decided to quit acting when you were here two years ago, but you did more roles after that."

"So, you *do* watch my stuff."

Bingo. I get a grin out of the guy. First time while behind the wheel.

I shrug, like I'm not pleased as punch. "I do tend to follow my clients' careers. I consider some of them friends. We exchange Christmas cards and birthday cards."

He pushes his lower lip out in a pout. "I didn't get any birthday cards."

After checking the map and telling him to take the next right, I explain, "One, you never gave me your address, and two, I don't know your birthday. All I know is that you're a Pisces. I read that in *Teen Beat* a bazillion years ago, and it stuck with me."

"And what's your sign?"

"Cancer."

"Does that mean we're a good love match? According to *Tiger Beat*?"

"No comment. Also, you need to take a left up ahead, so you should change lanes soon." I know he doesn't like being in the lane closest to oncoming traffic, so I return to the original question. "So, what made you want to quit after that show? Was the role that bad?"

My plan seems to be working, because even after he changes lanes, his breathing stays even. "It was, but it wasn't only that. I'd been doing roles just like it for several years at that point. I mean, I have friends who are series regulars on *Oz* and *Ally McBeal*, even *South Park*. While I couldn't land a guest spot on *Breaker High*."

He sighs. "Besides that, though? I think it was being here, away from my agent and my mom, from the whole business, really, I was able to accept that I'd aged out of the type I could play if I was just being myself. That I had no interest in getting better at acting."

"Take a left at this light up ahead." Once he flicks the turn signal, I ask, "Then why did it take so long to actually quit?"

After stopping the car at the red light, he looks over at me. "Have you ever had a piece of clothing that you loved, but was so worn that it really didn't serve the purpose anymore?"

Not sure where he's going with the question, I think about it as he makes the turn. "Oh, yeah. I had these cowboy boots—remember that time when cowboy boots were in? Because of that John Travolta movie?"

He nods. "With Debra Winger, about riding the fake bull in the bar."

"Yup. I thought I looked so cool in those boots. Wore 'em all the time, even when the heels wore down and the soles had holes in them."

He nods. "I had a pair of running shoes that I was super attached to because I won some celebrity 10K in them. Ran in them to the point I was getting shin splints. When I finally did get new ones, I had to make myself wear them. Even though they had better support and my shins stopped hurting, every time I put them on, they felt weird."

"Did they ever get comfortable?"

"It took some time, but yeah."

"So, is that how it is with you and directing instead of acting?"

He nods slowly. "I'd say I'm still in the breaking-in phase."

I point out the final turn that leads to crew parking, and after he turns off the car, he holds out his hand, palm up.

When I take it, he gives it a squeeze. "I'm sorry if I was an asshole back then. I was really afraid to let go of those shoes."

"You're forgiven," I say, before pushing the button to play the CD mix I made as another distraction for his driving time. When "Save Tonight" by Eagle Eye Cherry plays, I let the lyrics remind me to savor the time we have together, since it will inevitably end.

CHAPTER NINETEEN

DANI

I've been hoping for the right weather to take Luke out to Masonboro Island on a weekend, and we finally get a morning high tide on a Saturday. Back in the day, either Sully or Whitney could find us a powerboat to get across the intracoastal, but Sully no longer works part-time at a marina, and Whit's… well, not available.

I do, however, have a cousin who will lend me his kayaks, so I get up early and stuff a dry bag with towels and water and snacks. Then I wake Luke, tell him to slather on the sunscreen, wear board shorts and shoes he can get wet, and meet me in the car. Violet's agreed to take Peanut when she picks up Skye, so I put him in his crate with a puzzle toy, and we're off.

Less than an hour later, we're gliding through channels only a kayak could navigate, the only sounds the lap of our oars hitting the water, the wind in the reeds, and the cries of seagulls overhead. Luke's form could use some work, but he makes up for it with the strength of his stroke.

Which has me thinking about the strength of another stroke of his.

I had my pre-surgical appointment this week, and the recovery will take longer than I expected. Meaning, I won't be able to run for a week, no intercourse for a couple weeks, and kayaking will be out for at least a month, so I'm determined to enjoy all of those activities while I can.

Not that I've ever considered having sex on the beach. Even on Masonboro, an uninhabited island that you can only reach by boat, you're exposed unless you go into the dunes, which shouldn't be disturbed by human traffic. Plus, what would you do with the condom? Carry it back in a plastic bag?

Sighing, I refocus on the beauty of the day and the peaceful surroundings. When we get to the island, Luke loses his balance getting out of the boat. He yelps going down, but he's smiling when he pops back up, even though he's completely soaked.

"Just what I needed. Got a little sweaty with that workout."

As he helps me haul the boats onto the sand, he almost loses a shoe in the muck. "Why'd you tell me to wear shoes if they're going to get sucked into this mud?"

"You'll need them to get across the island, believe me. Especially when we come back later. The sand will be too hot to go barefoot."

I pull both boats well away from the water, telling him how I learned the hard way to avoid the high tide line. "My friends and I came out here in a tiny little flat-bottomed boat once. Pulled the boat onshore, but when we returned several hours later, the tide had come up, floating it hundreds of feet away. We had to swim out to it. We were lucky it didn't get pulled into the current because we'd have been literally up the creek without a paddle."

Luke pulls the kayak even further onto land after that story, and then we hike the hundred yards across the island to the Atlantic side.

I love bringing people to Masonboro, especially when it's their first time. I assume Luke's been to Hawaii or Mexico, but as we mount the final rise on the path, I glance over and am rewarded with a look of awe on his face.

He looks back, as if retracing our steps here in his mind, and then scans the wide, empty beach. "How is this place not crowded with tourists?"

"It's a lot of work to get here," I remind him, taking him by the hand and tugging him toward the ocean. "Ready for a swim?"

We drop our things on the beach and race for the water, both of us whooping with joy as we dive into a wave. When I resurface, swiping my hair out of my face, I grin. "I thought you might be a dive-in person."

"What's the alternative?"

"Some people wade in. Violet and Whit both take forever to get in the water. But I like to get it over with."

As we bob in the waves, diving under the big ones and floating over the small ones, all the tension fades from Luke's face. And then a sly grin appears. "We're all alone out here."

I roll my eyes. "Sex on the beach is highly overrated."

"Do you speak from experience?"

"I do not. I personally have no interest in getting sand up my hoo-ha."

Moving behind me and nuzzling behind my ear, he says, "We both know that intercourse isn't the only way to have sex."

"True," I say, pressing my ass into his hard length.

"We don't even have to leave the cover of the water." He slides his palms up to cup my breasts, tweaking my nipples through the thin fabric of my bikini. "Or even take off our suits."

Resting my head on his shoulder, I let my body float as he continues to caress my breasts and belly. His lips find my jaw while his hands slip inside my board shorts, stroking around and between my folds. I arch into him as his touch begins to drive me toward the edge, my hips buck as I get close, and as we float over a wave, I come, a breeze heightening the sensation on my wet, exposed skin.

Needing to feel him, I turn and wrap my legs around his waist, grinding against his cock even as my sex continues to shudder. Reaching between us, I press him against me, and he thrusts between my hands and my mound. I watch, entranced as his expression shifts from focused effort to the bliss of release, then I capture his mouth and his shout with my own.

Unfortunately, I also picture his little swimmers escaping into the water, and can't stop myself from pushing away.

His eyes pop open and he gasps, "What's the matter? Did something bite you?"

"I'm fine," I say on a pant, continuing to put distance between us. Once I process what I'm doing, however, I slap my hands over my face and then peek through my fingers to confess, "I'm running away from your sperm."

He laughs, his face a picture of disbelief. "You think my sperm are going to row in their own little kayak through the water and up your—what did you call it? Your hoo-ha?"

I nod, still hidden behind my hands. "I know I'm being ridiculous, I know sperm can't survive in salt water, but nobody ever said my fears were founded in reason."

"Will you tell me when it's safe for me to come kiss you?"

I swoosh the water between us away from me, assessing the amount of time since he came, the volume of water, and the current and the waves. "I think it's okay now."

"Are you sure? My sperm might be superheroes, able to leap great distances in a single bound." He swims toward me, doing the *Jaws* theme. "Or Great White Sperm. Able to consume vaginas in one bite."

To show him that he doesn't scare me, I let him put his

arms around me, and then I goose him, right in the sensitive spot he never should've told me about, and he squeals like a stuck pig.

CHAPTER TWENTY

LUKE

Dani thinks she's so sneaky, getting me to drive more and more, distracting me with music or tough questions to take my mind off the fact that I'm driving. I have to give her credit, though, because before I know it, I'm actually able to get myself from point A to point B. I need a few deep breaths before I turn the key, and I don't think I'm anywhere near ready to try a highway, but those are few and far between around here.

I could ask production to rent me a car, but I don't really want to be driving a rental for the next five or six months. Problem is, I don't have time to shop for one, and I hate to ask Dani for yet another favor. However, when she mentions something about getting her car fixed at a shop run by her buddy Ford's family, I get an idea.

Since I'm the only director who sticks around after his eight days of primary shooting, it's my job to direct second-unit days. These B-unit shoots can be anything from exteriors with a few extras, to an entire scene with dialogue. We're doing the latter today, and Ford is on tap as the sound mixer. He's young for a department head, but according to Dani,

215

he's been working in sound since college. Anyway, I'm hardly one to talk.

Unfortunately, the man has definitely got his guard up around me. Hard to tell if it's because I'm the boss, or he's new to the work, or if it's because I'm fake married to his friend. Banking on the idea that it's a combo of all three, and because a second-unit shoot is a smaller crew, I plan to ease up on the authority and double up on the charm.

When I'm on the lot, I usually spend the lunch break on the phone in my office, but today we're off in the middle of nowhere, so I'll use the time to get advice on buying a car.

After filling my plate at catering, I head for the table of gaffers and sound guys. "Mind if I join you?"

Luckily, there's a seat open next to Ford, and I don't waste any time. "I hear your family does auto repair."

His brow furrows. "Yeah?"

"Obviously you didn't join the family business, but do you know much about cars?"

"Some."

It's probably a good thing that the sound mixer—the guy whose job is essentially listening—isn't a Chatty Cathy, but I do hope I'm eventually going to get more than a one-word answer.

"I need to buy a car, and I know nothing about cars. I'm thinking a used car. Something safe, not flashy."

"Okay."

"I was wondering if you know anyone, in your family or otherwise, who'd be willing to do some legwork for me. Find me a couple of options so I could just do a test drive and then buy the thing."

Eyes on the table, he nods slowly. "I don't know anyone who does that, like, for a job, but I guess I could do it for you."

"I'd pay you for your time. My days are too long right

now, and I don't even have a way to get there to check them out."

"Because Dani's driving you?"

"Right."

"What kind of car do you drive now?"

"Actually—" I can't tell him the whole story, but maybe sharing a little bit of my dilemma will help. "I haven't owned a car for the past three years. I was in a pretty bad accident and am just now getting back to driving. Dani's been a big help with that."

I spend the rest of lunch answering his questions about what kind of cars I like, something I haven't thought about in a really long time. It's actually kind of fun reminiscing about the days before the accident, when my friends and I obsessed over cars. "I was so into my Ford Fox body. Thought it was da bomb."

"Oh, yeah. Those were rad," he says. "I was a Mazda Miata fan in the early nineties."

"But now, in my old age," I joke, "I want something reliable. And safe."

He nods, but he doesn't press further about the accident. "I'm off the rest of the week, so I'll see what I can find."

"That'd be great, man."

As we walk over to the tray bussing station, I have to ask about his family's shop, which Dani said was called Ford's Auto. "If you're not a mechanic or anything, how come it's named after you?"

"It's not named after me; I'm named after it. Ford is my mom's last name, and her grandfather opened the shop."

"Guess it's a good thing her last name wasn't Buick or Cadillac."

"True. Lincoln or Dodge would work, though."

He laughs, and I actually feel like I've made some progress with the guy. On the walk back to set, he says, "By the way, I don't know if you've thought this through, but you'll have to have a North Carolina driver's license to title and register the car. Which means you need a North Carolina address. Are you going to use Dani's?"

He's right. I hadn't thought this through. "I… I guess?"

"Yeah, well, unlike your marriage to my *friend*"—he waits to continue until I meet his eyes, where I can see clearly what he thinks about our marriage—"that stuff is not make-believe."

I always thought that everything you see in movies and on TV—including actions I've performed as an actor—is bullshit. Especially when it comes to anything having to do with sex or falling in love.

Problem is, movies and locker room talk are the only guides most of us have had on the subject. Unless you go to New Age workshops, I guess. But the point is, I performed the moves, and I thought they worked. Girls said I was sexy and acted like they had a good time.

Now I get that we were all acting. And I hate to admit it, but I'm pretty sure I was a wham-bam-thank-you-ma'am guy.

In my defense, I didn't know any better. But now, after slowing things way down with Dani, sex is a completely different experience. Sometimes I'm laughing moments before I'm rocked with mind-blowing pleasure. Some nights all I want is her cheek resting on my chest and her thigh hooked over mine while we talk.

Pillow talk. Now that was something I was sure only happened in movies.

As I run my fingers through her hair one night, I remember I need to ask her something, and it doesn't feel weird to do so. It feels like life.

"So, I got a call today."

"Sounds ominous."

"Well, I do want to get your blessing if I do this thing."

She rolls onto my chest and props her chin on her hands. "What is it you have to do?"

"The show's PR people want me to participate in a Where Are They Now story for *People* magazine."

"Do you want to do it?"

"At first, I didn't. Like, shouldn't all the focus be on the actors actually in the show?"

"And far away from you and me?"

"Exactly. But then when she told me more about it…"

"You got interested."

"More that it makes sense. They're hoping to get some positive press in a family-friendly environment. The article is all about people who started out as young actors and went on to direct."

"Who else are they featuring?"

"That's the thing. Ben Stiller, Jodie Foster, Ron Howard, people like that. I mean, I'd be an idiot to turn down a chance to be on the same page as them."

She shifts, and I realize I haven't exactly given her a real choice in the matter. "But if you're worried that it'll make it more likely that the world will find out about us, I won't do it."

"Do *you* think it will?"

"I already told the PR person that I won't answer any questions about my personal life, that I want it to be about the show. She said that wouldn't be a problem."

She wrinkles her nose for a beat, but then she shrugs. "If you want to do it, you should do it."

Kissing her nose, I thank her for understanding. I wish I could tell her that I love her. I wish I knew what that was. But I'm afraid that fake it till you make it won't work in this scenario any better than it did for me as an actor. If I lead her to believe I can make this work with her, but then bail when it gets tough, or can't follow through with the real feelings she deserves, she'll just be more hurt in the long run.

So I show her my gratitude instead.

Another night, snuggled up next to me, she asks, "I've heard a lot about your mother, but nothing about your dad. He's still around, right?"

"Yeah, he pretty much lets my mom run the show. At home and at the office. He runs the business side of things, but my mom calls the shots."

"Smart man," she says, snuggling in closer.

"Maybe, but she could use a little reining in. Someone to temper her."

"Maybe he does already."

A full-body shudder goes through me, and she giggles.

"You okay?"

"Just the thought that she could be worse." After a few moments of picturing what that would look like, I realize that there's no father in the images Dani paints of her family life, so I ask where he is.

"He died when I was three. He'd been in Vietnam before he hooked up with my mom. He was actually back in the States but still in the military. Died leading a training accident."

"I'm sorry" is all I can think to say. "That sucks."

"It might be one of the things that made my mom so nutty about babies. She was pregnant with my brother when he died, so she had to deal with two toddlers and a baby all by herself. After that, she went through men like you'd flip a Rolodex, none of them lasting more than a year or two. I always thought she was using them like sperm donors and kicking them out when they were no longer of use. But I don't know that for sure. Maybe they ran."

"Do you remember your dad?"

"I have a picture of him in uniform with me and my sister on his knees. He had a huge smile on his face. I think I remember that moment. It does feel like all the fun left after he was gone. Leaving me to play Cinderella."

I want to say something about being her prince, but it feels too hokey. And I'm not sure I can be that guy, or that she even needs one, so I say, "Yeah, but you don't need a prince to rescue you."

"Nah, but I wouldn't mind if a fairy godmother turned my old car into a fancier one. Or if some mousies and birdies cleaned up the house."

"All you've got here is a Pinocchio without a Jiminy Cricket, so I can't help you with magic."

She rolls over and touches my nose. "Seems like a normal size to me."

"I'm still a big fat liar. You pretend your whole life, you end up hollow inside."

Sliding her hand down my body until she finds my dick, she gives it a squeeze. "This part is some pretty impressive wood, though."

Rolling on top of her and pinning her beneath me, I say, "Think so? You want to check and see if it's real or just a toy?"

"Tempting," she says with a wicked grin.

"Even though this puppet has a few chips in his paint and is losing his hair?"

"I think I can see beyond a few flaws. If he knows how to handle himself."

"Oh, no. I'm the marionette, you've got to pull my strings."

"Challenge accepted," she whispers in my ear.

I may have missed my chance to be a real boy, but this woman makes me feel like it's still possible to find the real *me*.

CHAPTER TWENTY-ONE

DANI

I've heard about the bliss of having regular sex, and frankly I figured it was more bullshit fodder for women's magazines. But I'm finding it's not only real, it's even better than I imagined. Woodland animals aren't exactly flitting around me singing songs, but I do feel like I'm walking on air. Anything and everything is a potential turn-on, from shaving my legs to changing the sheets on the bed. My nipples seem to be permanently budded, thinking about what they want Luke to do to them. My sex clenches at the sight of him.

It'd all be annoying if it wasn't so freaking fun.

I'm humming along with The Lemonheads' "Into Your Arms," when I pull into my driveway after running a few errands—which may or may not have included a trip to the local sex shop. Turning off the engine, I'm surprised to see Violet's car in parked in front of my house. She still has a key, so maybe she's borrowing something for her engagement party.

But when I open the front door and find her hustling toward it, her expression makes it clear that something's wrong.

"There you are," she says. "I thought you were dead on the side of the road or something."

There's no way I'm telling her where I was. "Was I supposed to meet you for something?"

"You were supposed to pick up Skye early today. Nate and I had a doctor's appointment."

"I was?" The dog moseys in from the kitchen, and I gesture at her, confused. "But she's here."

Violet's sigh is loaded with exasperation. "Our assistant also made appointments for the afternoon, so I couldn't leave Skye with her. When you didn't show and didn't answer your pager"—she picks up my pager from the entry table and dangles it meaningfully—"I was not only worried, but we had to swing by here to drop her off."

I rub my forehead before pulling my planner from my messenger bag. Flipping it open, I don't see anything about picking up Skye. "When was I supposed to pick her up?"

"At noon," she sputters. "Four hours ago."

"When was your appointment?"

"At one."

"Then why are you here?"

"To make sure you're alive!" she yells.

Staring at my planner, I try to figure out what happened. Maybe I wrote it down, forgot about it, and the note fell out somehow. "I'm sorry, Vi. I have no memory of this conversation."

She blows out a breath. "It's fine. I wasn't late to the appointment or anything, but I was worried about you. I've never known you to forget anything."

"Yeah, I guess..." I trail off, wondering if I want to get into my sex life with Vi. She's shared a ton of her adventures with me over the years. But there's something about what's happening with me and Luke that feels like it might fall apart if I talk about it. Like if you tried to pick up a sandcastle, it'd spill through your fingers.

"Are you okay? Is anything wrong?" Vi places a gentle hand on my wrist. "You're making me worried."

I shake my head. "Nothing's wrong. I'm really sorry I put you out."

"It's fine, you just got me revved up." She pulls her blouse away from her chest. "But everything does that to me these days."

"Let me get you some ice water. Can't have the pregnant lady overheated."

"I do need to stay hydrated," she says as she follows me to the kitchen.

As I fill two glasses with ice and water, I ask, "Are you and Nate friends?"

"Huh?"

Handing her one, I repeat the question.

"Of course we are."

"But when did you know it was something else?"

She tips her head to the side. "Is this about you and Lukas?"

I shrug.

"Danielle Marie Goodwin. You owe me the truth."

"What do you mean?"

"Besides the fact that I'm your best friend?" She begins to tick a list off on her fingers. "I shared every one of my relationship disasters with you, I've known you your entire life, I just spent an afternoon worrying about you, I—"

"All right, all right. Don't get your knickers in a knot." Dropping my arms on the cool countertop and hanging my head, I sigh. "I feel like I'm in over my head a little bit."

"Meaning you're falling for your fake husband?"

Wincing, I peer through my hair. "Maybe?"

"Do you know how he feels?"

"I don't know how *I* feel."

After hiking herself up onto a barstool with a grunt, she leans forward to whisper. "Are y'all having sex?"

"It was not part of our deal," I add, not even lying because it wasn't part of the deal. And the new terms are about as clear as mud.

"But you are anyway?"

I shrug.

"Like actual intercourse?"

I shrug again.

"And you like it."

I wince, but then I nod.

Her shriek is so loud I about fall off the couch. "Jesus, Vi. Give a girl a heart attack."

Unrepentant, she claps her hands. "I'm so excited for you. And I want to know everything."

My shoulders creep up to my ears. "I... can't, Vi. It feels too, I don't know, fragile to talk about it."

She huffs out an impatient groan. "So, what's the friend question about?"

"I don't know. I don't think I'm, like, in love with him. I just really like him, and the sex is good."

"Is that enough?"

"Enough for what?"

"Enough to make you happy?"

"It kind of feels like it. But I don't know if it'll last. Or if it's enough for him."

She reaches out and squeezes my hand. "At some point, you might have to have this discussion with him. But I say, enjoy what's happening now and don't worry too much about the future. These things have a way of working themselves out."

I'm not sure I believe her, because my memories of all the relationships she went through involved some drama, including the early days with Nate. And a few minutes later, when she tells me about the plans for Nate's family to buy Carolina Casting, I about fall out.

"What? But that's the exact opposite of what you wanted a year ago."

She shrugs. "Things are different. If I'm under their umbrella, then my health insurance will be better and cheaper. That makes a difference when you're having a baby."

"Are they going to swoop in and take over?"

"Of course not. Me and Nate's sister are like this." She holds up two fingers twisted together. "And I know his dad respects me and the work Nate's doing with the foundation. It'll be fine."

"If you say so."

What I'd like to know but am afraid to ask is, does love make you look at *everything* with rose-colored glasses? And if so, how do you know what's real?

CHAPTER TWENTY-TWO

LUKE

It's not that I don't get along with my brother, but Dani's guess about our relationship hit close to home. We are competitive, but mostly because other people set us up to be. The list of people who do this includes—and probably should be headed by—our mother.

But my sister Gabriella is another story. Named after my mother's favorite Italian aunt, Gabi's a couple years older, never had any interest in acting, and has managed to create a remarkably conventional life for herself despite the fact that her two brothers are household names. She's also incredibly levelheaded and lacking in resentment, considering the neglect she must have suffered when my mother took on managing our careers.

Even though she's never worked in the business, she did grow up in Hollywood, so when I call her to check in the first thing she does is ask for a funny story.

"Well, something wacky happened today on set."

"Did one of the actresses have a hair emergency?"

I do wonder whether she'd consider my new look an emergency, but I say, "Come on, Gabs. I'm better than that."

"It just kills me how they're supposed to be typical teens, but they're effortlessly styled and have a New York model's taste and access to the latest styles."

"That's showbiz, sis."

"So, what happened?"

"I'm not directing at the moment, but I was on set because we have a new stunt coordinator, so I was there to make sure everything was on the up and up. In the scene, Leif, who plays Lawson—"

"Layf? That's how you say that name?"

"That's how he says it."

"Ha."

"Anyhoo, Lawson is mad at his buddy Parker again, so he comes storming into the high school gym—"

"Mm, I can smell it now."

"Are you gonna let me tell this story, or what?"

"Sorry. Zipping lips now."

"Lawson is so angry, the minute he sees Parker he hurls a basketball at his face."

"Boy needs therapy."

"Tell me about it."

"So did he break the other actor's nose?"

"This is supposed to be a funny story."

"That could be funny."

"You are one sick puppy, Gabs."

"Takes one to know one. What did happen, then?"

"The ball bounced off his face and hit the camera."

"Whoa. Did it break the camera?"

"No, no. It was a beach ball painted to look like a basketball. Props did a nice job on it."

"What's so funny, then?"

"Well, the kid playing Parker is the one doing the stunt, right? Getting hit in the face with a beach ball isn't awesome, but the hard part is hurling yourself to the ground—to the hard-as-hell court floor—without hurting yourself. I wasn't sure we could use a take with the ball hitting the camera—"

"Because it'd break the fourth wall?"

"Exactly. But we did take after take, poor Toby bouncing up every time saying, 'I'm good, man, I'm good.' The beach ball hit the damn camera every single time."

"So, what did you do?"

"Gave up. Toby was so sweaty the makeup people couldn't cover the red spots the ball made on his face, and the stunt guy was afraid the kid could break a wrist or something, he was getting so tired. We did one take where it hits him in the stomach for safety, and then just sent the dailies to LA."

"I'm so glad I'm not an actor," my sister says.

"I'm with you on that," I say, truly meaning it. "What really killed me was how much fun Leif was having smacking his co-star in the face with that beach ball. I mean, it wasn't going to do any permanent damage, but it had to smart."

"So, things are good? You kicking ass and taking names, Mr. Producing Director?"

Do I tell her what's happening with my life at the moment? Do I even know how to describe it? Because what started as a little favor to a friend has snowballed into: I might be falling for the person I'm pretending to be married to.

Probably not. My sister may enjoy a good romance novel, but to her, blurring the lines between what's fake and real is never a good idea. And she should know, since she's had a front-row seat for the lives my brother and I lead. Ones that have a lot more fiction in them than fact.

Instead of getting into it, I ask if she's had time to stop by my house. Since she lives one town over from me in the Valley, Gabi offered to water my plants and forward my mail while I'm in Wallington.

"All's good at your place," she says. "Did you want me to send all your mail or what?"

"Not the junk mail, but yeah."

"There are a few where it's hard to tell. Okay if I open them?"

"Sure, just tell me what they say."

Paper rips and shuffles on her end of the line. "Weird."

I'd been pacing my office as I talked to my sister. Dread hits me square in the gut at her words and I sink into the nearest chair before asking, "What's weird?"

"SAG insurance wants your signature to confirm that you want to add your wife to your plan." She laughs. "Like you're ever getting married."

"Yeah, about that."

The list of who knows about this not-so-secret, not-so-fake secret fake marriage just keeps getting longer.

CHAPTER TWENTY-THREE

LUKE

I am determined that everything will go well for Dani's upcoming surgery. I found the doctor's notes on the counter after her bloodwork appointment, which made it clear that she needs someone to drive her home after the tubal.

She also won't be able to drive me to and from work that day, so to get behind the wheel all by my lonesome sooner rather than later. The problem has been getting up the nerve to actually do it.

Just as I'm telling myself that it'll be like jumping in the ocean rather than wading it, I get a 911 page from the first AD. I don't recognize the number, so when I get him on the line, my first question is, "Where are you?"

"On location," he says, his tone hushed. "I'm using the restaurant's phone. We need you here ASAP."

"What's the matter?"

"This director is out of control. He wants to choreograph a dance scene. You need to come rein him in, or I'm afraid the actors are gonna walk."

"For fuck's sake." Checking my watch, I realize there's no way I can go with Dani on the scout we have planned. She'll have to go and bring back Polaroids, because we've got to sign off on a place today, so we can get permits by next week. "Fine. I'll be there as fast as I can."

"Faster than that, Luke. Meanwhile, I'll tell Leif and Cara that you're on the way."

After I hang up, I debate whether I should pull the office PA to get me there or drive myself.

It's like that old Nike campaign, Luke. *Just do it.*

Before I can talk myself out of it, I grab the keys for one of the production rental cars, leave a message for Dani with the PA, and march out the door.

Fifteen minutes and a hell of a lot of deep breathing later, I make it to the set.

Forty minutes and a long talk with the director, both praising his talents but knocking down all his crazy ideas, and I've got him back on track.

An hour later, I've helped him block the scene without seeming like that's what I was doing, received a furtive thank-you from the actors, and I'm back at the car.

When I get back to my office two hours later, I call Ford. "How are you doing on the car hunt? I'm ready to buy."

I manage to get away from the office in time to get to the Volvo dealership before the end of a normal person's workday and come away with keys to a decidedly unsexy— but by all accounts very safe—Volvo station wagon.

After thanking Ford profusely, I bundle Peanut into the car, memorize the directions to Dani's house, take five deep breaths, and drive home.

Home for now.

Part of me wants to ask Dani if we can do this for real. Be a couple for real. But a bigger part of me worries that I'm not capable of that. I mean, it's not like I have any kind of track record actually being in love with someone. I *think* I know what it means. Putting her needs above my own. Taking her into account when I make big decisions. Sticking by her side no matter what. But I'm not sure, and I don't know if it's right to convince her to give us a chance when I'm still not convinced that I'm capable of sticking around through thick and thin, especially when our marriage has a planned divorce built in.

I wish there were something I could do to show her how much she means to me. I've offered to replace any number of aging appliances and equipment that have obviously been in her house since her aunt was alive, and probably for many years before that. But from the wall phone to the toaster to the stereo, she won't hear of it.

It's hard to tell whether it's pride, attachment to her aunt's things, a thrifty nature, or all three, but she's rebuffed all my efforts. She won't even let me pay for a cleaner to come in or to have someone detail her car.

I really got lucky with those sticky notes. I wonder if it's possible to purchase a lifetime supply.

When I pull up and park in front of her house, it's suddenly clear that hiring someone else to wash her car is a terrible idea, because not only is she obviously very good at doing it herself, she's also hot as hell while going at it. Leaning across the front seat for a better view, I soak up the way her cutoffs cling to her round ass cheeks when she leans over to finish wiping the car wax. When she stretches up to standing, my mouth waters with lust as I take in sweet curves highlighted by a thin, damp tank top.

"Arf! Arf-arf-arf!" Peanut yaps from his spot in the front seat when Skye gets up from the porch.

Unfortunately, as Dani whirls to face the sound, she neglects to remove her forefinger from the spray nozzle and a stream of water shoots through the open passenger side door, hitting me square in the face.

"Oh, shit!" she cries, pointing the spray at the ground. "Luke? What are you—whose car is that?"

Scooping up Peanut, I exit the vehicle and step around to the other side. "Thanks for christening my new car. Any chance you have a towel handy?"

She can't stop apologizing, even as she helps me dry off the car's interior. "Good thing you didn't get leather."

"Because it'd be ruined?" I ask, before whipping the end of a towel at her.

Yelping, she hops away. "No, you jerk. Because it'd fry your ass off after sitting in the sun all day. Every Yankee that moves here makes the mistake."

"Eh, rookie move. I'm from SoCal, remember?"

She nods slowly. "Right."

I roll up the windows and lock the car, and we both stand there looking at it. "So, you bought a car."

"Your buddy Ford helped me find it."

"Where did you register it?"

"Here."

She shields her eyes from the sun to peer at me. "At my address?"

I wince slightly. "I hope that's okay."

She swallows, before saying, "I don't know what you're— what we're—doing here, Luke."

Taking her hand and giving it a squeeze, I say, "I don't know either. All I can say is, this"—sweeping a hand, I take in her house, her yard, the dogs, and the woman herself—"this all feels more like real life than my supposedly real life back in LA."

My confession echoes in my head as I lie in bed next to Dani later that night. Could this be my real life?

It took me getting away from Hollywood to face the fact

that I'm a mystery to myself, that the kid from *Our House* isn't me, at least isn't all of me. I suppose it could take another ten years to tease out the threads of who I am from the character I played on screen for a third of my life. If I have to wait to be in a relationship until I figure out who I really am, I could be dead.

When I was a kid, I was always told that I should just say the lines and be myself. But if your words and actions define you, and I spent my formative years doing and saying things other people wrote, who am I?

I've never said this to anyone, but when a situation is awkward or confusing and I don't know what to say, I look around for my script, hoping they've written something funny that'll get me out of it. Because anything I come up with on my own feels less like the me that everyone knows.

Dani seems to accept me as I am, even if I feel half-baked. We make each other feel… all kinds of things. Lust, giddiness, frustration, wonder.

Can you put all that in a blender and make a love smoothie?

CHAPTER TWENTY-FOUR

LUKE

The next morning, we end up heading off in separate directions and in separate cars for the first time. Even though it's the weekend, we both have a lot to do to get ahead before her surgery. The doctor said Dani will need to take it easy for at least two or three days. She already asked Violet to drive her to and from the appointment, but I'm hoping to leave work early.

Unfortunately, those plans are upended by a call midday Saturday with news from on high. Rewrites for episode two in combination with our current shooting schedule mean that I'm going to be directing second unit the day of her surgery. Ford, Sully, and Helen will all be working that day too, so only Violet and Nate will be around to watch out for Dani.

Too worked up about the situation to sit still in my office, I take a break, head back to Dani's, and go for a run. It's too hot to take Skye with me so I'm alone with my tangle of thoughts as my heels strike the pavement of the streets surrounding our house. While my lungs struggle to suck in the humid air, neighbors wave as I pass little house after little house.

After I've hit my limit, I'm thankful for Dani's outdoor

shower, where I step under the cool stream of water still in my running clothes, still wrangling with guilt and frustration that I can't be there for the woman I've come to care about more than I ever expected. But it's not until I turn off the stream of water that I have the epiphany.

I don't think I'm the only one who'd like to show Dani I care about her. I have a feeling I just ran by a whole slew of people who'd jump at the chance. After dressing quickly so I can act on my idea before the woman herself gets home, I knock on the door of the next-door neighbor I've seen Dani talk to the most, an older black woman who seems like she might know everything that goes on around here.

The woman who answers the door is much smaller than I'd realized. The dog in her arms is tiny too, a Chihuahua that makes Peanut seem like a giant. After I introduce myself, the woman shifts the dog to her hip to look me up and down.

"I know who you are. Another one of the pretty boys coming and going from Danielle's house."

"Oh, I'm not—we're not—" I sputter, even though I am and we are.

She waves a hand in my face. "I don't give two hoots what you're getting up to, but the way you protest, it makes me think it ain't anything good. Or it's too good if you know what I mean."

The look she lowers at me is so disarming, I feel like I've been stripped.

"I didn't mean she's a lady of the evening, young man. Not that I judge. Sometimes a woman's got to make a living however she can. What I mean is, she's got all these friends, including big strapping boys like yourself, but does anyone ever take care of her? She out here washing her own car and painting her own house and fixing her own fence. All by herself."

Even though she's completely dressed me down, I muster enough gumption to stand up for Dani. "Forgive me, but from what I know about her, it seems like she wants it that way."

"Sure, she wants to be independent. But everybody wants other people to step up sometimes."

"Well, as it happens, that's why I'm here. Could we step inside and speak for a few minutes? I don't know when Dani will be home, and I'd kind of like this to be a surprise."

DANI

I spend the day getting ahead on work and errands as much as possible, so I don't have time to go home before heading to Violet and Nate's engagement party Saturday night.

When I pull up in front of the bride and groom's new house, I finish making a few notes from the afternoon's meetings, keeping the car on for the air- conditioning, and so I can hear the end of "Dreams" by the Cranberries. Then I grab my sundress and sandals from the back seat so I can change out of my summer work uniform—khaki Bermuda shorts and white short-sleeved polo shirt.

In the olden days, I'd just walk in Vi's house, so it feels weird to stand on the porch waiting for my best friend to let me in, but this is their space, and I don't want to violate that.

"Why didn't you just come in?" Violet asks after opening the door and pulling me inside the heavily air-conditioned foyer. Waggling her eyebrows, she answers for me, "Afraid we might be doing it on the kitchen counter?"

"Ugh, thanks for the visuals. And no, I wasn't worried about that. You're pregnant."

Leaning close, she whispers in my ear, "Girl, pregnant sex is the best."

"I'll have to trust you on that."

I hand her the bottle of wine and a gift bag with a selection of hand towels with snarky sayings on them like, "Best friends don't care if you cleaned the house, best friends care if you have wine," both of which I nabbed during my travels over the course of the day.

"Oh, you didn't have to," she coos, before adding, "But I'm glad you did!"

I hold up my dress. "Is there somewhere I can change? I came straight from appointments."

She leads me to the guest room and stays to chat while I change clothes. I guess some things will always be the same between us. "Yikes, I just realized. Should I have invited Luke?"

"My marriage is fake to the general public, remember? So, no. But you should've invited Whitney."

Collapsing across the end of the bed, she sighs. "I did. She made up an excuse. I guess she hates us now."

"I don't think that's what's going on."

"Come on, Dani. Her parents always said we weren't good enough for her. Now that she's hanging out with the so-called right people, she probably agrees."

"When I talk to her—"

"You talk to her?"

"Yeah, I figured out a time of day when asshole won't be home, but she will. She's let slip some shit that has me worried."

"About?"

"It kinda seems like she's afraid of him. I've tried to keep the line of communication open, let her know I'm here."

"Maybe we should just show up at her house."

"What, and abduct her?"

"We could bluff our way through something. Make it all about her being a bridesmaid. I mean, he can't say no to that, can he?"

"He might. Can't have her hanging out with the trailer trash."

"I beg your pardon. Neither of us is trailer trash."

"Barely one step up."

"Well, I'm going to do it. I need to know if she's going to stand up with me or not."

"I can't do it till I'm recovered from my surgery, so if you want backup, you'll have to wait."

She twirls a finger in the air in front of my face. "And you, missy. I'm keeping my eye on you too."

"What's wrong with me?"

"Are you still getting laid?"

At that moment, her grandmother calls for her. After I help her up from the bed, she says, "I know you don't like to talk about this stuff, but I'm here if you want to."

A few hours later, I'm sitting outside on the front porch with Ford, doing my best to reconcile the wild girl I thought I knew with the nesting momma-to-be putting leftovers in Tupperware.

Slumping down in the wrought iron chair, I take in the front yard and the white picket fence separating one identical property from the next. "I can't believe they bought a place in this ticky-tacky development. I'd be afraid that I'd come home late at night and go to the wrong house. Did getting pregnant fry their brains?"

Ford stretches out his long legs, crosses his feet at the ankles, and tips back his beer before answering. "It makes sense that Vi would want her kids to have a normal childhood with the way her parents left her. She loves her grandparents, but growing up in an inn had its challenges. I don't think Nate had much stability growing up either, so I get why they'd go for something traditional."

I slide a look over at him. "When did you get so smart?"

He flashes a grin at me, but it's not as bright as it used to be. "I'm the sound guy, remember? I spend a lot of time listening to other people's conversations. You learn a lot about human nature that way. Especially when people forget that they're wearing a wire."

I take a sip of my own beer before asking, "Where's your flavor of the week, by the way?"

"Eh, taking a break. Getting a little tired of that."

"Please don't tell me you believe in the one true love bull-shit, too."

Instead of answering me, he asks, "Why do you call it that?"

"Because it's a line of goods they've been selling us—girls, at least—since we were little."

"I don't believe in the Disney version with fairy godmothers and magic. I think it takes work. Most of which involves getting your own head out of your ass."

Not the wording I was expecting. "Do tell."

Sitting forward, he sets his beer on the ground, rests his elbows on his knees, and stares out over the yard. "No couple's in a perfect place from the get-go, and it's easy for your head to get stuck in that place. Meanwhile your heart and body have other ideas. If you're lucky, the head isn't too stubborn or stupid to catch up before it's too late."

"Too late?"

"Before the other person gives up and moves on."

He slumps back in his chair, leaving me to wonder if he's talking about who I think he's talking about.

Before I can figure out how to ask, he taps my knee. "So, where are you with Luke? Head still up your—"

I hold up a palm. "Stop, that's a gross analogy."

"However you want to say it then. What's up with you and Luke?"

I don't look him in the eye, just cross my legs all casual-like. "That's not real, I told you."

"Uh-huh," he says, his eyes not letting me escape. "You're married, you live together, and you spend all your free time together."

"He's not here tonight," I point out. "And now that you found him a car, I don't have to be at his beck and call anymore. So, we'll be seeing a lot less of each other. I mean, after my surgery he'll probably move out and file for divorce."

"Really?"

"Really," I shoot back, meeting his gaze.

He breaks first and tells me he's going to head out. Before heading inside to say his goodbyes to the happy couple, he says, "Take it from someone who knows. Don't let fate fuck you over while you're working up the courage to ask for what you want."

CHAPTER TWENTY-FIVE

DANI

When I wake up in my bed, I'm not quite sure what day it is. Light coming through the gaps in the curtain tell me it's daytime, but is it still Tuesday? A general ache in my belly tells me that the surgery probably happened, and when I peek under the covers and pull up the nightgown Vi must've gotten me into, I find one bandage over my pubic bone and another near my belly button. The view of my swollen abdomen brings on a rush of nausea, so I push the nightgown back down and sink back onto my pillows.

Skye appears at the side of the bed with a whine. After staring at me for a few moments, she barks and then exits the bedroom. Some nurse she is.

"Dani?"

Blinking my eyes open again, I think I see Whitney in the doorway, but I'm probably dreaming.

"Oh, I didn't mean to wake you," she says. "The dog barked, and I wanted to make sure you're okay."

"Are you—how are you here?" I ask, or try to. My voice is so creaky I can barely make sound.

"Miss Ida let me in. I guess Vi had to go back to work, so

she was watching out for you. She recognized me from when I used to live here. I told her to take a break and I'd sit with you."

Realizing that I need to pee, I swing my legs to the side of the bed, but when I try to stand, I almost fall over.

Whit swoops in and grabs my elbow to steady me. "Whoa, girl. That anesthesia must've knocked you for a loop."

The nausea hits again, and my shoulder and neck suddenly hurt more than the incision sites. "I feel like shit."

Whitney takes over, helping me to the bathroom, starting the shower, which she says will help ease the pain in my upper body, which she explains is caused by the gas they used to inflate my belly. When I ask how she knows this, she tells me that she read my exit instructions while waiting for me to wake up. She also makes me eat a couple of crackers and sip some ginger ale.

"You need a little somethin' on your stomach, or the nausea will get worse."

After she helps me into the shower, she sits on the toilet and natters away while I stand under the warm stream, telling some story about how she pretended she had a dentist appointment so she could come by and see me, and how she's slowly getting Hardy used to the idea of her being brides-maid for Violet, and that she's hopeful he'll let her do it.

She helps me out of the shower and into a clean night-gown, makes me eat and drink a bit more and take a pain reliever, and then tucks me back in bed. The minute I'm horizontal, sleep pulls me down so fast, I don't have the chance to ask why she has to lie to her husband to get out of the house.

When I wake up again, I *really* have to pee. This time I'm not nauseous, I'm ravenous. After a visit to the bathroom, I wander into the kitchen, hoping I can find something to eat.

I'd intended to stock up the kitchen before the surgery but spent the weekend getting ahead on work instead.

I guess I'm still a little out of it because it takes me a minute to notice the bakery box on the kitchen island. Pulling the neon green sticky note off the top, I read, "In case you wake up while I'm running Skye, I'll be back before work. Luke."

Opening the box, I find oversized muffins inside. After devouring one of them, I notice other boxes and foil-covered dishes lining the kitchen counters. And a beautiful arrangement of flowers in a jar. Stumbling to the refrigerator, I open it to find that it, too, is full.

That's when I get it. Lifting up one of the Tupperware containers, I find one of my neighbor's names written in Sharpie on the bottom. When my aunt set up the phone tree all those years ago, she suggested that people mark their dishes so that they'd be easy to return, and everyone's done it ever since.

I stuff the rest of the muffin in my mouth to keep a sob from escaping. The last—and only—time these counters arrived filled with the love of my neighbors in the form of food was right after Aunt Gracie died.

I suddenly miss her.

So, so much.

Dragging my ass back to bed, I crawl under the covers and let sleep take me again, hoping that when I wake, the grief will have passed.

CHAPTER TWENTY-SIX

LUKE

Getting her tubes tied was supposed to be minor surgery, but Dani doesn't exactly bounce back after forty-eight hours of taking it easy. I try to get her to check in with the doctor, but she refuses, claiming that she doesn't have any of the symptoms that warrant it, like a high fever or "foul-smelling" discharge.

I'm certainly glad that's not the case, but something's off, and I really hope it's not regret. Maybe it's hard for someone as capable and independent as she is to let other people take care of her. In fact, I can attest to that fact, since my spy Miss Ida reports that she's had to shoo Dani away from doing house and yard work multiple times over the past few days.

I'm struggling too. With knowing how to give her the space she needs to heal—both physically and emotionally—without losing her entirely. Every time I think I've broken through her protective walls, she's shoring them up again. She probably senses that my ability to remain at her side isn't to be trusted, and I hate to convince her otherwise only to disappoint her in the end.

Still, I miss her. Miss riding in the car with her, miss our sexual experimentation, but most of all, I miss the closeness we'd found. I'd hoped that activating the neighborhood phone tree would show her how many people truly care about her, including me. But while she dutifully eats the food and writes thank-you notes to send back with every dish once it's been cleaned and dried, she doesn't seem to absorb the love packed into the contents.

We're also not sharing a bed at the moment. I wanted to be close in case she needed something, but she was in such pain at first that she asked me to sleep elsewhere. Now, the dogs get to be in her room, but not me.

I'm in my office, staring off into space, wondering how to get back to the fun and sexy times we'd shared only a couple weeks ago, when my phone buzzes.

Hoping it's Dani wanting to talk or needing something from me, I press the button eagerly, but instead of announcing that my wife's on the line, my PA says that it's the Brothers Werner's PR department.

Figuring it's a follow-up from the *People* magazine interview I did last week, I shake off my worries and answer in my best professional voice.

The publicist wastes no time getting to her point. "Is it true that you're married to your driver on *Lawson's Reach*?"

Uh-oh.

"Uhhh, sort of?"

"You're sort of married?" she asks, her voice tight.

Figuring it's best to stick as close to the truth as possible, while revealing as little as possible, I say, "I mean, she was my driver, but only for two weeks."

"Did you fire her?" she shoots back, pitch and volume shooting up. "Because that could be a big problem."

"No, no. The budget only allowed for me to have a driver for two weeks, and that was established up front. I knew her from working in town a few years ago, and we... reconnected."

The woman sighs. "All right. I'm going to have to keep an eye on this. We might have to revisit the *People* spot if this spreads any further."

"If what spreads? Further than where?" I'd assumed she was calling to grill me because someone on the crew had figured it out and had tattled on me to the studio.

"Further than the *National Enquirer*. Right now, it's only a grainy photo of you with your arm around a tall, dark-haired woman with a caption describing you as newlyweds. They also included a shot of you and Ms. Kingston and are playing up the possibility of some sort of scandal. I'm trying to figure out if any other outlets have the photo, but I'm really hoping that someone else blows up and this just fades away."

Unfortunately, that's not what happens.

CHAPTER TWENTY-SEVEN

DANI

Two days after Luke comes home with a copy of the *National Enquirer*, I come home to find him packing a suitcase.

I guess this is it. He's outta here.

It's fine, I tell myself. *I got the tubal, my problem is solved.*

I'm fixed, I don't need him anymore.

But when I find out why he's going back—that not only his job but my own is on the line—my heart drops, and not with the grief that's become an unwelcome presence for the past week, but in panic.

"They can't fire you," he says as he stuffs running shoes into the outer pocket of his bag. "You're not an employee."

He's going back because the story didn't die. Someone decided that everyone in the world should know that America's sweetheart has been displaced by a big nobody. Just as I'd feared, I'm the bitch that broke up Loolie.

"But Luke, that's not the point. My reputation is all I have as a contractor. Everything I've worked to build can all disappear if people think I'm a big liar. Homeowners need to trust that I'll protect their property, and producers need to trust that I'll deliver."

"I know, I know," he says, obviously stressed.

"Could *you* lose your job?"

"I need to talk to Max in person. Maybe stand up myself to the powers that be. In any case—" He breaks off, his hands still, and when he meets my gaze, with those blue eyes focused on me, god help me, I'd believe him if he told me he was setting off to buy me the Brooklyn Bridge. "I promise I will fix this one way or another."

Suddenly too tired to stand—a feeling that won't seem to go away, despite the fact that I should be feeling better by now—I park my butt on the bed. "But this was all my idea."

"I went along with it. And getting married was my suggestion." After zipping up his duffel bag, he grabs a sticky note and writes a telephone number on it. Holding it up, he says, "This is my home number. Call if you need me."

I follow him to the door and assure him that I don't mind taking care of Peanut while he's gone, but when I grab my keys, he holds up his own set. "I can drive myself, remember?"

"Yeah, but it's silly to waste money paying to park. I'll drive you."

We don't say much during the short drive. I'm stuck between saying what I think I *want* to say and what I think I *should* say. The want feels a lot scarier than the should, and I'm not stuffed full of courage at the moment, so I go with the should.

"You should start the divorce proceedings while you're home." Even though I have to push the words past an aching throat, I know it's the smart thing to do. For me and for him. "And then move out when you get back."

"Is-is that what you really want?"

He seems truly mystified. Like we aren't two people on two separate rafts caught in two different rip tides. Even if we are capable of doing the work to make a real marriage work, our lives are always going to pull us apart. "Luke, come on. It was always going to end. This is fate making sure we know that. You might not have another opportunity to go back to LA anytime soon, and if you don't file for divorce in California, that'll just drag everything out."

His gaze on the messenger bag in his lap, he asks, "But we're friends, right?"

Swallowing past the hurt, I nod and make myself take his hand to squeeze it. And then I make myself let go. "Yes, but your loyalty's with Kellie, and I get that."

LUKE

It's been a very long travel day involving three flights with a middle-of-the-night layover in Chicago, but I don't have time to sleep. I have to talk to Max, but I need to talk to Kellie first.

After a blessedly short cab ride to my place, I drop my carry-on bag and head up the street toward Kellie's house, hoping she's home. It takes me a block to remember that I can use my cell phone to find out, so I flip it open and hit the number at the top of my speed dial.

Should that tell me something? Would Dani be in that spot if I could use my cell in Wallington, or would Kellie remain at the top of my list?

"Wow," she says upon answering, obviously recognizing my number. "I didn't think you could use this phone where you are."

"I can because I'm here. A block from your house."

"What? What are you doing here? Why didn't you tell me you were coming?"

"It was kind of a last-minute thing. We, uh, need to talk."

"Yeah, I guess we do." I hear a muffled yell and then, "Okay, I'm back. Are you walking? Oh right, of course you are."

"Actually, I've been driving again, but right now I'm walking up—"

Her squeal sounds in my ear as well as down the street. I look up to find her jumping up and down and waving one hand, the other pressing the phone to her ear. Laughing for the first time in what feels like weeks, I say, "I missed you, Kel."

"I missed you too, ya big lug."

We both hang up, and then she runs to meet me, hurling herself at me. When I catch her, she wraps her arms around my neck and her legs around my waist like a monkey. Like she always does. I always forget how tiny she is. As preteens, she was taller than me, but when I got a growth spurt in my late teens, I left her far behind.

As she chatters about how she loves my new look, I'm struck by how different it feels to hold Kellie as compared to Danielle. I'd always thought I'd never be as close to a woman as I am with Kellie, but with Dani… it's like she's under my skin and deep inside my heart.

After a few beats, Kellie sighs and hops down. "I suppose I shouldn't be photographed jumping you like that."

I glance around the quiet neighborhood, and thankfully, no paparazzi seem to be running away, cameras held aloft in triumph. They could be lying in wait, however, so we head inside.

"Sorry to ambush you like this," I say once we're settled on comfy couches. Everything at Kellie and Janette's house is cozy and inviting. One reason I spend so much time here. "But I need to find out exactly what happened and put out some fires."

Her brows knit together. "Are you really married?"

"Sort of."

"It's fake?"

"I mean, I legally married her, but only to help her out with a situation."

"But it's not totally fake?"

"We started out pretending, but now… I don't know how to untangle what's real from what's make-believe. Or if I'm even capable of maintaining a real relationship."

"Luke, you've got to stop undermining yourself like that. You are an amazing person. You'll be an amazing real boyfriend if you ever get out of your own damn way. Who is she, anyway? The girl in the picture?"

"Do you remember the driver I had the last time I was in Carolina?"

"The one you gave the sticky notes?"

"That's her."

"Omigod, Loo. You're in lu-u-urve!"

She uses the silly term from our show, the bit our characters would use to taunt each other when they had a crush.

"How did you get from sticky notes to lurve?"

"It's obvious," she says, all know it all. "The way you talked about her."

"Then you know more than I do." Suddenly exhausted, I rub both hands over my face. "But what's important right now is fixing this situation. Dani's worked hard to build her resume as a location scout, and I don't want this blowing up her reputation. And the *Lawson's Reach* PR people are worried about blowback for the show. But I wanted to check in with you before talking to either them or my mother."

Kellie bites her lip, her gaze tracking to a window. "I've been dodging her calls."

"Why?"

Turning to face me again, she suddenly looks older. "I think I'm done."

"With acting?"

She laughs, but without much mirth. "No, silly. With this." She waves a hand in a circle between us. "Our fake relationship is putting a strain on my real relationship."

I know what you mean.

"And I'm tired of having to play a role in my real life."

Again, sounds familiar.

"So, I'm coming out."

"Of the closet?"

She nods, but I need to know. "Are—are you sure? Is this what Janette wants? Is she sure?"

Kellie leans back on the couch and yells over her shoulder. "Babe? Are we sure?"

Janette's low alto bellows back, "We sure the fuck are."

"Wow. Okay. Do you have a plan?"

She explains that her agents have been pushing her to start up Loolie again to give her a leg up next pilot season.

"But I want to live my life. I'm ready for that. So is Janette. Thing is, it is a risk, and I'm not sure Angie or my agents will be on board with it. I'm not Ellen. I'm America's so-called sweetheart. What if I fess up and then never work again?"

"Well, I mean, *Will & Grace* is doing pretty well. They got renewed for another season."

"But the guy playing Will isn't even gay!"

Thinking about what Dani said about fate, I say, "Maybe this is all for the best. I mean, you're the best actor I've ever worked with. I hope you—and your representatives—can trust that. Maybe you need to be looking for different kinds of roles. Fuck being America's sweetheart." Before she can protest, I add, "I know it's easier said than done. I can't imagine being in your position."

When my stomach rumbles, Kellie tows me into the kitchen and puts out snacks while she tells me what she'd like to do. By the time my belly's full, my mind is too.

"I need to run this by Max and the *Lawson's Reach* people, but I'm in if I can do it without blowing things up for Dani back in Wallington. If they fire me, so be it. But I don't want her hurt."

As Kellie walks me to the door, she hooks an elbow

through mine and leans her cheek against my arm. "You need to tell Dani how you really feel about her."

Stopping at the door, suddenly so tired that I'm not sure I can drag myself home, I lean against the nearest wall. "How do I even know? I've spent my life doing things other people want me to, saying things they tell me to. To the point that I don't know who I am. So how do I know I can be the man she needs for the rest of her life?"

Kellie takes my hand. "*I* know, Luke. I know the real you. You love her. You just have to tell her. Not what you think she wants to hear, but what's in here." Pressing my own hand against my heart, she pats it a few times before kissing me on the cheek and shooing me out the door. "Go get some rest and call me when you have news."

CHAPTER TWENTY-EIGHT

LUKE

I don't expect my mom to be excited about what Kellie and I are planning, but even I don't expect her to forbid it.

"She can't do this," she says, picking up the phone in her home office and angrily punching in numbers. "This is career suicide."

Pressing a finger on the plunger before she can finish dialing, I hold out my other hand. "Mom. Think about what you're saying."

"You two are the ones who aren't thinking," she says, swatting my hand out of the way and slamming the handset down. "You have no idea the work that has gone into maintaining your image as America's favorite couple."

Hands braced on the edge of her desk, letting the weight of my head drop, and blowing out the frustration that's been building over the past couple of weeks, I do my best to calm down.

I know my mother means well. That she truly cares about her children and her clients. Maybe it's that she has a hard time extricating what's real from what isn't too.

My mom is petite, so I sit my ass down and make myself

smaller before saying what I have to say. "I truly appreciate everything you did for me when I was a kid. I'm well aware that there were stage parents who fucked their kids up. You protected me and Tomasz and Kellie, and I think we're all grateful for that. I know I am."

She opens her mouth to speak, but before she can, I reach across the desk to take her hand. "I can't speak for the others, but I'm asking you to let me go. Let me make my own decisions, even if they might be mistakes. I feel like I'm starting to figure out who I am for the first time in my life. I'm doing work that I really like, living in a place that feels right, and—"

"All while living with a woman you're pretending to be married to."

"That's a mistake I've got to deal with."

"You'll end it with her? Get a divorce?"

"I need to fix the problems that are endangering her career."

"*Her* career? What about yours?"

"She has fewer options than I do and has more to lose."

"So, you're throwing away everything we've built for you."

"No, Mom. I'm taking what I learned and applying it. Can you please try and hear me? I think I might be good at this."

"At directing TV?"

"Yeah, but also at life. Real life. The real life I'm starting to build in Wallington. I just hope I haven't screwed things up so badly that I lose it all."

She rubs her index finger up and down the center of her forehead, a gesture that started when she was worried about developing wrinkles. Now, it means she's struggling with something, so I keep my mouth shut and let her work it out.

Finally, she blows out a breath and picks up the phone.

Shit. "What are you doing, Mom?"

She shoos at me impatiently. "Hush. Let me do what I'm good at. We're going to fix this."

CHAPTER TWENTY-NINE

DANI

I haven't heard a word from Luke since he left for California and I'm afraid to admit even to myself how much I miss him. I also haven't been able to leave the house. It's not that I'm afraid that people will point at me and talk. It's that I am so tired it takes everything I've got to feed the dogs and let them out in the backyard.

When the doorbell rings, I ignore it. Ida and my friends will knock, but they'll come in without me answering the door. So, when I hear footsteps coming down the hall, I don't even turn over in bed.

"Well, you're looking like ten miles of bad road," an unfortunately familiar voice declares.

"Thanks, Ma," I say, without moving. "Appreciate the support."

"Am I your mother?" Without waiting for an answer, she adds, "You'd hardly think so. When I have to find out from a supermarket aisle magazine that you're married."

"I didn't tell you because it's not real," I say, still not rolling over to look at her. "We got married so I could—" Not sure if I have the energy to get into this, I almost fib about what I've done. But what would be the point of that? "So I could get my tubes tied."

She gasps. "I can't believe she got to you."

I play her words over in my head a few times, while she knocks the dirty clothes I've let pile up on an armchair onto the floor, but they still don't quite make sense. With some effort, I push myself up to sitting and ask, "What are you talking about?"

Dropping into the chair, she shakes her head, her bottom lip trembling. "Aunt Gracie. She got to you."

"Got to me?" Despite my mother's claims, Aunt Gracie never said a bad word about my mother, or her parenting. It was easy enough for me to figure out on my own.

"She tried to get me to stop having babies," she says, jabbing at her own chest to emphasize her words. "She wanted *me* to get my tubes tied."

Normally, I wouldn't take her bait, but I'm not letting her blame my aunt. Not when she's the one at fault here. "Is that so? Maybe you should've listened."

She gasps again, a hand flying to her chest. "What if I'd done that before I had you? You wouldn't exist."

I'm as unmoved by this stupid argument as I was when doctors tried using it to talk me out of sterilization. "You sure seemed liked you regretted having us."

"That is not true." Jumping up, she begins to pace back and forth, her hands gesturing wildly. "No matter what your aunt told you. But she didn't understand. She couldn't. It's not like she ever had a baby or lost a husband. She was just tired of taking care of you all."

"When did she take care of us?"

She stuffs her hands into her armpit and her pacing slows. "She helped me out after your father died and I... had a nervous breakdown."

All of this is news to me. "I don't even remember her being at our house."

"You were little, you and your sister. She came over every day to look after you until I got back on my feet. But the only thing that made me happy was holding a baby in my arms. Even before your dad died. As soon as you weaned yourself, I was so devastated I could barely eat. It wasn't until I got pregnant again with your sister that I felt back to myself."

"Did you ever talk to anyone about this? It sounds like you had postpartum depression."

"I tried, but everyone said I just needed to get over it. One doctor gave me Valium, but that made things worse. Then your aunt tried to talk me into getting fixed—like I was a dog, for heaven's sake. When I refused, she wouldn't come back to help."

"So you recruited me instead."

"Not right away. I tried to be a good mama, Danielle, I really did. But I'd get so irritated. Babies are so easy. Babies don't talk back, and I know what to do with them. Meanwhile, your sisters and brothers minded you. You were so cute taking care of them. Teaching them how to use the potty and cross the street. Read, even. You should've been a teacher, I swan. Only babies love me, but you were so good with children."

Before I can process all this, she continues. "That's why this is so awful. Your aunt wanted to turn you into herself. A lonely old woman."

"At least she looked out for me. All you ever do is take from me."

The wounded look on her face is real, but I can't find the energy to feel bad for telling the truth.

"I worry about you all the time, Danielle. I worry about you ending up all alone. And now look at you. My worst fears have come true. You're lying in bed in the middle of the workweek looking like something the cat dragged in. And where's this so-called husband of yours?" She pulls a tabloid paper out of her shoulder bag and drops it on the bed like she's playing an ace. "Run off to his real girlfriend in California."

I can't argue with her on these points. I'm sure I do look terrible, and I have been left alone. But I also know that I did the right thing. For me.

I lift my chin, meet her aggrieved gaze, and speak directly. "I want you to listen to me and hear what I am saying. I can take care of myself. And that's what's important. I don't need anyone else. If you can't accept that, then I need you to leave me the hell alone."

The one thing I do get out of bed, showered, and clothed for is my follow-up at the gynecologist's office. As I'm on the way out the door, the phone rings, but I don't answer or stick around to hear the message. I don't have the time or emotional capacity to deal with anyone right now, whether it's Luke or someone's manager or agent, or another damn magazine wanting to dig into my life.

The good news I get from Dr. Burrows: I'm recovering fine physically, so I can go to the beach and have sex if I want. Presumably at the same time, but I don't ask for clarification.

The bad news: she sees through my bluster, and presses until I admit that I'm still feeling fatigued, and that daily tasks feel overwhelming.

"It's not talked about enough, but it is very common to have to deal with depression after any kind of surgery."

Despite the fact that I find myself fighting tears, I protest, "But I don't regret getting the tubal, I swear."

She holds up a hand. "I'm not talking about that. I'm saying that it is totally normal to have a strong emotional response to surgery. I mean, on an elemental level, it's an invasion of your body, so that alone can be traumatizing. It can be worse for people who are quite fit."

Hands clasped on her desk, her smile kind, she continues. "We like to think we're invincible, and evidence of the contrary can stir up all kinds of feelings, of vulnerability and mortality. Even grief."

If I continue to meet her eyes, I'm afraid I'll lose it, because everything she's saying rings true. I nod and promise that I do have people I can talk to, and that if the feelings persist, that I'll either come back to her or talk to a therapist.

"And what about your husband?" she asks. "Has he been supportive?"

Instead of telling her that my "husband" is probably filing for divorce right now, or that pretending to be married to him may be the end of a career I've worked hard for, I say, "He's traveling for work, but yeah, he's supportive."

It is nice, I have to say, to be able to exit the office without paying a dime. I'll credit Luke for making that happen. But on the drive home, I decide that I need to suck it up and get back to the originally scheduled programming.

Even if my reputation is sullied to the point that I can't do locations, I can always bartend to stay afloat. Maybe working in the entertainment business is a bad idea, anyway. Even when things are good, it isn't stable. There must be other careers that I could get into that use my skill set and connections. Real estate, management rentals. Heck, I could go back to school, finish my degree, or get some other kind of job training. I wasn't a terrible student, after all. I didn't finish because I needed to take care of my aunt.

And because I was grieving.

I'm not going to let emotions drown me this time. I'm done with wallowing. My mom's problems are her problems; they have nothing to do with me. My aunt died, but she left me a house and values I can live by. I am part of a community I care about, and I live in a town that I love.

I just need to get back in the saddle. In more ways than one. The minute I get home, I ignore the answering machine and call Ford and convince him to meet me at the Rumrunner Hotel's bar to celebrate.

"Celebrate what?" he asks.

"Being alive," I answer.

An hour later, I'm as pulled together as I can be. Wearing mascara and lipstick I found in a bathroom drawer—left behind by one of my roommates at some point, I'm sure—and the shortest skirt I could find, I belly up to the bar and order a gin and tonic.

When Ford joins me and asks why I'm not drinking beer, I shrug. "Changing things up a bit."

He leans in to peer closely at my face. "Are you wearing makeup?"

"Like I said, I'm turning over a new leaf."

But when I start flirting with the guy next to me at the bar, Ford kicks my shins. And when the guy excuses himself to visit the bathroom, Ford gets in my face. "What the hell are you doing?"

"The thing y'all have been trying to get me to do for years, duh."

"Be an idiot?" he asks.

"Have casual sex," I say. When he just stares at me, I spell it out for him. "A one-night stand? Get jiggy? Bang it out with—"

"All right, all right, enough. I know what you meant, but I don't get why you're doing it. Aren't you married?"

"I told y'all that was fake."

"I thought you were into him."

"Even if I was, I mean, the guy's famous line is 'I'm outta here.'"

"That was his character."

"Still, that's the reality I have to face. He's in LA right now, filing for divorce. One way or another, the whole world is going to find out that our relationship was a sham." I gesture to the bar's clientele, like they're included. "Then all I'll get is a pity fuck. Or a guy who wants to brag that he slept with Lukas Keith's wife. I need to get this done before everyone knows."

He takes a moment to digest this before saying, "I think you're going to be disappointed."

"Says the king of picking up girls."

"Says the guy who's always disappointed by them."

"Maybe you need to do something about that."

"I wish I could."

"While you're figuring that out, I'm going to have sex." I've been keeping an eye on the hallway that leads to the bathrooms and despite the fact that he's nowhere near as sexy, or even as interesting to talk to, as Luke, I am relieved to see my guy emerge and head back our way.

This is just ripping the Band-Aid off after all. Jumping in the water instead of wading in. It's not like I ever have to see the guy again.

Ford places a hand on my forearm as I slide a five across the bar for my drink. "Don't you think Luke will be upset?"

"Shh," I hiss. "Anyway, Luke married me so I could do this very thing."

Ford shakes his head, like he's disappointed in *me*. Which is so hypocritical, it fuels my determination. Before the dude's butt hits his barstool, I ask, "Want to get out of here?"

For some reason I thought he was staying at the hotel, which would have been convenient, but apparently, he's staying at a house with friends on the island. When we get to his car, he crowds me up against it, cups my face with his hands, and… and I can't do it.

"I'm sorry. This isn't going to work."

"But you said—"

"C'mon, man. You've got to feel it too." I motion back and forth between us in the air. "There's nothing here."

He frowns. "But I can make it good for you."

"I don't think you can, actually."

"But—"

When he reaches for me, I take a step back. "Dude. Don't make me use my pepper spray."

Hands up, he blows out a breath. "Fine. Whatever. You're not that good-looking anyway."

Any hurt I might feel from his attempt at a dig is eclipsed by my own frustration. Luke said he was helping me. With his tantric touch, and his scent that's somehow dirty and heavenly at the same time, and the way he looks at me like I'm the only thing in the world. But apparently, exposure therapy with Luke didn't get me to a place where I can have sex whenever and with whomever I want. It apparently emptied the playing field.

So I can only have sex with him.

Him and his magic penis that makes me feel like jumping his bones even when I had a bad day. Him and that runner's physique that can go for hours. Him and those clear blue eyes that see into my soul.

Totally bogus.

After stomping back into the hotel bar to let Ford know that I'm alive—and avoid his questions about what happened —I stomp to my car and stomp on the gas all the way home.

Once there, I stomp into the house, slam the front door, and hurl myself on the couch with such force that it slides into a side table. The teetering lamp flickers, but a crash has me sitting up with a gasp.

My aunt's candy dish, a beautiful flowery china bowl that she always kept filled with peppermints, lies on the floor in pieces.

Just like me.

CHAPTER THIRTY

LUKE

I have to give it to my mom. When she decides to do something, it happens.

Less than forty-eight hours after she started making calls, Kellie and I are on the set of *Entertainment Tonight*, taping an exclusive interview to be aired the next day.

You'd think Kellie would be the nervous one here, since she's about to out herself to the world, but it's me who's a wreck.

Maybe it's because my mom demanded that we do the interview with a guy who isn't one of the show's primary hosts, but a journalist who came out publicly a year ago. Or that the questions she's agreed to answer are as respectful as they could be.

Meanwhile, despite the fact that I am not the main focus here, I've got marching orders from my mother and Max to maintain a squeaky-clean reputation. For myself, and the show.

I'm just not sure how to do that without slighting a woman back in Carolina who I think I might have fallen in love with.

Despite the fact that I'm not quite sure how I'll manage to juggle all these demands, the AD's countdown means I have to pack it all away and put on an appropriately happy face.

After introducing us, the reporter makes a joke about how that probably wasn't necessary since we've been America's favorite couple for so many years.

"I understand you have something to share about that relationship," he says. Our focus is supposed to be on him at this point, but out of the corner of my eye, I catch the red light on the camera focused on Kellie, and I give her hand a quick squeeze. She shoots a grateful smile at me, and then I let go.

"Luke has been my hero," she begins. "But not in the way most people think. We care about each other deeply, but our relationship has only ever been as friends. The best of friends."

The camera pointed at me lights up, and I do my best to look supportive and calm, even as worries somersault through my stomach.

Kellie takes a shaky breath before continuing. "I've kept my true feelings—my true self—hidden for far too long, out of fear. Fear that you'll judge me, call me names, that I won't be able to work anymore."

There's a slight tremor in her voice, but she lifts her chin and presses on.

"When the latest story hit the news, Luke offered to quit his current job to take the spotlight off the show he's working on and off me. But I wouldn't let him. He's been the best friend a girl could have, but our romance has never been real, because I'm gay. My life partner is a woman."

She lets that hang in the air for a few moments as the camera zeroes in on our interviewer's kind expression. "Luke has already sacrificed a lot to help protect our privacy and my career, but I won't let him do it anymore. I love him like a brother, and I always will, but he's never been my lover."

Turning to face the camera, she adds, "If that means I can

no longer be America's sweetheart, I'm okay with that, because if people don't love the real me, that's their problem, not mine."

The journalist thanks her for sharing this with their audience before turning to me, so that I can share the scripted response my mother helped me craft.

"I couldn't be more proud of Kellie. Too many people in this country get caught up in judging other people for loving who they love or how they want to live their lives. Like if you don't want the picket fence with two-point-three kids, and you don't want to be married to someone of the same race, or opposite gender, you don't deserve happiness."

That's the end of my planned speech, but instead of shutting up, I turn to the camera. "But why? What's the harm? And meanwhile, the rest of us are ignoring what's really going on behind those picket fences. I mean, what's that movie quote, 'Let he who is without sin cast the first stone?'"

Rolling with it, the interviewer quips, "I'm pretty sure that's from the Bible."

Hoping my error won't make things worse, I soldier on. "Well, it was probably in a movie too. In any case, do we really want to be casting stones here? How about we practice acceptance, empathy, and love instead?"

I've veered from the narrow subject of the interview, but the director isn't slicing a hand across his throat, so I keep going.

"I think this is why we tell stories. To try and understand human relationships, which are endlessly and fascinatingly complex. Like the ones on the program I'm helping to bring to the airwaves. *Lawson's Reach* isn't about good guys and bad guys, or even happy endings you can tie up with a bow. It's about smart young people trying to figure out how to grow up without losing their friends."

Turning to face the camera, I continue. "About how you have to work to hang on to the people you love. You might get hurt—most likely, you *will* get hurt—and you might hurt the people you love, because humans make mistakes. But that doesn't mean you give up."

Taking a deep breath, I reach for my friend's hand, and she takes it. "I fell in love with Kellie when I was just a kid. Romance wasn't in the cards for us, but I still love her. And I wish her the very best."

The journalist thanks me for my honesty and then asks, "What about the marriage that we've heard about?"

I'm supposed to say that my marriage is one of convenience, that Dani is also just a friend, beginning with: "There's nothing to tell."

But I find I can't continue with the planned speech, because the words now feel like lies. "What I mean to say is, I hope you'll respect my privacy with regard to my marriage. I know that's often not how these things work, but I hope that you can recognize that my life choices shouldn't affect your opinions about the show I'm working on."

After the taping, Kellie gives me a ride home, avoiding the highway as she drives us from Hollywood back to Studio City without even asking. When I turn down the volume on the Spice Girls' "Wannabe" to ask if she's free for dinner later, she tells me that she and Janette have plans.

"Anyway," she says, "you've got work to do."

When she stops at a red light, she reaches in the back seat.

"What's this?" I ask after she drops a tote bag on my lap.

"Research."

"For what?"

"For your speech."

"What speech?"

"The speech you're going to give when you see Dani again."

Holding up one of the many VHS tapes crammed into the bag, I ask, "How am I supposed to watch all of these? My flight leaves at six tomorrow morning."

"You don't have to watch the whole movie. Just skip to the end for the groveling part."

"You think that's what I'm going to have to do? Beg for forgiveness?"

"With the way you left things so vague in the interview? And the fact that she hasn't called you back?"

"I guess you have a point." I go through them as she takes the curves of Laurel Canyon Boulevard. "Have you watched all these movies about men and women falling in love?"

She shoots me a get-real look. "Buh doi. Of course I have."

"Why?"

"Love is love." She shrugs, before releasing a heavy sigh. "But also, there aren't a heck of a lot of movies about two women falling for each other."

"Maybe we should do something about that."

"Maybe we should," she says, nodding slowly. "But in the meantime, you need to get your girl."

CHAPTER THIRTY-ONE

DANI

I wake up the next morning on the couch feeling hungover. I only had the one cocktail, so I'm pretty sure it's an emotional hangover. I'm not used to so much feeling, and I don't think I like it.

When I drag myself into the bathroom and catch sight of my face, with the dried remains of mascara tears running down my cheeks, I'm sure I don't like it.

I feel slightly better after showering and ingesting caffeine. Still, I have to make myself play back the answering machine. When I finally sit myself down and press the button, it turns out Luke wasn't the only person trying to reach me yesterday.

There are quite a few so-called news organizations wanting comments from me. Them I ignore.

There are also multiple work calls, from homeowners as well as a line producer on a new show coming to town. Thankfully, none of them say, "Liar, liar, pants on fire, we never want to work with you again."

By the time I hear Luke's voice, my hand is cramping from all the notes I've been taking, so I shake it out as I listen. Unfortunately, he must've called from a cell phone with a bad connection, because the only words I get clearly are *"Entertainment Tonight...* Wednesday... favor... Kellie," and a few numbers.

Then the machine cuts off, having run out of tape.

I try calling the home number he gave me, but no one picks up, and the outgoing message on his machine says that he's out of town and to call his agent or manager with any work inquiries. I leave a message telling him that I couldn't hear half of his message so I'm not sure what's going on.

It seems he's going to be on *Entertainment Tonight*. Maybe on Wednesday, which is today, and... what? Explain to the world that he was only doing me a favor, and all is well with him and Kellie? I guess that would save her reputation as well as the show's, but it kind of leaves me up shit's creek without a paddle.

He promised to save my job, but if he couldn't do both, I suppose he'd side with Kellie. Sadness washes over me, then anger, then resolution. I know better than to rely on a man—or anyone, really—to take care of me.

The best way I can save my reputation is to do the very best work I can. To prove that no matter what life throws at me, I can be relied on to find the perfect Wallington location for any production, and I can be trusted to take care of a homeowner's property.

I get out my planner and get to work.

When I get home later that day, feeling better about my employment situation after knocking out a bunch of meetings, Peanut is more than ready for his dinner, so I get that taken care of before checking the answering machine. There are fewer calls from reporters, and a handful of work calls.

Then there's a call with no sound at first, and I almost press fast forward to skip it, assuming that it's either a prank or a misdial, but Luke's voice stops my finger from hitting the button.

"Sorry, Dan, I was trying to listen to the flight announcement. So, hi. Um, I haven't heard back from you, and I'm not sure what that means. Anyway, I'm in Dallas on the way back to Wallington. My flight gets in at nine thirty, but don't feel like you have to pick me up or anything. I can get a cab if I need to. Just wanted to give you a heads-up. I hope it's okay that I sleep at your place tonight. I guess if it's not, leave me a message on my cell. Oh, shit. They're calling my name. I gotta go."

I play the message again, my heart squeezing and my gut tightening as I listen for clues. I can't say for sure, but it sounds like he's worried that I might be upset, which makes me think that my guess was right. That he's going to—or he did, since if he's in transit, they must have pre-taped the interview—tell everyone that our marriage is fake. I'm not sure if he's saying he wants to stay here but doesn't feel welcome or that it'll be too late to find a hotel.

My brain begins to ache along with my chest and stomach, but there's nothing I can do to fix it. When I can't fix things, I go for a run.

After putting Peanut in his crate with a puzzle toy, I head out. Even though it's early evening, it's still pretty hot, but I set a fast pace anyway, needing to pound out my feelings and sweat out my worries. After I've circled Wallace Park a few times, I remember that Violet will be dropping Skye off at my house, so I head home.

Her car's in the driveway when I get there, and when I stumble into the house still sucking wind, she jumps up from the couch. "Oh my god, are you okay?"

Waving her down, I head for the kitchen, needing water. "I was running; don't worry. Did you feed Skye?"

"Yes," she says, following me.

"Why are you still here?"

"Can't I hang around to say hi to my best friend?"

"Yeah, but you usually don't." After gulping down some water, it hits me. "Do you know something I don't?"

She bites her lip before answering, "Depends what you know."

I flick water at her. "Just spit it out."

She makes a face like she's afraid I might throw the whole glassful at her. "Do you know that Luke and Kellie are going to be on *ET* in, like"—she glances at the clock—"oh shit. Like two minutes?"

I blow out a breath. "I suspected as much, but I wasn't sure."

She glances at the living room worriedly. "Do you want me to watch it and report back? Or do you want to record it and watch it later?"

I shake my head. "If you know they're definitely going to be on, we might as well get it over with."

She sprints to the living room, moving pretty damn fast for a pregnant lady, flicks on the TV, and then changes channels till she finds the right one. The moment she does, a still of Luke and Kellie appears and one of the hosts teases the interview.

"I guess it really is happening," I mutter.

She pats the couch next to her. "Do you know what he's going to say?"

I shake my head. "We haven't talked since he left."

"He didn't even call you?"

"He did, but I wasn't here."

"And where are things between you?"

I shrug. "It was always going to end. It's probably better that this scandal finished it off before I, you know, got attached or something."

She takes my hand. "Are you sure you're not… attached?"

"I know better than to do that, Vi," I lie.

Because of course I'm attached.

Even though I know that when you let yourself love people, they leave.

"Is that really how you want to live your life, Dani?" Vi asks, her voice uncharacteristically gentle, like I need handling with kid gloves.

"I don't know that I have a choice. I mean, my mom won't leave me alone, but the aunt who was more of a real mother to me"—my voice hitches, but I power on—"the woman who taught me how to live? How to garden? Take care of your neighbors? Be a good friend? She kicked cancer, and then she still died. And all I got was a damn house."

Vi squeezes my hand. "And memories. You have so many memories of her, of how you made that time better for each other." She looks around the living room, like she's seeing it for the first time. "Every part of this house, and even parts of you, are a testament to how much she loved you."

"I guess."

"Anyway…" She elbows me, hard. "What about me? And Sully and Ford and Whit? We haven't left."

I sink further into the worn couch cushions, just like I'm sinking into self-pity. "But you have your own lives. You're in love. I get it. And then you'll be wrapped up in the baby. Which is normal. I wish I wanted to be normal, but I don't think I'm made that way."

"Danielle Goodwin." When I don't look up, she pokes me in the thigh until I meet her eyes, lit with determination. "No matter what life changes I go through, no one will ever know me the way you do. No one else has stood by me through all the stupid shit I've done. When I couldn't decide what to do with my life. When I dated all the wrong guys. When I started my own company. And I've been there for you too. I'd help more if you'd let me. Sometimes you make it hard."

When she takes my hand again, I focus on how they fit together as I whisper, "I'm just afraid to rely on anybody. That they'll up and die on me."

She bumps me, shoulder to shoulder. "I'll try not to do that."

When I just nod, because my head is too full of snot to say anything more, she adds, "And I promise I won't ask you to babysit. Like, ever. But I might ask you for advice, if that's okay."

"Sleep training."

"Oh, okay." She shifts away from me. "You're giving advice right now?"

"I've been waiting for permission. Do the sleep training. It's worth it."

"I'll put it on the list."

"I'll get you a book."

When I meet her eyes again, I'm rewarded by the look I see in her face. Violet loves me. And I believe her. She's not going anywhere.

"And now the interview you've all been waiting for," the TV guy says. "We've got an exclusive with America's favorite couple, Lukas Keith and Kellie Kingston."

CHAPTER THIRTY-TWO

LUKE

Despite the fact that I did my best, I still feel guilty that I couldn't fulfill my promise to protect Dani's job unilaterally and definitively.

Since I haven't been able to get her on the phone and she hasn't returned any of my calls, I have no idea what she's thinking. Or feeling.

During my two layovers, I've talked to Max, who promised to quit if the studio tried to fire me or blackball Dani. I talked to my mother, who reassured me that my Bible gaffe wasn't too bad. And I talked to Kellie, who gave me the unfortunate news that *ET* cut me off after I said, "There's nothing to tell."

So when I emerge from the Jetway, even though I told her that I'd get a cab, I'm very worried when I don't see her face in the small crowd greeting passengers from our flight.

But I'm not giving up. Best case scenario, she didn't get my messages and didn't watch the interview.

Worst case scenario, she watched the interview, she's pissed, she's locked me out of the house, and I'll have to track down a boombox to serenade her John Cusack in *Say Anything*-style.

At least I finally know what I want to say. Or, more accurately, some ideas for a script. Between *Four Weddings and a Funeral, Sleepless in Seattle, Dirty Dancing*, and *When Harry Met Sally*, I've learned I should say something about how she's my north, south, east, and west. That a million tiny things add up to mean we're supposed to be together. That I don't want to go the rest of my life without feeling the way I feel when I'm with her, and since I know that, I want the rest of my life to start as soon as possible.

Unfortunately, she's not here, so I can't tell her any of these things.

Bucking up, I head to baggage claim, telling myself I still have a chance. Going over the words in my head as I wait for my bag, determined to not let the moment pass me by, like the guy in *My Best Friend's Wedding* warned, I grab my bag from the carousel, turn, and plow right into someone.

Who barks at me.

"Whoa, Peanut—I'm sorry, buddy. Did I squash you?" Looking up at the woman holding my dog, the woman I've held in my heart and my head since I left her side five days ago, all the words I was supposed to say evaporate. Instead of begging her to love me, I ask, "How long were you standing behind me?"

Instead of answering, she asks, "Did you file for divorce?"

Blinking, thrown by her sharp tone and blank expression, I tell myself that maybe she missed the broadcast. "Did you watch the interview?"

Setting Peanut on the ground between us, she crosses her arms. "I did."

"Do you still *want* a divorce?"

"That was the plan."

"But I—" All the romance words have left the building, so

an action seems required. The only thing I can think to do: get down on one knee. Unfortunately, Peanut takes this as an invitation to jump on me, so I have to put him in a football hold before looking up at the woman I love. "Danielle Goodwin, will you consent to not divorce me?"

"So, you didn't file for divorce?" she asks.

I have a sense that people have stopped to watch this scene, but I can't stop now.

"I did not. I don't want to divorce you. I want to be married to you. I want to wake up next to you, cook with you, talk shop with you, run on the beach with you, do all the little things with you for the rest of my life." Leaning forward and lowering my voice, I add, "Also, have lots of good sex with you."

She does not squeal and pull me to my feet for a passionate embrace. Instead, she frowns. "What if I'm mad at you?"

"Mad? What else did I do?" I'm sure I did something wrong, but if I know what it is, I can hopefully fix it.

She flings a hand in the air. "You broke me, dammit. The whole reason for the fake relationship was so I could get the tubal, so I could live happily ever after without needing anyone else, except for occasional casual sex with, like, whoever. No strings attached. But I can't even kiss another guy now." She flings the hand again. "So, you know, thanks for nothing."

She's right, of course, but I'm sure I can come up with ways to try and make it worth it to only have sex with me for the rest of our lives, except—"You know you can't kiss another guy how?"

Crossing her arms and lifting her chin in the I've-got-my-walls-up Dani way, she says, "Because I tried. I went to a bar and picked up a guy."

She shrugs, like she's not killing me right now. "He was

good-looking and all, but I couldn't even kiss him. Because he wasn't *you*."

A surge of relief combined with a wriggle from Peanut almost tips me over. My knee's also starting to hurt, so I put him down and stand. We've got a larger crowd watching now, so I try to take her elbow to steer her toward the car. "Dani, I—"

Swatting me away, she begins gesturing wildly in the air. "You ruined me for everyone else. Now I only want you. I want sex with the man who saw me two years ago—like, really saw me like no one else ever has—and bought me the perfect gift. The man I watched overcome his fear of driving. The man who cares enough about his best friend to race across the country and throw himself on a sword for her. The man who makes me feel things I never thought possible."

Reaching out slowly, because it feels like any quick movement might make her run, I take her hand. "Just to be clear, you're talking about me, right?"

When she finally meets my gaze, she tries to frown, but I can tell she's pretending. Especially when she wraps her arms around my neck. "It's not fair, you know."

I nod, sliding my hands around her waist. "You're right. Life isn't fair."

"I mean, I wanted sex one way, and now…" Her hands spread wide as they slide over my chest, feather across my ribs, before gripping my hips to reel me in.

I meet her hungry gaze with my own. "You have to settle for sex with me?"

Her hands drop into my back pockets as she presses into me. "I mean, is it even a choice if I can only choose you?"

I dip my lips to her ear to whisper, "Well, I am an actor. I could pretend to be other people. If that's what you're into."

A full-body shudder goes through her in response to my suggestion. Filing that away for later, I cup her cheeks and find her gaze again. "I love you, Danielle Goodwin, and I'd be honored if you choose to love me."

When she kisses me, I'm not sure if the applause and swell of music is real or imagined, but I don't really care.

EPILOGUE

DANI

September 25, 1999

When Violet and Nate decided to get married, their initial plan was to have a small ceremony at the inn that her grandparents used to own, followed by a party at the beach. Once Nate's family got involved in the planning, however, the guest list ballooned, and the couple were convinced to move the event to the Rumrunner Hotel.

My friends and I worked and played at the beachfront hotel the last summer we were all together, while living like a pile of puppies all crammed together in my house.

Bittersweet memories for me, but looking at the happy couple on the dance floor now, it doesn't seem that the change of venue has put a damper on their celebration. Violet's belly makes it clear that she's almost six and a half months pregnant, but you'd never know it otherwise. She's not only radiant, but she's full of energy, flitting from the dance floor to working the room and back again. Nate looks like his smile is about to break his face, it's so wide, and I'm happy to see that he's making sure that his bride is staying fed and hydrated.

I wish I could say the same about our friend Whitney.

To her credit, she's here. Thankfully, her husband is not. None of us liked Hardy McRae in high school. The nasty kind of bully that always covered his tracks so that only his victims knew their tormentor, even thinking about the guy makes my skin crawl. We were all shocked when Whit up and married him a year ago and got sucked into the Wallington upper class her parents always aspired to.

But even though she's here, she looks like she wishes she wasn't. Thinner than ever, obviously pale despite perfectly applied makeup, she hasn't moved from her seat at the reception despite being asked to dance multiple times.

Speaking of which, my husband is—surprise, surprise—an amazing dancer. The kind that makes his partner look good. Which has *my* smile wide enough to break my face, even if I'm a little worried he might up and lift me over his head at any moment, *Dirty Dancing* style.

The band shifts to a slow number, and he pulls me close. "I love you, wife."

"I love you too, husband." Words I can't seem to say enough these days.

His hands warm on my lower back, he adds, "And I love that I can call you my wife in public. I love that I can dance with you and not worry who might be watching."

Shifting so that we're swaying back and forth with our foreheads touching, I murmur, "Another win for capitalism, I guess."

"Huh?"

Smiling at his goofy expression and threading my fingers together behind his neck, I lean back slightly to meet his eyes, the beautiful blue reflections of the sea and sky that I get to stare into lovingly without worry or shame. "The Morality Memo was basically struck down by the show's surge in ratings, right? It's a win for capitalism over all those people who want to tell other people how to live."

He tips his head side to side. "I guess you're right, though I was kind of thinking it was a win for us."

"We are the lucky beneficiaries, that is true."

Enjoying myself at a wedding is a brand-new concept for me. I didn't mind the years I spent bartending in this space, chatting to the lonely hearts who avoided the dance floor the way I would in their shoes. But I, too, love being able to publicly kiss and hold hands and dance with my husband. My Pinocchio, who escaped the circus with his real-boy heart intact, who turned out to be the perfect prince for this Cinderella.

But when we return to our table for a breather, the expression on Ford's face presses pause on my dream sequence. Grabbing his coat jacket from his chair, he growls, "I was just about to pull you off the dance floor."

"What's the matter?"

"A woman came and found me. Whit's in the ladies' lounge, shivering so much that her teeth are literally chattering, but when I touched her forehead, it's on fire. I think she needs to go to the hospital."

"What are you standing here for? Did you call Hardy?"

He shakes his head, his jaw ticking with emotion. "She told me not to call him, not to call her parents. I called 911, but she's asking for you."

AFTERWORD

That's a wrap for Dani and Luke's love story, y'all, but there is a bonus epilogue, available only to Karen Grey VIPs, along with the prequel novella to this whole series. Sign up at followkarengrey.com. (If you're already a subscriber, don't worry, you won't be subscribed again.)

If you're as worried about Whitney as Ford and Dani, her book *When I Come Around* releases February 29, 2024 and you can preorder it now at your favorite book retailer.

If you loved this Carolina Classics story, leaving a review is the absolute best way to support an author. You can leave one wherever you downloaded the book, or on Goodreads or Bookbub.

ALSO BY KAREN GREY

What I'm Looking For: *The course of true love never did run smooth*, but in this smart and sexy retro rom-com with a finance-nerd heroine and a drama-geek hero, returns on love can't be measured on the S&P 500.

Forget About Me: An underwear model, a best friend's little sister, and a dog who steals the show make for an unforgettable mix in this bittersweet romantic comedy.

You Spin Me: If two lonely people fall in love over late-night phone calls, will meeting face-to-face make them, or break them? In this heartfelt, slow-burn retro romcom, it may be the end of a decade, but it's the beginning of a love story.

Child of Mine: A single mom gets a job offer she can't refuse but has to work side-by-side with the one-night stand that doesn't know he's a father. Of her daughter.

You Get What You Give: When a fiery redhead and the guy she thought was a one night stand turn out to be rivals, his family feud causes shockwaves bigger than the surf stirred up by the latest hurricane.

Hold On To Me: In this slow-burn, boss-assistant, entertainment biz romance, a bad cop movie production chief takes on a sexy assistant who challenges her every assumption.

When I Come Around: When two besties work together on a movie out of town, a secret friends-with-benefits deal seems like a good idea. Until their friends weigh in.

For Fork's Sake: Grumpy, nerdy soil scientist Sam finds passionate, idealist Diane interviewing his grandma for her YouTube channel. Feathers fly between these farm business rivals!

The Single Dad's Guide to Recreation: He's the new-in-town single dad tasked with cutting costs at Climax Parks & Rec. She's the program director with classes on the chopping block. It should be easier for them to keep their hands off each other.

ACKNOWLEDGMENTS

As always, many people helped me get this book from the far reaches of my imaginations to the page, but the top of the list has to be author Liz Alden, who not only answered my many questions about getting a tubal ligation under the age of thirty frankly (and brought a friend to do the same - thank you too, Sarah LaPrade) but she did a last-minute critique read that made this a much better read. So please thank her by reading her books!

Editor Sarah Pesce of Lopt 'n Cropt and proofer Kimberly Dawn did their bit as well.

As for other research, fellow Brandeis alum and producer-director extraordinaire Jason Ensler patiently answered my questions about his job. All errors are my own. Dear friend Robin Holmes very generously talked to me about being in the car when a tire crashed into the windshield on an LA freeway. *Come as You Are* by Emily Nagasaki was invaluable resource for Dani's journey of sexual awakening.

Author friends in various Facebook groups have been awesome with advice and general cheerleading, but I have to specifically thank the members of regular Zoom meetings and WhatsApp chats: Erin Mallon, Sarah Ready, Jill Brasher, Sara Whitney, Jordan Bloom, Lainey Davis and Danika Bloom.

Most of all, I couldn't do it without y'all! I love thinking of you as I dig these stories out of my brain and I hope you love them as much as I do.

ABOUT THE AUTHOR

KAREN GREY is a *USA Today* bestselling and award-winning author of vintage romantic comedies with smart heroines and hunky heroes. Drawing on a long career as a performer, her retro 80's and 90's romances are populated with characters working both on- and off-stage in theater, TV and film. When not reading or writing, she's lounging at the beach or hiking in the mountains. Or dreaming about both with an IPA in hand and a dog or a cat nearby.

(Author photo: Celestial Studios)

For the latest news and bonus materials, join her free VIP club at: followkarengrey.com

facebook.com/karengreyauthor

instagram.com/karengreyauthor

goodreads.com/karen_grey

bookbub.com/profile/karen-grey

tiktok.com/@karengreyauthor

www.ingramcontent.com/pod-product-compliance
Lightning Source LLC
Chambersburg PA
CBHW011208190726
48288CB00013B/3377